COOL WEATHER, WARM HEARTS

A ROMANCE ANTHOLOGY

T.L. COULTER   ROSA LEE JUDE   IAN D. SMITH
ANN SWANN   MELISSA GARDENER   PEGGY PERRY
MORGEN BAILEY   RENEE MARSKI
MICHELLE PRESLEY   BETH BAYLEY
KAROLINE BARRETT   PEARL BUTTERWICK
SHAWN MARIE GRAYBEAL   DONNA WALO CLANCY

DWC
PUBLISHING

Autumn Winds of Change by T.L. Coulter
A Little Grace by Rosa Lee Jude
Ditched by Ian D. Smith
The Sweet Scent of Home by Ann Swann
Sanctuary by Melissa Gardener
Sweet Talking Man by Peggy Perry
A Very British Autumn by Morgen Bailey
A Season for a Second Chance by Renee Marski
Harvest on the Mountain by Michelle Presley
The Ugly Pumpkin by Beth Bayley
The Best Next Thing by Karoline Barrett
Harvest Moon Dance by Pearl Butterwick
Dreamscape by Shawn Marie Graybeal
Never Again, Maybe by Donna Walo Clancy

Cover Design: Melissa Ringuette
of Monark Design Services

Interior Design: Rogena Mitchell-Jones
RMJ Manuscript Service | www.rogenamitchell.com

Printed in the USA
First Edition

AUTUMN WINDS OF CHANGE

T. L. COULTER

Dedicated to those who have ever felt the sting of love loss. To those who never thought they'd find love again. To those who are jaded and those who have hardened their hearts against love.

Love can find you again in the most unusual circumstances. It's never too late in life. Don't give up. Keep living your life, and as surely as the autumn winds come blowing in year after year, love will blow your way again...

— T.L. COULTER

1 THE STING OF DIVORCE

*R*ebecca Williams had always believed in love. To her, love was forever, love was a true partnership and working through the hard times. So, after eighteen years of marriage, she could only stare at the divorce papers still in unbelievable shock. Rebecca had always thought that she and Mark could work through anything. Even after they'd separated, she thought they'd eventually patch things up until Mark announced he was in love with another woman and wanted to go ahead with the divorce.

Rebecca's hand began to shake as she painstakingly read through and signed each section of the divorce papers. The thing that hurt the most was having to tell their son. He was the apple of both of their eyes, and they would do anything to make sure that Jace felt loved. Even with the difficulty of divorce and the painful feelings that Rebecca harbored, one thing she and Mark could agree on was co-parenting and working together to provide Jace a loving environment.

Once the papers were signed, Rebecca left the lawyers office in a frenzied hurry. She needed to get as far away from town as she could. Rebecca hated living in Utah, but she was stuck there until Jace graduated from high school. It was better to have both parents in the same area. It was the deal that Rebecca and Mark had made. But, Rebecca knew it would be an everyday struggle to stay. It wasn't that Utah was bad, it just wasn't home for her.

Rebecca had made a name for herself writing romance under the pen name R.L. Williams. She'd done so well, that she'd been able to quit her full-time job and spend more time with Jace. Writing was her therapy and saving grace, and she needed it now more than ever.

As Rebecca sped out of town, she followed the signs for Causey Reservoir. The sun was beginning to go down as she finally reached her destination. She breathed in a sigh of relief that there was no one else around.

Rebecca placed a blanket on the bank of the reservoir and collapsed onto it. It wasn't long before the gut-wrenching tears began to fall. She was now thirty-eight years old. Everything about her life had just changed in the blink of an eye. She had no idea where to go from here. She had already found a new home, but it felt empty, like she was missing something. Her career was going well, but how was she supposed to write about romance when she couldn't make her own marriage work? So many thoughts spun through her mind making it impossible to put a coherent one together. The only thing she could do was to look up towards the night sky for answers.

As Rebecca stared numbly into the night sky, she heard nothing but silence. No one and no creature was stirring about. Not even the twin-kling stars were able to give her broken heart the solace she was seek-ing. She cried out to the night sky with every ounce of pain she carried in her now broken heart...

"I will never love again. It is time that I harden my heart once and for all. No man will ever have the power to hurt me again. I am now the master of my own destiny."

Aphrodite was watching the scene before her as she let one solemn tear run down her face for Rebecca. The tear found its resting place in Aphrodite's fountain. As the goddess looked into the water, she smiled. She approved of what she saw and whispered a message through the winds to Rebecca...

"Oh, my dear sweet child. The Autumn Winds have a way of blowing in the most amazing surprises. Beware the changing winds of autumn."

Rebecca sat up startled. She knew her mind had to be playing tricks on her. She'd thought perhaps she'd finally snapped. She looked around to ensure that she was in fact still alone. There was nobody as far as she could see through the moonlight. She could have sworn she'd heard a woman's voice in the wind that seemed to carry a message for her. Something about the autumn winds and change, but the night was still again. No other strange winds appeared. It was unsettling to her, and she knew her friends would think she'd finally lost her mind. There was only one friend she knew she could count on to tell. She knew she had to tell someone she could trust, and her best friend and fellow author Kendra Jackson was just the person.

Once she was back in the car, Rebecca immediately phoned Kendra.

"Hey, it's me."

"Thank God! I've been trying to reach you all day. Are you okay?"

"Sorry, I turned my phone off. I just needed some time away from everything."

"If anyone understands that, it's me."

"Kendra, I need a favor."

"How can I help?"

"It's cabin time."

"No need to say another word. When can you leave?"

"Is tomorrow too soon?"

"Nope, tomorrow it is."

"Thank you!"

"Anytime lady, anytime."

Rebecca and Kendra would often meet at Kendra's cabin at Lake Almanor in California for writing retreats. This time, Rebecca just needed her best friend and tree therapy. She quickly made her flight reservations. Jace would be at Mark's this weekend, so all she needed to do was pack and head the hell out of Utah.

---

2 HARDEN MY HEART

Kendra picked Rebecca up at the airport in Reno. They didn't say much to one another, but words weren't needed right now. Kendra could sense that Rebecca needed some silent time. She knew that when Rebecca was ready, she'd talk. Instead, Kendra put on some upbeat music and drove as fast as she could to the cabin.

After unloading the car, Rebecca started organizing the cabin and putting the groceries away. Anything to keep her mind off the upcoming conversation. She knew the minute she sat down, the tears would begin again. She was lucky enough to have a friend like Kendra who could understand her need for space. All her other "so-called friends" couldn't wait to get the scoop on the divorce. It was an endless probing of questions. Of course, they'd caveat it with, "we understand if you don't want to talk about it," but the lust for gossip was written all over their faces. She felt as if Kendra was the only friend she could trust.

After a light dinner, Rebecca joined her friend on the couch. She let out a heavy sigh, pushed back the tears already threatening to fall, and braced herself to retell the story of how her marriage had ended.

"I knew we had problems, but I always thought we could work them out. We'd hit hard times before and so I didn't think this time was any different. The initial decision of separation crushed me, but I thought fine, we'll separate, and it will do us both some good. I always thought we'd end up back together. I thought the time apart would only help us both realize how much we needed one another."

Kendra listened intently, never interrupting, and only moving to grab tissues for her friend. She waited for Rebecca to continue.

"One day after I moved out, he called me to tell me he'd met someone. Someone from work and they were going to make a go of it. How do I compete with someone younger and more attractive?"

Kendra creased her brows. "Younger yes, more attractive, no way!"

Rebecca actually let out a little laugh. "You're my friend, and you're biased."

"Not biased, just telling you the truth. You're beautiful inside and out. Any man would be lucky to have you."

"Again, you're biased. Sweet, but biased."

"So, what now?"

"Well, we signed the divorce papers, and according to Utah law, in three months it will be final."

"That sucks!"

"To me, it doesn't matter. I'll probably die an old maid."

"No, you won't. You'll love again."

"That's just it, I don't want to. I'm going to do whatever it takes to harden my heart. I won't be hurt like that again."

"You can't mean that?" You're too sweet. Don't let this turn you into something you're not."

"I don't have a choice. It hurts too bad. I feel like I can't breathe. I feel like my heart has been ripped out of my chest, shredded into a million pieces, stepped on, run over a few times for good measure and then roughly stuffed back into my chest. Besides, I need to be strong for Jace."

"That's the problem, Rebecca. You don't have to be strong for anyone. You need to process through your feelings."

"I am, I'm just going to do it privately. I can do this on my own."

"You don't have to you know."

"I know, but it's the best way for me."

"Well, I know it's way too soon, but when you're ready to date…"

"Whoa, let me stop you right there. I'm not going to be dating."

"But someday…"

"No, never!"

Kendra didn't argue with her friend as she knew better. She also knew that someday her friend would eat those words. She wouldn't rub it in. Well, maybe she would, a little. In the meantime, she knew how to cheer her friend up.

"How about I make us a drink? We can then watch Supernatural. What do you say?"

Rebecca smiled at her friend. How could she be so lucky as to have such an amazing friend? No matter what was going on in her life, Kendra was always there. She hoped she was as good of a friend to Kendra as Kendra was to her.

"Now, you're speaking my language. Although I'm swearing off men, Dean Winchester is still a sight to behold."

Kendra chuckled as she made her way into the kitchen to fix their drinks. "I couldn't agree with you more. That man has no right to look that good."

They talked, laughed and drooled over Dean until Rebecca could no longer keep her eyes open. Kendra covered her dear sweet friend with a blanket and looked down on her with worry. She knew her friend would be all right. She knew how strong and resilient she was. It broke her heart to see her friend like this. But, she also knew that one day Rebecca would love again. In the meantime, they had Dean Winchester to keep them company.

---

3 THE DREAM

Two years later, Rebecca was struggling to put the finishing touches on her current romance novel. However, lately, she'd felt like a fraud. How could she write about romance when her own life was devoid of it? She couldn't see dating on the horizon anytime soon, if ever. She'd spent the first year after her divorce eating salted caramel ice cream and binge-watching the Hallmark Channel. Then one day she was tired of feeling sorry for herself. She put the spoon down and then spent the next year working out and eating better. Things were looking up these days. The one thing that hadn't changed was her thoughts on dating. No, she was going to continue to remain single. It was what was best for her.

Even though she'd had an awakening, she still wasn't pushing herself to look good for a man, it was to look and feel good about herself, and for the first time in years, she felt amazing, and it showed. She noticed the appreciative eyes of men here and there when she'd go out with her girlfriends. It felt good to receive the attention, but that's as far as it went. It wasn't that she hadn't been asked out, she had, but she just wasn't interested. She sure as hell wasn't going to go to online dating. Not that she felt there was anything wrong with people who did, but it wasn't for her. She wasn't up for scrolling through half-naked pictures of men or constantly hearing "hey baby, want to hook up?" No thank you. If she did eventually meet someone, she wanted it to be the old-fashioned way. A shot in the dark she knew, but as a hopeless romantic, very necessary.

Rebecca finished combing through the last chapter of her book, and as she saved the document, she yawned. She was shocked to see that it was after midnight. She'd been so engrossed in editing her novel that she hadn't realized it had gotten so late. Occupational hazard of an author. She was surprised to find herself so tired. Even though she'd moved on from the divorce, she still had insomnia most nights. She wasn't going to let this newfound gift of sleep pass her by. As soon as her head hit the pillow, she was out.

She boarded the plane, and she was shocked to find that she wasn't alone. However, when she turned around to find out who her companion was, his face was blurry. She found it strange, but still continued on in search of her seat. As she began to sit down, she looked across the aisle and spotted an old friend. There sitting across from her was Preston Barnes, a good friend from college. She and Preston had been inseparable during the first few years of college and kept in touch a few years after graduation, but as the years passed, they grew distant and eventually lost contact with one another.

"Preston, how the heck are you?"

"Rebecca! It's so good to see you."

Preston awkwardly reached over his companion to give her a hug.

"Rebecca, I want you to meet Natalie. She's my girlfriend's mother."

"So, you travel with your girlfriends' mother?"

Preston and Natalie both laughed. It was Natalie who answered her. "Actually, we are on our way to surprise my daughter Cheryl. Preston is going to propose to her in Ireland."

Rebecca smiled. "Oh, my goodness, Preston, this is fantastic news. Congratulations!"

"Thank you. There's something I need to tell you though."

Rebecca raised her eyebrow. "What is it?"

Preston turned his head towards her mysterious passenger. "I told you that you'd meet the love of your life during the fall."

Before anything else could happen in the dream, Rebecca awoke and sat straight up in bed. The dream had felt so real. She hadn't spoken to Preston in years. What the hell was that all about? She looked at the clock and couldn't believe she'd slept the whole night. She had no idea what the dream meant, but she was going to track down Preston and ask. Right after coffee of course...

Aphrodite smiled to herself. She'd known about Rebecca's connection to Preston and used it to her advantage. Rebecca was right where she was meant to be, and if Aphrodite had her way, which she always did, then Rebecca would be meeting her soul mate in the fall, October to be exact...

4 PRESTON

It didn't take Rebecca long to find Preston on Facebook. She wasn't sure why she hadn't thought to look him up sooner. In all honesty, she was hardly ever on Facebook unless she was posting for her books. Her private page had been sorely neglected. She sent a generic message of, "it's been awhile. How are you doing?" etc., and then sat back to patiently await his response.

Okay, she was actually pacing, and when it didn't immediately ding back with a response message, she began to fidget with her fingernails. What was she so anxious about? She decided she was being silly and that he would contact her when he was free, so there was no need to hover over the phone.

Rebecca got halfway down the hall when she heard her phone ding, and she moved faster than lightning to retrieve her phone. The problem was she had hardwood floors, and her socks were slick, so she ended up flat on her back before she could reach her phone. She felt like such an idiot that she couldn't do anything except laugh at herself. She was seriously contemplating getting an alert bracelet. She started thinking about when her son wasn't with her, nobody would know if she fell down the stairs, or if she had knocked herself out acting like a silly teenager racing for the phone.

She just lay there letting her mind drift to the possibilities of what could happen to her living alone that she'd forgotten about her phone until it dinged again. She carefully got up and walked slowly to her phone. No need to take another chance at slipping and falling.

She laughed at her foolishness when she saw that the first message had been from Jace. He was texting to say he loved her and missed her. She smiled with pure happiness to see his words. The second message was from Preston.

"Hey there! Great to hear from you, it's been way too long. Things are going great, and I would love to catch up with you sometime soon. Here's my number, please give me a call any time. Too much to tell you over messenger, so please call me. I hope you are well."

Rebecca didn't want to seem too eager, but something in her gut kept pushing her to call him, so she did. It rang twice before he picked up.

"Hello."

"Preston, hey it's Rebecca."

"Hey there! It's so good to hear your voice. How the heck are you?"

"Doing okay, but I want to hear all about you."

Preston laughed. "Same Rebecca. You forget that I know you well. You always try to hide what's on your mind by talking about everyone else. So, let's hear it. What have you been up to these past few years?"

Rebecca sighed. "I could never hide anything from you. I guess that hasn't changed."

"Nope, so spill it."

Rebecca filled him in on everything from the divorce to her latest book.

"Are you happy now?"

"Yes, thank you."

"Now, what about you?"

"Whoa, hold on a minute Ms. Impatient."

"First of all, I'm sorry about you and Mark. I really thought you two would go the distance."

"Thank you!"

"Second of all, your message said you had a question for me. I'm all ears, ask away."

"This is going to seem weird, but I had a dream about you last night."

Preston laughed. "I always knew you secretly dreamed about me."

"Preston, I did not!"

"Yes, you did, but that's not what we're talking about right now. Go ahead, you had a dream about me."

"Yes, like I said before I was rudely interrupted by your ego, is that I did have a dream about you."

Rebecca told him about the dream and what he'd said in it. When he went quiet, she got worried.

"Are you still there?"

"I am, I'm just trying to process this information."

"Why? It was just a crazy dream, but it felt so real that I couldn't get it out of my head. I felt this strong need to call you."

"I'm glad you did. I don't know how to tell you this, but your dream is pretty factual. I met someone who is absolutely amazing. After my divorce, I didn't think I'd ever find love again, but she walked into my life, and I knew from the moment I saw her that things were going to change for me. The funny thing is, right now she's in Ireland for work, and her mother and I are flying there to surprise her. I'm going to propose. I haven't told a soul except for her mom. This is really weird, Rebecca. I'm a little freaked out right now."

"You? Imagine how I feel right now. You're not messing with me, are you?"

"I swear to you that everything I've just said is all true. I might joke around a lot, but I'd never lie to you, ever!"

"I don't know what this means."

"I think it means that you're going to meet someone this fall. Not just anyone, but the one."

"But I'm not looking for anyone. I don't think I can give my heart away again."

"You can, and you will. Do you have anything specific going on in the fall?"

"Just a book signing in Dublin."

"So, wait a minute. You're traveling to Ireland, too?"

"Yes, in October."

Preston laughed. "Oh man, this is certainly interesting."

"What is?"

"I'm traveling to Ireland to propose to my soulmate, and it seems that you'll be traveling to Ireland to find yours. How cool is this?"

"It's not cool. Not cool at all. This is all just a weird coincidence."

"Come on, Rebecca, what are the odds? You have a dream about me proposing to my girlfriend, and you didn't even know I had one and again I haven't told anyone else about the upcoming proposal. Coincidence or no coincidence, you're going to meet your soulmate very soon."

"No way!"

"Yes, way! Let go, Rebecca. What can it hurt? I know it's scary, but you don't want to end up alone, do you? One day you'll wake up, and Jace will be gone living his own life, and you'll be all alone. Take a chance woman!"

"I'll try, but I can't promise anything."

"Oh hey, remember that bet we made years ago on that Oklahoma University and Oklahoma State University game?"

"Oh, my goodness, that was so many years ago."

"Yes, but do you remember our bet? If Oklahoma State won, you had to do whatever I asked you to do. If I recall right, I never claimed on that bet. You ready to pay up?"

"No."

Preston laughed. "Too bad, time to pay your debt."

"Ugh, fine! You know I don't like being in debt to anyone."

"Oh, I know."

"What do I have to do?"

"When you're in Ireland, you have to go up to an Irishman and kiss him. Nothing else, nothing more, just kiss him and walk away."

"Are you out of your ever-loving mind?"

"Maybe, but that's what I want you to do. I want you to throw caution to the wind and live a little. Pay up, sister!"

"I hate you!"

"No, you don't."

"Ugh, no I don't. I miss you though."

"I miss you, too. Let's do a better job of keeping in touch. I really want to find out how my punishment turns out and I can't wait to hear all about the man you meet in Ireland."

Rebecca and Preston talked a little while longer and promised to stay in better touch. Even though she was mad at Preston for making her pay up her debt, she couldn't help but smile and feel light-hearted. It really was great catching up with her old friend. However, the dreaded task of kissing an Irishman and complete stranger loomed over her head, and she had to tell Kendra all about the dream, Preston, and the bet.

---

5 DUBLIN

"Ladies and Gentlemen, this is your captain speaking. We'll be landing in Dublin in approximately thirty minutes. The current temperature in Dublin is sixty-two degrees with a seventy percent chance of rain later today."

Rebecca nudged Kendra awake.

"What? Are we there already?"

"Just about, we're landing in thirty minutes."

"So why are you waking me up now?"

"So that you're not all cranky pants when I wake you as we're landing. Remember what happened when we went to New York?"

"Are you always going to throw that in my face?"

"Well, you did almost get us kicked off the plane."

"I was hungry. Don't judge me."

Rebecca laughed. She loved giving Kendra a hard time. She looked over at her friend and thought she'd fallen asleep again. Kendra's eyes didn't open, but her mouth certainly did.

"So, how long are you going to wait to kiss your Irishman?"

"I knew I should've never told you about that."

"I'm so very glad you did. I will totally make sure this happens. I can't wait."

"Well, I can. First things first, we have a book signing to do."

Kendra finally opened her eyes. "Oh yeah, I forgot about that. I'm looking forward to traveling around the next two weeks. Oh, how I've missed Ireland."

Rebecca had only been to Ireland once before, and it had stolen her heart then. She knew it would only take more of it now. Kendra who was single with no kids got to travel more often, and frequently traveled to Ireland and other exotic places that Rebecca could only dream about.

She wasn't jealous, just happy for her friend. She knew once Jace left the house, she'd finally get her chance to travel.

Thankfully, their luggage made it in one piece, and they made it to the hotel in time for breakfast. Rebecca was starving, and she knew how hungry Kendra got when she didn't eat. They grabbed a quick bite to eat, checked into their rooms, and headed to the ballroom that would be their home for the next two days.

The ballroom was alive with authors from all around the world. Rebecca was excited about the event, while Kendra scowled at everyone. Rebecca knew that eventually, Kendra would return to a normal human being. She just needed the food and coffee to kick in first.

After settling in at their tables and getting their displays set up,

Rebecca went to find the restroom. She was marveling at the beauty of the hotel when she ran smack into the back of someone.

"Whoa there, lass, tis best you be watching where you're going."

"I'm sorry sir. I was just in awe of the woodwork and detail of the hotel. It's amazing."

"Ah, tis grand isn't it? The hotel has been a family business for over a hundred years now. Be sure to check out the underground pub. My son runs it you know."

"You have an underground pub here? I didn't see that on the website."

"Ah, that's my lad for ya. He wants to keep the pub for locals only. A bit of a gruff fellow, but once you get to know him, he's a bit bog."

"I'm sorry, what is bog?"

"Ah lass, it means soft. He's a bit soft around the edges."

Rebecca laughed, and the man smiled at her. He was a nice-looking older gentleman.

"I will certainly check out the pub... Mr.? I'm sorry, I didn't catch your name."

"Flannigan. Kerry Flannigan."

Rebecca put her hand out for him to take.

"Rebecca Williams. Nice to meet you."

"Likewise, lass. I best be getting back to it now."

He tipped his head toward Rebecca, and she gave him one last smile before going on her way. She just loved the Irish charm.

Later that night, Rebecca remembered the pub but was too jetlagged to go. She told Kendra about it, and they both promised to suck it up tomorrow night and check it out. For now, she lay there and prayed that sleep would find her.

---

6 THE KISS

As much as Rebecca loved signing books and talking to fans, she was relieved when they finally shut the book event down. After two straight days of sitting in the ballroom, she was ready to get out and see the town. She and Kendra found a nice pub to grab dinner in and walked around the city until it got too cold to continue. On their way back to the hotel, Rebecca once again remembered the underground pub. Kendra didn't argue about going. She could use a shot of something to warm her up. Besides, she remembered the bet and how Rebecca had to pay up. It was time to kiss that Irishman.

Mr. Flannigan hadn't been exaggerating, the place was hidden well. It wasn't accessible through the hotel, you had to go around back. It felt like one of those forbidden 1930's prohibition clubs that you had to give a secret knock to get in the door. Once inside though Rebecca could see the appeal to the place. It was warm and cozy with a rustic and antique feel. Definitely masculine with its leather couches by the fire and leather bar stools. It was what she imagined a high-class man cave to look like, but yet, so much more inviting.

The man at the door took their jackets and pointed them in the direction of an empty couch off to the corner. Rebecca was surprised to find the pub so packed. After talking to Mr. Flannigan, she thought she'd find the place empty. Kendra headed to the bar to order drinks while Rebecca watched as a band began to take the stage. Live music in a pub that wasn't supposed to be popular was puzzling but welcome. As Kendra returned to their seats, the music started. The band was surprisingly good, and the drinks were extremely strong.

Kendra kept eyeing the singer and then Rebecca.

"What are you up to? I don't like the way you're looking at the singer and then me."

Kendra just smiled mischievously and winked.

"Oh no. No, no, no."

"Oh yes. Yes, yes, yes. You promised Preston you'd pay your debt. I'm here to make sure it happens. That singer is hot. That's the guy. Get to it, missy!"

"I don't think I can do it."

"You can, and you will."

"Let's wait until I've had enough liquid courage first."

"Woman, we don't have all night. Here, down this shot and get to it.

If you don't do it in the next five minutes, I promise you, I'll do something extremely embarrassing."

"You mean more embarrassing than me kissing a total stranger?"

"Way more embarrassing. You know I'll do it, too. You've witnessed it firsthand."

"I hate it when you're right."

"I know you do, but I also know you love me. Pucker up buttercup."

Rebecca eyed the stranger now seated at the end of the bar talking to the bartender. She downed the shot, mustered up her courage, and did her best to remain confident and calm as she went to meet her fate.

"Excuse me." Rebecca lightly tapped the stranger on the shoulder.

When he turned to face her, he had this cocky grin on his face. It said to her that he was used to strange women coming up to him in a bar. And truth be told, he probably was.

"Well hello there, lass. What can I do for you?"

Rebecca noticed that his accent wasn't as strong as she'd grown accustomed to hearing. It was almost a mix of American/Irish if that makes sense.

"I have a few questions for you."

"I'm all ears, lass."

"Are you married?"

His eyebrow shot up intrigued. "No."

"Do you have a girlfriend?"

"No."

"Do you have any reservations about kissing me?"

He opened his mouth to answer, but Rebecca didn't want to lose her nerve, so she made her move. At first, she felt all awkward and was sure she was screwing this up big time. However, all thoughts left her as his arms wrapped around her waist to bring her in closer as he kissed her back. She let herself get lost in the feel of him.

The kiss had started out rushed and hard but soon became soft and passionate. Rebecca would've been content kissing him all night, but the patrons in the bar began to whistle and clap at the show before them. This brought Rebecca back to reality as she quickly ended their kiss.

The full rush of embarrassment was written all over her face. She was sure her face was glowing bright red. She couldn't seem to find her voice. All she managed to croak out before bolting from his arms was, "thank you!"

Rebecca then ran out of the bar, passing quickly by a gaping Kendra, and the guy at the door who winked at her as she left. In her hurry to escape, she hadn't noticed the complete baffled look of the stranger, nor had she noticed that Mr. Flannigan had been in the bar. Kendra grabbed their jackets and ran out after her friend. She didn't have to go far as she found Rebecca hyperventilating near the entrance of the hotel.

"Are you okay?"

Rebecca just shook her head and then she began to laugh like a crazy person. She laughed so hard that she had tears flowing down her cheeks and she snorted. Kendra couldn't help but laugh with her.

"Did I really just do that?"

"You not only did that, but you also did it with sass! Girl, the whole room stopped to watch. When I say that was one heck of a scene, I mean it. That's the stuff romance novels are made of. Bravo my friend. So, tell me, how was it?"

"I can't even describe it. I've never felt anything like that before, and I mean never. I could've kissed him all night long."

"So why not go back and do just that? The night's still young."

"I can't. We're leaving here tomorrow to go site seeing, and I don't want to be thinking about Mr. Dreamboat Irishman in there. No, it's better to leave it as is."

"Are you sure?"

"Yes. Let's go try to get some sleep. Our driver will be here for our early morning departure."

Kendra elbowed her friend and winked at her. "Something tells me you won't be sleeping tonight."

Rebecca just smiled, but she had a feeling her friend was right.

When the alarm went off the next morning with no sleep for her, she was cursing Preston, Kendra and that darn sexy Irishman. The only one celebrating was the Goddess Aphrodite.

7 THE IRISHMAN

Kendra knew better than to give Rebecca too much of a hard time about the kiss last night. She could tell by looking at her friend this morning that she didn't in fact sleep at all. She couldn't help but giggle as they headed out of the hotel.

"You better stop giggling right now or else."

"Come on, just let me giggle. I promise not to say anything else."

"I swear to you that if you snicker, giggle or…"

Rebecca was cut off short when she ran into the back of her friend who'd stopped abruptly.

"What in the world Kendra?"

"You're not going to believe this."

"What?"

"Brace yourself."

"For what?" Rebecca peeked around her friend.

"No, no, no this is not happening."

"Oh, it's happening."

Rebecca peeked around her friend again to see a very smug and sexy Irishman leaning up against their hired car, arms and legs crossed, with that same cocky grin on his face from last night. Her cheeks flushed bright red.

"Top of the morning to you, lasses. I've been out here waiting on you both for quite a while. You ready for your journey?"

Kendra just burst out laughing. "You're our driver? This is freaking priceless."

He only smiled and nodded which only infuriated Rebecca but only because of her embarrassment over last night. She somehow found her voice.

"You're not our driver. I was specifically told by Mr. Flannigan that his son would be driving us this week. He's the owner of the pub, and you're a singer."

"Pleased to meet you, lass. Aidan Flannigan at your service. Pub owner, singer and now your driver."

"No, you're not."

"Last time I checked I was most certainly Aidan Flannigan."

About that time, Kerry Flannigan joined them.

"Ah, I see you've met my son, again."

Rebecca wasn't having it. No way could she be in the car with this guy for two weeks.

"I'm sorry, there must be some mistake."

"No mistake, lass. Aidan is your driver. I would say, by the looks of things last night, you two will get along just fine."

Rebecca put her head down mortified.

"Now, don't you be worrying your pretty little head lass, he'll be a true gentleman."

Rebecca wasn't worried about him, she was worried about the way he made her feel just by looking at him.

Kendra was still laughing as they headed towards the car. Rebecca did her best to ignore Aidan, and when she went to get into the back seat, Kendra wouldn't let her in.

"I'm sorry my friend. I need the whole back seat to stretch out. Do you mind riding up front? Thanks, you're a peach", Kendra said with a fake sarcastic southern drawl.

Rebecca wanted to throat punch her friend. She'd just put her in a bad situation. If she refused, then Aidan would take it personally, but if she did as her friend asked, then she didn't know how she would keep from embarrassing herself again. She glared at her friend and shut the door a little harder than she'd intended to and climbed in the front seat; arms crossed.

Aidan got in but didn't look at Rebecca. Before he started the car, he asked, "Want to talk about that kiss last night?"

Rebecca kept her head forward. "No."

"Fine by me, lass."

Aidan didn't say another word, he just drove off whistling. Kendra was smiling to herself as she got comfy and nodded off to sleep. Rebecca was fuming and plotting all the ways she was going to murder her friend.

8 ROMANCE BLOOMS

It was four days into their trip when Kendra got an emergency phone call from home. Her dad was admitted into the hospital for tests, and she needed to get back home immediately.

Rebecca was worried. "I should go with you."

"No, it's nothing serious, but I need to be there to help my mom with the business so that she can be with dad. You stay here and finish out the vacation. As a single mother, you don't get to do this very often."

"Are you sure? I feel bad staying."

"You just don't want to be alone with Aidan."

"No, that's not it. I mean no, I don't want to be left alone with him, but I really feel bad about staying."

"You shouldn't. You deserve this vacation. I'll make it back to Ireland, you can count on that. I love you, my friend. Go enjoy yourself. I'm going to go get my flight arranged and pack."

After saying goodbye to Kendra, Rebecca still felt guilty about staying behind, so she took a short walk on a path close to their bed & breakfast to clear her head. The trail ended at a lovely pond. She found a bench and sat down to take in the beauty surrounding her. The air was cooling off a bit as she wrapped her blanket tighter around her body for warmth.

Rebecca's peace and tranquility were shattered by approaching footsteps. Thinking it was another guest, she didn't bother to turn around, until she heard his voice.

"Evening, lass. Mind if I join you?"

"Do I have a choice? I'm sorry, I don't know why I just said it like that."

Aidan just shrugged and chuckled. Rebecca liked his laugh. Truth be told, she liked everything about him. They hadn't talked much in the last few days, but she would catch herself observing him when he wasn't looking. He was polite to everyone, played with the children wherever they went, held open doors for everyone, and just seemed like an all-around nice guy. Besides, she had been the one to kiss him, so why was she punishing him for her actions.

Not waiting for an invitation, he sat down next to her. She looked over at him, and he smiled back at her.

"Mind if I ask you a question, lass?"

"Sure."

"You promise not to bite my head off?"

"I promise. Sorry if I've seemed like a crazy person on this trip. I don't make a habit of going around kissing strange men."

"Well, that's what I want to ask you about. Why did you kiss me?"

Rebecca sighed. Now was a good time as any to tell him the truth. She told him all about her friend Preston, the bet and Kendra choosing him in the pub.

"I'm glad. I'm glad she chose me. I quite enjoyed it. I just couldn't understand why this beautiful lass would want to kiss me when she had her pick of the lads in the pub."

"Somehow I find that hard to believe. I bet women come up to you all the time."

Rebecca liked that he'd called her beautiful, but she chose to ignore it.

"You flatter me lass, but you're wrong."

"I bet it's that gruff exterior you put off. You do realize you scowl a lot."

Aidan laughed. "Aye, I do."

"Why?"

"To keep people away. It's just for the best."

"Ah, is that so you don't get hurt again?"

Nobody had ever gotten Aidan like Rebecca seemed to. The way she kept her distance yet observed him when she thought he wasn't looking. She had gotten under his skin the moment she walked up and tapped him on the shoulder.

"I was married once."

"What happened?"

"When she found out I couldn't have kids, she left me. She'd wanted to be a mum her whole life. It was the one thing I couldn't give her. Kind of makes a man feel like a failure."

"I'm so sorry."

"It's been five years now. I just don't want to disappoint another woman, so I keep to myself."

Rebecca told him about her marriage, about her son and how she herself couldn't have any more children. Aidan listened attentively. They continued to talk as the night sky fell upon them. It wasn't until Rebecca started to shake from the cold that Aidan offered to walk her back. Without realizing it, he'd put his hand on the small of her back to guide her. The touch was electric for both of them. Aidan removed his hand and followed quietly behind her.

The bed & breakfast was quiet, but the fire in the parlor was going full blaze. Aidan asked if Rebecca wanted to join him to warm up. She knew she should say no, but she went against her better judgment and joined him.

Rebecca put her hands close to the fire. "This feels amazing."

Aidan was smiling down at her.

She smiled back. "What are you thinking about?"

"I was thinking of something else that felt amazing."

Rebecca raised her eyebrow. Aidan moved to face her, grabbed her blanket and pulled her closer to him.

"Would you mind if I kissed you, Rebecca?"

She just shook her head and bit her lip in anticipation.

"Good, because I don't think anything could stop me from doing just that."

The tension between them was thick. He leaned in and gently kissed her. It was sweet at first, and then it became something more. At that moment they felt more connected by that kiss than anything else had in their entire lives. The kiss went on until Aidan reluctantly pulled away. He knew if he kept kissing her, he'd never let her go.

Rebecca was light-headed. The kiss had completely relaxed her and had her wanting more of him. All she could do was sigh and lay her head on his chest. He pulled her over to the couch where they stayed just holding one another until they both dozed off into a peaceful sleep.

9 ALL GOOD THINGS MUST END

The next few days were a blur for Rebecca and Aidan. After falling asleep on the couch, they both agreed that they'd see what the rest of the week brought with no obligations, and at the end of the trip she'd go home, and they wouldn't make a big deal out of it. They decided not to talk about specific things in their life, just what they both did for a living, hopes and dreams and future goals. When Aidan told her that he spent half of his time in Ireland and half in America, she was shocked, but that explained his accent. She didn't want to know where in America as they said no specifics. She just wanted to spend as much time with him as possible before saying goodbye. Their quick connection was something straight from a romance movie, but there was no denying that it was there.

They spent the next week traveling around Ireland. During the day, Aidan showed her things off the beaten path, and at night they drifted off to sleep in one another's arms. So, when the day came for the trip to end, Rebecca did her best to toughen herself up for the goodbye that was looming in front of her.

Aidan was feeling it too. Before Rebecca had abruptly come into his life, he'd felt hallow, as if he was missing something. He now knew what that was. He'd only known her less than two weeks, but he wanted more. He didn't want her to go, but he knew she had to. But, he had a plan. He just had to have faith that it would work out as nicely as it did in his mind.

Aidan drove her to the airport. He knew what she was feeling because he felt it, too. As much as she promised she wouldn't cry, she did just that as he kissed her goodbye. They had promised to let one another go, but it was the hardest thing she'd ever had to do. He kissed her one more time and watched her walk away from him and out of his life, but not for good.

and Kendra were by her side as she and Aidan promised to love and honor one another till death do they part.

Later that evening with Jace having a ball with his grandparents, Rebecca and Aidan escaped to their honeymoon suite.

Aidan took her in his arms. "I love you, Mrs. Aidan Flannigan. From the moment you walked up and kissed me, you had my heart. I'll never let you go or let you down. You have my solemn promise, lass."

"I love you too Mr. Aidan Flannigan with all my heart and soul."

The wedding party wasn't the only one celebrating. Aphrodite was certainly congratulating herself on a job well done. She needed her next victim, and it didn't take her long to spot her. Sitting alone was little Ms. Workaholic herself Kendra. Yes, it was time for Kendra to learn a lesson or two about love herself. Aphrodite smiled to herself. This was going to be a challenge, but hey, she absolutely loved a good challenge. Game on!

The End

A LITTLE GRACE

ROSA LEE JUDE

*M*elonie fumbled in her purse to find the front door key. For an anxious second, she thought she might have left it on the counter in her apartment, three thousand miles away. The moment of anxiety was quickly dismissed as her fingers found the fuzzy chain she knew was on the other end of it.

"Gracious," Melonie spoke aloud and looked at it closely. "It would have been embarrassing to try to break into a building so soon after inheriting it."

Inherit. The word made a twinge pass through her heart. Only three months earlier, Melonie had received the sad news that her maternal grandmother, Gracelyn Treemont, passed away. Melonie was the sole heir to her grandmother's sizable fortune. *Baked with Grace* was a household brand best known for the fruit pies that the founder first created in the building that Melonie was about to enter. A sadness filled Melonie's heart. She thought about all the lost years she was not in contact with her grandmother.

"There's no sense in dwelling in the past. I'm here to start a new chapter, and it begins when I get this building open."

"It's been several years since anyone has been inside." A male voice coming from behind Melonie startled her. "You might not want to go in there alone."

A feeling of apprehension began replacing the sadness. As a cold fall breeze rustled a few stray leaves in the doorway, Melonie felt the chill of change. She knew that getting used to small-town life would take time. She did not want people to enter her business before she had a chance to grasp what she was doing. She turned to face the person.

"Thanks for your concern, but—" Melonie stopped in mid-sentence.

Her gaze landed on the man's royal blue eyes. They were beautiful. Looking at the face that surrounded them, she realized it matched his eyes. He might have been the most handsome man she had ever seen. It was not just his looks. It was like there was an electric field around him. She quickly turned back to the door to regain her composure.

"I'm sure I will be just fine as soon as I can get this key to work."

Her hands shook while she fumbled with the key. She took a deep breath and softly laughed to herself.

"Allow me."

The man reached around her and held out his hand for the key. Without making eye contact, Melonie dropped the key into his open palm and took a couple of steps back from the door. The man slipped the key into the lock with ease. Melonie heard the clicking sound of the lock turning. Before she could say anything, the door was open, and the man walked inside.

"I'm not sure if the electricity is on." No sooner did Melonie speak; the overhead lights came on. Melonie could see that the man knew exactly where the light switch was located. "Have you been in here before?"

"Many times. I worked here when I was a teenager. Of course, Mrs. Treemont closed the place not long after that. She didn't need to make pies anymore, did she?"

While Melonie knew that the story of her grandmother's success was common knowledge, she did not expect a total stranger to start talking about it.

"I'm sorry. Have we met before?"

"Excuse me. I've forgotten my manners." A smile appeared, and the man extended his hand. "I'm Gus Lowe. I'm the local building official. I was getting ready to inspect a building down the street when I saw you out front. I thought you might need some help."

"Certainly. I apologize for my reaction. I've lived in a large city for too long. We tend to question people's motives. Living in a small community will take some getting used to."

"I'm sure you will get used to it quickly. Miss Grace's granddaughter must have some of her welcoming personality."

The man's smile was as charming as his eyes. Melonie would need to control her composure. She didn't want to embarrass herself with a schoolgirl reaction.

"How did you know that I was her granddaughter?" Melonie broke her gaze with Gus and began looking around at her surroundings. "I haven't been here in years. Neither had Grandma, from the looks of this place. I had forgotten that the locals called her Miss Grace. It's sweet."

"It's a small town, remember? Word travels fast. Anyone who ever spent more than ten minutes with Miss Grace saw the latest photo she had of you. You're Melonie, right?"

"Again, my manners are atrocious." Melonie made eye contact with Gus. Those two pools of blue were captivating. "Yes, I am Melonie Peters. Grandma Grace only had one grandchild. Unfortunately, I did not get to see her as much as I would have liked while I was growing up."

"Miss Grace never got over the passing of your mother. I don't suppose a parent ever recovers from losing a child, even a grown one." Melonie watched Gus walking around the large room. "What do you plan to do with the building?"

"Something crazy." Melonie let out a nervous giggle. Few people knew the reason she returned to her mother's hometown. "I'm going to reopen the bakery."

"Really? That's fabulous. It doesn't violate the *Baked with Grace* brand? I remember that Miss Grace didn't willingly close this place. Even though she certainly didn't need the income any longer."

"All that corporate nonsense is ridiculous. I let the lawyers handle it. I'm planning to start a few charities in my grandmother's name. This little bakeshop is going to come back to life under a new name. Gracelyn Treemont will certainly still be in the building. I have all the recipes that she never made for America, and a few of my own."

"I'm listening."

Gus pushed away a couple of old boxes that were sitting on a long counter that faced the front door. Jumping up and sitting on the counter, he offered his hand for Melonie to do the same. She was so surprised by his actions that without thinking she followed his lead and joined him.

"I was still in middle school living away from here when my grand-mother sold her recipes to the corporation who created *Baked with Grace*. It was during that time I didn't get to see her much."

"Can I ask why?"

Melonie noticed that Gus' eyes appeared to alter their color and intensity as his mood changed. The royal sparkle that she first saw with his friendly manner was now a dark blue that matched the seriousness of his expression.

"After my mother died, my father was quite angry. It was how his grief manifested itself. My grandmother tried to get him to allow me to stay with her and go to school here. He felt she was trying to take me away from him. I don't agree with what he did. As a child, I hated it. But, as I've gotten to know him better as an adult, I understand it. He had lost my mother. He was afraid of losing me."

"We can't live inside another person's skin. We don't know what they fear." Gus jumped down from the counter and began to walk around the open floor space. "I remember when this place was everyone's favorite hangout."

"I guess it would have been a fun place to hang out. Grandma seemed to enjoy having kids around." Melonie studied what was left of her grandmother's shop. Beside the counter was one of several large display cases. Scattered throughout the large room were tables, some with chairs resting upside down on top. A layer of dust rested on every-thing. "I've not been in here since I was about nine. Minus the dust, it's as I remember it."

"I think I was in early high school when Miss Grace closed the place. My friends and I were in here just about every day after school up until then. When we were younger, our mothers would give us enough money to stop for a cookie after school. I liked your grandmother's cookies a little too much. I was a little chunky in middle school. I ran it all off playing sports in high school. Those packaged versions of Miss Grace's pies and cookies weren't nearly as good as the real thing."

"Preservatives, nasty preservatives; that's what Grandma would say. Every once in a while, I would sneak away and call her before my father got home from work." Melonie smiled at the memory. "I thought I was pulling one over on him. I forgot that he paid the phone bill."

"Did you get in trouble?" Gus walked back into the kitchen area and yelled back his question.

"No. He never mentioned the phone charges. I guess that was his way of compromising."

"Well, this is still a great location. We've needed a bakery on this street for a while. You're going to have to do some work to get it to meet code though."

"I think I have a friend who might help me." Melonie felt a surge of excitement. "He's a new friend. I was a little apprehensive about the stranger at my door at first, but he seems kind of nice."

The royal blue sparkle returned to Gus' eyes. There was no use fighting her feelings.

"I'm serious, Cassy. He just appeared out of nowhere."

"Like a knight in shining armor."

Even through the phone, Melonie could imagine her friend shaking her head and rolling her eyes in disbelief. Cassy was a true romantic. She liked to put up a tough exterior by making jokes.

"I wouldn't call him a knight. But, he might be a prince or a king, perhaps. Remember how your grandmother used to go on about how blue Elvis' eyes were?"

"Oh, girl. Gramma made me watch his movies all day, all summer.

I've still got those stupid songs in my head." Cassy paused. "I've got to admit though; the man could sing and those eyes of his. Heartbreaking."

"Well, this guy Gus has his eyes, but there was more to it than that. It was like magnetism. I felt drawn to him."

"This is going to be more than a new business venture for you. It's about time that you allowed yourself to be interested in someone. Keith has been gone a long time. He wouldn't want you to be alone."

A freak accident on a construction site had taken Melonie's high school sweetheart just a few months before they were going to be married. It was a strange situation for a young woman to be in—a widow who was never married. Right after high school, Keith went directly to work for his father's large construction business while Melonie went off to college an hour away. They were set to marry just two weeks after she graduated from college. She was so consumed with the whirlwind of planning that she let his last phone call go to voicemail. It was a decision she still regretted.

"If the tables were turned, Keith would have had a girlfriend before the funeral was over. You know how popular he was." Melonie tried to make a joke. She knew her friend would hear the emotion in her voice.

"Keith *could* have had a girlfriend that quick. He would *not* have. He would be like you have been. It doesn't mean he would want you to live a life of solitude. Didn't you say this guy, Gus, has something to do with building? Maybe that's a sign from Keith."

"Gus is a building official. He's the one who makes guys like Keith follow all the rules."

"Gus sounds like a nice guy. Let him help you get that building of yours straightened out so that you can open. You have to become instantly successful so that you can hire me, and I can stop missing my best friend."

"Like you would leave the city life. This is a small town, Cassy. No coffee shops on every corner."

"You will sell coffee. That's all I need. I think I could stand for my life to slow down a little."

Melonie could hear Cassy swearing under her breath; the sound of something breaking in the background.

"Listen. I've got to get off here. My ability to do more than one thing at a time isn't working. Send me a message later today. Preferably one with a photo of Blue Eyes."

"How am I supposed to get a photo of Gus?"

"You mentioned in a message yesterday that the fall leaves were beginning to turn. Get him outside and pretend to be taking photos. You can tell him you're also a travel writer and you've got a new assignment. You are supposed to be the creative one. Why am I always coming up with the stories?"

"Because you are the one that needs them. I think I just heard a knock. I'll catch up with you later."

"Photo. I want a photo!" Melonie heard Cassy giggle before the phone clicked.

Taking a deep breath, Melonie thought about what her friend had said. Cassy was right. Seven years of being alone were enough. She walked from the back of the building to the front door. As she hoped, she saw Gus peeking in the window.

"If you are trying to tell me something, Keith. Show me a sign."

Melonie put on a smile and opened the door. She heard the jingle of the bell that was attached. It reminded her of her grandmother.

"Are you going to make apple pie?" Gus blurted out the question.

"Good morning to you, too, Gus." Melonie was amazed at the quick sign. Keith loved her apple pie. "I haven't developed the menu yet, but since it's fall, I would say that apple pie would be a good choice."

"I'm sorry. That was rude of me. I dreamed last night that I was sitting at the counter in there eating a slice of Miss Grace's apple pie."

"That must be an important memory for you to dream just after being back in this building a few minutes."

"Miss Grace was an important person in my life. She treated me like a member of her family."

"I didn't realize that you knew her so well. There's a lot I didn't know about her or this business."

"Then, it's great that you are here now. You will find out how loved she was in this community. The town is already buzzing with the news that you are planning to reopen her shop. That's why I stopped by."

Melonie took a moment to look past the blue eyes and see the person behind them. There seemed to be something quite genuine about Gus Lowe. She would need help to get her grandmother's shop open again. It appeared that help was sent to her.

"I'm all ears. I'm sorry I don't have any apple pie to offer you now. I did manage to find a coffee pot in the back. I'm not sure if I have water though."

"Your lawyer called a couple of weeks ago and inquired about the utilities here. They have remained in place for minimal insurance reasons. There will be a few things you'll need to do for a certificate of occupancy. The codes have changed a little since Miss Grace ran this place."

"Does that mean my coffee maker doesn't work?" Melonie laughed. "I don't suppose there is a coffee shop nearby."

"I bet that coffee maker saw better days. There's a diner about two blocks from here. Why don't we take a walk over there? I can tell you a little more about what the place will need to come up to code."

"Let me get my key." Melonie turned to walk back into the shop.

"No need. I have one."

"You have one." Melonie stopped in her tracks and slowly turned around. "Why do you have a key to my building?"

"Don't be alarmed, Melonie. Remember, it has only recently become your building. Miss Grace gave me this key years ago."

Gus pulled a key from his pocket. It was attached to a fuzzy key chain identical to Melonie's. Her heart skipped a beat. She had made two identical keychains at camp one summer and mailed them to her grandmother. When the lawyers gave her the key to the building, she was happy to see that it was attached to one of them. Melonie assumed she would later find the other one in some of her grandmother's belongings. She never imagined that the keychain would be in someone else's possession.

"She told me that you made this." Melonie's eyes travelled from the keychain to Gus' face. "She gave me this key when I worked for her when I was a teenager."

"And you still have the key?"

"I told you she was an important part of my life. After your grandfather passed away and her business started taking off, she needed someone to help her keep up with the maintenance of this place. I was in college by then, and I would come home on weekends and look after things. I tried to give the key back to her several times after she closed the place. She would always tell me to hold on to it and that I might need it one day. I guess that day has come."

"I hope you aren't sorry you held on to it."

Melonie pulled the door behind her. She lingered a moment and looked at the sign on the door. Just like on all the boxes of frozen pie that were sold in grocery stores across the country, there was a photo of a young Melonie in the logo of *Baked with Grace*.

"I thought you might have remembered."

"Remembered?" Melonie turned around from the door. She saw a serious look on Gus' face. "Remember what?"

"Nothing. Let's walk to the corner. The diner is two blocks behind us."

Walking side by side, Melonie took in the surroundings. The town had changed little in the years since she last visited. Some of the shops she remembered were now replaced by offices, but the little town's Main Street was still busy—full of business occupants and their customers.

"The business community will enjoy having a bakery again. I'm sure you know about the manufacturing plant that is associated with *Baked with Grace* that is a couple of blocks in the opposite direction."

"Yes, I've heard of it. It was important to Grandma for this community to benefit from her success."

"And indeed, they have. Last I heard there were about nine hundred people employed there."

"All making Grandma's apple pie." Melonie laughed. "It's not as good as hers."

"It's good for frozen pie. But, it's nowhere near as good as one of Miss Grace's after it came right out of the oven."

"You mean a slice."

"No, I mean a whole pie. This boy could eat a whole pie. It's one reason why I have to exercise every day." Gus patted his stomach. "I like pie too much."

"I remember a little boy who used to live here who got in trouble for eating one of Grandma's fresh pies. He took his first bite from the middle. I don't know whatever happened to him. He's the boy in the picture with me on the logo."

"The little boy that was giving you a peck on the cheek?"

"Yes. That was all an accident. Grandpa was taking photos of some of the pies to use for promotion. It was back when Grandma started selling her pies to a restaurant chain. A.J. lived down the street. We used to play sometimes when I would visit. I think it was mostly his way to get pie. I found out later that Grandpa paid him five dollars to kiss me on the cheek."

"A.J. was a lucky boy. He got to kiss a pretty little girl."

"And he got five dollars and that pie I am holding in the picture."

"I bet he remembers that kiss more than that money or pie."

"It was a long time ago." Melonie paused and studied several of the trees that were beginning to show their autumn leaves. "I have forgotten how beautiful fall is here. Why don't you stand over there next to those trees and I will take your photo?" Melonie pulled out her phone.

"Why would you want my photo?" Melonie noticed a sly-looking grin crossing Gus' face.

"Before you let your ego get ahead of you, you don't know that for the last five years I've been a travel writer. I intend to keep working freelance. I want to gather as many photos this autumn as I can to write stories to pitch to travel publications next year."

"Why would I agree to be a model for your photos?"

"Because you want apple pie."

"You got me there," Gus grinned.

Without another word, Gus began posing next to the tree. His height made some of the leaves of red and gold lay on the top of his head of chocolate brown hair creating a quite unique look. Despite her made-up story, she decided she might use the photos for a future article.

"You're a natural."

Gus reached up to pluck a leaf from a tree not realizing that a squirrel was just six inches from his hand. Melonie quickly snapped the photo. She wished she had a better camera with her

"Have you done this before?"

"Guilty. I did a little modeling while I was in college. It helped pay the bills."

"Thanks for the photos. Is that the diner up ahead?"

"Yes. You can see that place from a mile off." Gus laughed. Melonie looked at the bright pink and blue structure. "It was originally owned by the great-grandfather of a friend of mine. I helped them paint that place a couple of times—pink paint in my hair for a week."

"Who don't you know around here?"

"Small town, remember? If you are a kid, who doesn't mind working, you are in high demand. My father wanted me to stay out of trouble. In the summer, he expected me out of the house by sun-up and not home until dinnertime. Every evening, he made me empty my pockets to show him what I'd made."

"Wow. Sounds like he ran a tight ship."

"He did. I'm thankful for it though. I got some real experience with life before I had to live it on my own."

They arrived at the door of the restaurant. A young woman was coming out; Gus held the door open.

"Hi, Gus. I haven't seen you around in a while. What have you been up to?" The woman batted her eyes. "I was hoping you might call."

"Always busy, Renee. Let me introduce you to our town's newest resident. This is Melonie Peters. She's re-opening Miss Grace's bakery."

"I heard that Miss Grace's granddaughter was returning. Gus, you were always close to that family. It's nice of you to show Melonie around. I hope to hear from you again soon." Renee gave Melonie a forced smile before winking at Gus and then walked away.

"Renee seems nice." Melonie held the menu in front of her and didn't make eye contact with Gus. "I guess being a bachelor in a small town has its advantages."

"What makes you think I'm a bachelor?"

"I assumed since you aren't wearing a wedding ring. I'm sorry if I—" Melonie gave Gus a big-eyed look.

"No worries. The only Mrs. Lowe around here is my mother, and she would be thrilled to see me dining with Gracelyn Treemont's granddaughter."

"I certainly didn't want the reputation of being a homewrecker. That would be bad for business."

"Oh, I don't know. That might add a little mystery to the whole bake shop scenario," Gus smiled. The server placed steaming cups of coffee in front of them. "They make a mighty good breakfast here, Melonie. Would you like something to go with your coffee?"

"All I ate this morning was a banana. It is long gone. I will have the ham and cheese omelet with hash brown potatoes and raisin toast." Melonie handed the menu back to the server.

"That sounds pretty good to me, too. I'll have the same."

As the server took Gus' menu and began walking away, Melonie decided to ask the question that was burning inside of her.

"This is probably too personal a question to ask someone I recently met. But, since you have a long history with my family and possess a key to my building, I'm going to ask it. Why is the charming and kind Gus Lowe still a bachelor?" Melonie took a swig of her coffee concealing her nervous energy.

"I met my princess a long time ago, and I lost touch with her. My romantic heart will not settle for anyone else."

"I could give you some of the advice that's been given to me. You can't live in the past. You probably wouldn't follow it any better than I have."

Gus remained silent.

"Keith was a special man. I miss him." Melonie smiled and stared into her coffee cup. "He joked that he was lucky I decided to accept my second proposal."

"Second proposal? I think I remember Miss Grace mentioning that you lost someone quite tragically. That's rough."

"Yes. The little boy in the photo with me, he was my first proposal. A.J. made me this little wire ring and got down on one knee." Melonie looked down at her hand. "I was all giggly."

"Did you accept?"

"Yes. Both our mothers were there. It happened inside the shop. They told us we would have to wait until we were thirty. I'm thirty now, I guess I'll have to look him up."

They were both silent for a moment. The server walked up and placed their plates of food in front of them. Melonie watched Gus cover his potatoes in ketchup. She searched her memory trying to recall who she knew that did the same thing.

"Do you still have the ring?" Gus' question broke her chain of thought.

"No. Unfortunately, I do not. My sad little heart decided that I should give it to my mother. It's in her casket with one of my hair ribbons and a picture I drew of our dog."

"Oh." Gus set down his fork and stared at Melonie.

"I remember asking my father if I could send something with her. He said he thought she would like that. My dog and that ring were my most prized possessions. I knew I couldn't send Sheba. My mom used to put a ribbon in my hair every day. I included a ribbon in her favorite color."

"What color was that?" Gus smiled.

"Lavender." Melanie paused. "Enough about that. This food looks yummy. I can tell that I will be spending some time here."

"That's good to hear." Gus picked up a piece of toast. "Now, let me tell you how much work you are going to need to do on your building. Don't worry, I'll be gentle."

"I'm amazed about how quickly it's all come together."

Melonie walked around the seating area of her new bakery and coffee shop with a broad smile shining from her face. The previous month was a whirlwind of activity, but the remodeling breathed new life into her grandmother's shop. Melonie kept as much of the furniture, fixtures, and layout as she could to honor her grandmother. She added her own style to it with a new coat of paint and décor that took it from an old-fashioned style to a modern look.

"I love the name." Melonie's friend Cassy had arrived in time to help with the opening. "*A Little Grace*—those three words say so much."

"All the things I would have imagined for my life did not include owning a bake shop in my mother's hometown." Melonie straightened a lavender tablecloth on one of the tables. It was one of the touches to the décor that honored her mother.

"What about Gus? Did you imagine him? He has all the charm and charisma you so aptly described with a goofy schoolboy side that I was not expecting." Cassy sat down on one of the high stools located near the coffee bar.

"Don't all men have that?"

"Perhaps, but it usually doesn't reveal itself so easily after they have hit thirty. There's definitely a chemistry between the two of you."

"I think I would call it more a comfortableness. It's like I've known him for a long time. I must remember, he must've helped me out of respect for Grandma. After today, he might be only a customer."

"Oh, please, Melonie. You are not that naïve. He will certainly become someone different to you after today. His job will be complete, yes. But, I've seen how he looks at you. He will be far more than a customer if you let him."

"Look at the time!" Melonie glanced at the clock on the wall. "The ribbon cutting is scheduled for eleven. People will be arriving any minute." Melonie walked to the window that separated the dining area from the kitchen. "Claire, Mandee, let's get the coffee brewing."

Two young women appeared through the swinging door carrying large trays of pastries. Melonie was fortunate that there was a culinary school nearby that specialized in baking, another benefactor of the Gracelyn Treemont legacy. Melonie's entire staff would be students from that school.

"You are so blessed to find these students." Cassy moved out of the way where a third student, Henry, began brewing coffee. "It will be great experience for them."

"It will be great experience for me. Claire knows more about baking than I do. She's going to put a wonderful new spin on Grandma's recipes."

"Where's the apple pie?" Gus' voice boomed through the front door. Melonie turned to see him with an older couple behind him. "There's a crowd forming out here. I want to make sure that I get dibs on my own pie."

The same sparkle that shone from Gus' blue eyes lit up his smile. He walked toward Melonie. Butterflies danced in her stomach when their eyes met. Quickly, her attention was diverted to the door when she saw the crowd.

"Who are all those dressed up people?" Cassy came up behind Melonie.

"The Mayor, the Chamber of Commerce people, a few business owners from down the street. The whole town is excited about this. I've been trying to tell Melonie." Gus squeezed Melonie's arm, causing her to look back at him, and she, again, noticed the couple. "Melonie, these are my parents. They were good friends of Miss Grace. They wanted to be here today."

Melonie smiled and extended her hand, first to the woman. She could see that Gus got a lot of his handsome features from the beauty in the woman's face—a face that looked vaguely familiar.

"We are so pleased that you have opened Gracelyn's shop again." The woman's voice was warm. Her smile sincere. "She would be so proud and pleased."

"Our stomachs thank you and our bathroom scales cringe." Gus' father's handshake was quick and firm. The man's strong jaw and body structure was an aged duplicate of his son's. "Our families have been connected for a long time. So glad to have you back in town."

"Miss Peters, I'm Taylor Pennington with the Chamber of Commerce. Are you ready for us to begin the ribbon cutting?" The woman seemed anxious to begin the ceremony. Melonie smiled, nodded and followed her outside.

"What a whirlwind of a day!"

Eight hours later, Melonie finally sat down. A steady flow of customers entered the shop from the moment the ribbon was cut until the mid-afternoon. It was so busy that Melonie lost track of Gus and his parents. She was surprised to see them enter the shop again just as Mandee was getting ready to flip the door sign around to say they were closed.

"May we come back in?" Gus peaked around the door, causing Mandee to look in her boss' direction.

"It's okay, Mandee. You guys finish what you are doing and go on home. You've worked hard today." The girl gave Melonie a smile and walked to the kitchen.

"I'm so sorry that I didn't have time to talk to you earlier." Melonie extended her arm toward one of the tables, inviting Gus and his parents to sit down. "Once that ribbon was cut, the place took on a life of its own."

"We understand. It was wonderful." Gus' mother was the first to sit.

"The coffee is top notch." Gus' father sat down next to his wife. "I had a tasty éclair. I can see that I will have to include this as a stop on my morning walk."

"Thank you. Those were made by one of my intern bakers." Melonie sat down across from them. "I bet you didn't get your apple pie." Melonie turned to speak to Gus and found that he was kneeling on one knee in front of her.

"No. I didn't. But, I know one way you could make it right."

Melonie's heart started beating rapidly. She watched Gus open a small box as he moved it toward her. Her eyes looked down at the contents. It was a wire ring; made like the one A.J. had given her years ago. This one had a lavender ribbon entwined through it. Melonie's eyes pooled with tears. She looked up and saw that his eyes were glistening with emotion.

"How did you know? I didn't tell you what the ring looked like."

"I've been trying to figure out a way to tell you this, Melonie. I thought you might figure it out on your own. I thought you might eventually recognize me."

In an instant, Melonie's mind raced back twenty-five years. She saw a dark-haired little boy standing before her with the most beautiful blue eyes. The tears that were in her eyes rolled down her face, followed by new ones.

"You're A.J. How in the world did I not know that?"

"A. J. stands for August James. My friends started calling me Gus sometime in middle school after you moved away. It stuck." Gus took a deep breath before he continued. "We were young. We've changed a lot, at least on the outside. My heart would recognize you anywhere."

"I felt so comfortable with you from that very first moment we met again. There was something familiar about you—so much like home."

"You can ask her now, son." Gus' father smiled in encouragement.

"You both were five when Gus first proposed. You're thirty now," Gus' mother spoke. "I think your mother would approve."

In that very room, A.J. had proposed to her, and their mothers had told them to wait until they were thirty. Melonie could almost feel her mother's gaze upon her. After a quiet moment of reflection, Melonie returned her focus to Gus.

"I never answered you the first time, did I?" Melonie smiled. She felt a rush of emotion fill her.

"I hope I don't have to try a third time." Gus held out the wire ring to her. "This one is symbolic. There's a real one with a diamond in my pocket."

"When I gave the original to my mother, I didn't realize that it was the person who gave it to me who was the real prize."

Melonie held out her hand for Gus to slip on the wire ring with ribbon onto her finger.

After sealing the vow with a kiss, Melonie whispered in his ear. "Grandma planned all of this, didn't she?" Melonie leaned back and looked into his eyes.

"I believe she did. Right from that first pie."

DITCHED

IAN D. SMITH

*F*lying fast jets usually gave me an adrenaline boost from exhilaration, but I'd just discovered that an unexpected engine shutdown did, too. The near-silence was really striking after the usual constant background noise. I immediately did everything I'd been trained to do. No engine. Then did it again. Still no engine.

At low altitude and with decreasing airspeed, my aircraft would crash within a few seconds, and all I could do was choose roughly where. Being close to the coast of south-west England, I quickly decided the sea was a better option than the hills covered with small fields below me.

I hit the transmit button. "Mayday, mayday, rafair four two seven, engine failure, attempting forced landing in the sea, fifty twenty-one north, four twenty-seven west."

I followed a wooded river valley and was struck by the riot of fabulous autumn hues in the sunshine. I passed low over a small port town on my inexorable descent to the sea. I remembered seeing rows of houses, boats aground in the tidal river, a bridge, a car park, people looking up, a beach. And finally, the calm, empty sea, getting ever closer.

Ditching would probably be fatal but would damage my aircraft less than a crash landing. I was far too low for safety but knew I'd probably survive, even if injured. I pressed the "eject" button.

I woke up feeling confused, in a hazy, green world, filled with out-of-focus bubbles, my exposed skin felt cold, and my back really, really hurt. Then I remembered.

I surfaced under my parachute and struggled to get free of the lines and canopy, close to panic. Finally, I could unclip my face mask and take a deep breath of fresh air. My aircraft had sunk, but my life-raft had inflated itself. I splashed over, but couldn't climb in. My back was screaming at me to stay still. I could only hope my distress call had been received, and that help would be on its way. Surely someone in the town had guessed I was in trouble.

While everything was still fresh in my mind, I tried my best to remember exactly what I'd done and noticed before the engine failed. For that test flight, there were additional flight data recorders and video cameras in the cockpit, which should be recovered soon. I was confident the inquiry wouldn't conclude that I'd done anything dumb.

As I bobbed about, I saw the small Cornish coastal town I'd not crashed on, then spotted an orange inshore lifeboat bouncing across the waves towards me at an impressive speed. A small crew of volunteers from the Royal National Lifeboat Institution had dropped everything and run to their boathouse, hoping to rescue me rather than recover my body.

The crew were great. They pulled me aboard, clearly relieved that I wasn't badly injured. We were back in the port almost before I knew it, but the bumpy ride didn't help my back pain. They carefully helped me onto the slipway, where I sat, feeling weak and useless.

"Hey, doc, over here," one of the lifeboat men shouted.

A woman of about my own age hurried towards me, carrying a large medical bag. She was slim, wore black trousers and a white blouse under a waxed cotton jacket, and looked very anxious. She knelt beside me. "Any injuries?"

"My back's killing me." I tried to pull my flying helmet off, but she stopped me.

"You might have neck injuries."

"I don't care, it's making me feel trapped."

She looked annoyed. "Okay, I'll do it. Lie down." Two lifeboat men held my shoulders steady while she carefully eased the helmet off.

I immediately felt free, and far less stressed. I relaxed and closed my eyes. "Thank you."

I heard her ask the lifeboat crew if they had a spinal board and the sound of someone running.

"I heard you'd ejected, always a risk of spinal injuries." She had an upper-middle-class accent, like a character in an Agatha Christie production.

"I probably pulled over 12 G," I said. "I blacked out."

I opened my eyes to see the doctor scanning my face intently. And I noticed she was pretty, had lovely brown eyes, some freckles, and long ginger hair, pulled back in a ponytail. A few wisps had broken free, and I wanted to reach up and smooth them back. Hers was a face I knew I wouldn't forget and wanted to see again when I wasn't nearly crippled with pain.

She asked me to wiggle my toes and fingers, then to squeeze her fingers with mine, and flashed a small, bright torch in my eyes. "Nothing obvious, but you need to be in a hospital. A rescue helicopter will be here soon. Sorry, but I'd better not give you any pain relief until you've been assessed."

A couple of minutes later, I was strapped to a spinal board with blocks of foam immobilising my head. I felt stupid, but I knew the doctor was right. The pain was now taking over my mind like a grey fog.

She asked the lifeboat crew to cut off my lifejacket and one sleeve from my immersion suit. She checked my pulse and blood pressure. "You're fit," she murmured.

My inappropriate sense of humour took over. "Thanks. You're pretty, too."

She looked surprised, then blushed. "I meant your blood pressure and resting pulse are healthily low." Then her professionalism gave way to a shy smile, and she gave me a playful jab in the chest with one finger.

I decided I really liked her. Cheeky, bright and good-looking. I felt touched that she knelt beside me, one hand firmly on my arm in a comforting gesture. I wasn't so distracted by pain that I didn't notice she kept looking at me, her eyes meeting mine.

When we heard the unmistakable beating sound of a large helicopter approaching, she grinned at me. "They're taking you for a ride. Won't that be fun?"

"Yeah, like they're not going to rib me mercilessly?"

She leaned in close. "Shouldn't go around crashing planes, should you?" she whispered.

"Said they'd be here dreckly," the lifeboat crew Cox said. "On a training exercise."

The doctor looked puzzled. "Dreckly?"

"Directly," I said. "Cornish version of *mañana*, but without the same sense of urgency."

The Cox grinned. "Pegged you for up country," he said. "Local boy, eh?"

"From Truro."

He nodded, turned to his crew and waved a hand at the beach. "Come on, me *ansums*, clear a landing spot."

"Local vernacular," I told the doctor, who was looking puzzled again.

With the tide out, the nearby beach was the obvious choice. Despite the early October sunshine, it was too cold for most visitors, and the lifeboat crew only needed a minute to clear a suitable area. The huge red-and-white helicopter settled, a crewman hurried over, the doctor quickly briefed him, and he nodded. "We'll be at Derriford in no time."

I had to shout to be heard above the engine noise. "Doctor, thank you. I'm Paul Treleaven. I'll be back to thank everyone personally, but please let them know I really appreciate their help."

"Amy Hesketh," she said. "I'm at the local surgery if you want to say hello." She squeezed my hand briefly, then I was hoisted by four willing pairs of hands and carried over to the helicopter.

A minute later, I was strapped in, and we lifted up into the air. My adrenaline rush had worn off, and I felt weary and in pain. But remembering Amy's smile made life a bit better.

The next day, I perched cautiously on the edge of my hospital bed and watched my little misadventure on the local TV news. Everyone said I was a hero, which was a gross exaggeration and kind of embarrassing. There were some snatches of mobile phone video of my brief flight over the town. Seeing the splash, I made when I hit the sea hard explained my back pain.

The day before, I'd had blood samples taken, been assessed, scanned, interviewed by an air accident investigator, and finally prescribed some drugs. I was eventually told I'd be discharged the next day. The drugs worked a treat, but after a night of really weird dreams. I decided to be a big boy and cope without them.

One of my friends on the squadron, Jennifer, had set off ridiculously early to collect me and had thought to bring me some clothes. She'd gone to load the remains of my flight kit into her car, and I was waiting to be told I could leave.

"Good morning."

I almost jumped with surprise and turned my head too quickly, which caused a stab of pain. But it was a lovely surprise to see Amy beside the bed, smiling at me. She wore jeans and a waterproof jacket with droplets of water on it, and her hair framed her face beautifully. I'd feared I'd never meet her again.

"Hi, thank you so much for helping me yesterday," I said, holding out my hand.

She shook my hand and held on to it for a few seconds. "Thanks for not literally dropping in on my town," she said quietly.

"And I apologise if I embarrassed you. My sense of humour can get me into trouble."

She laughed. "I wanted to apologise for being abrupt with you. I was having an awful morning, which wasn't your fault." She sat down on the edge of the bed beside me. "Now we've got that out of the way, how are you? Be honest."

"My current choices are pain or strong but unpleasant drugs."

She nodded. "What've they told you?"

"All muscular injuries, probably from hitting the sea too hard. With physiotherapy and rest, I'll be back to normal in a few weeks. I was remarkably lucky."

She beamed and patted my forearm. "That's wonderful."

"It is. I'm being discharged today."

"What'll you do then?"

"One of my colleagues from the squadron's driving me back to Lincolnshire."

A look of disappointment flashed across her face, and I saw her swallow. "That's rather a long way from here."

"I'll take some leave to come back and buy you a drink to say thanks. I want to thank the lifeboat and air-sea rescue crews, too."

She flushed slightly. "Thank you, that'd be lovely." She pulled a slip of paper from her pocket and passed it to me. "My number and email."

I heard footsteps and loud conversation, then two people walked around the corner. My colleague Jennifer, leading the way, as usual, and the senior doctor treating me.

Amy let my hand go and stood up quickly as if she felt guilty.

Jennifer grinned. "Sorry, didn't know Paul had a visitor."

I gestured to Amy. "Flight Lieutenant Jennifer Stevens, Doctor Amy Hesketh. Amy was my first responder yesterday."

Jennifer shook Amy's hand vigorously. "Thank you so much. Paul can be a plonker. I mean, he just lost a bloody jet, but he's fun to have around. You're an emergency doctor?"

I really liked Jennifer. Well-built, full of life, sporty, and with a heart of gold, but she could easily be a bit overwhelming.

Amy wasn't fazed. "No, a GP. We were told a plane had crashed in the sea and the pilot ejected, so I was at the lifeboat station when they brought him in."

The doctor hovering in the background took the opportunity to give me my prescribed medication, letters for my own medical officer and various forms to sign. A minute later, I was discharged from his care.

I thanked him and managed to stand up without wincing. Jennifer led the way to the car park, while Amy walked beside me. I reckoned she was only a couple of inches shorter than me.

"Sorry, hope I didn't upset her," she said quietly.

I guessed she thought Jennifer was my girlfriend. "Not at all, Jennifer's a good friend and a sort of honorary sister."

Amy gave me a shy smile. "You absolutely sure you're okay?" she asked quietly. "I'd rather you didn't put a brave face on for me."

"I'm feeling really bloody uncomfortable, and it hurts if I move without thinking," I admitted. "But I'll get over it in time."

We emerged into a grey, drizzly day, and walked over to Jennifer's car, chosen primarily to carry people and kit to sporting events. Amy nodded. "You should be able to sit comfortably enough. Must be a long journey."

"Six hours," Jennifer said. "But I'll stop more often on the way back for Paul's benefit." She shook Amy's hand and went around to the driver's side.

Amy gave me a slightly wistful smile. "Take care."

"I will. And I'll keep in touch."

She reached out and squeezed my arm. "I'd like that." Then she opened the passenger door for me. As I passed her, she leaned in, quickly hugged me and kissed my cheek, then turned and hurried away.

I watched her for a couple of seconds, feeling pleasantly surprised, then climbed in, shut the door and put on the seat belt.

Jennifer started the car. "Well, what are we going to talk about on our drive?" She grinned as if she'd just had a great idea "How about you and that cute doctor fancying each other?"

"Me? I wouldn't be that lucky."

Jennifer snorted. "She thought you're cute, Paul. Why else would she blush when she kissed you? And you like her, too."

I did. I knew I'd never forget her, even if we never met again. If we didn't live on opposite sides of the country, I'd be very interested in seeing if we could have a relationship. "Yes, she's attractive, but we live a six-hour drive apart. Now, can we talk about something else than my non-existent love life?"

"What's more fun than teasing you? She's cute, bright, professional, posh accent. Perfect girl to impress the family. And nothing like that daft cow who ditched you."

She was right. I felt sure Dad and my brother's family would approve. Mum would have too if she'd lived long enough. "Would you woo someone so far away?"

She shrugged. "Maybe, if he dinged my bell. But since she's clearly off-limits, let's talk about yesterday, instead."

I sighed. It would be a long, long journey home.

Two weeks later, I was hunched in my jacket against cold breeze whistling across the medical surgery car park, but grateful the rain had stopped. We were having an autumn of highly changeable weather.

I'd explored the ancient town that morning, a lovely place which most definitely did not need a large, smoking hole in the middle of it. I also realised I'd almost flown over Amy's surgery on route to my impromptu sea dip.

I was there to take her out for the thank-you drink I'd promised. I was also doing my best not to feel first-date nerves. Despite exchanging friendly texts, emails and even a couple of phone conversations, I was trying not to start a 'what if' game. The confidence I had about every other aspect of my life completely failed me when it came to meeting women, and I was pretty hopeless at reading the signs. Amy's scrutiny of my face and eyes might have been something medical rather than finding me attractive.

But, as Jennifer had eloquently put it, I'd be a complete moron not to see if Amy fancied me, and that even I shouldn't find it hard to spend a few hours behaving like a sensible, well-balanced guy.

The door swung open. "Sorry," Amy said. "Always like to get everything sorted before I leave, saves awful panics in the morning." She fiddled with the alarm system in the lobby, then shut and locked the door.

"Still up for letting me treat you to a drink or two?" I asked.

"That would be lovely, thank you. How's your back?"

"Not perfect, but on the mend, thanks."

She nodded. "Perhaps my favourite pub? It's only a short walk." She looked around the car park. "Did you drive?"

"Parked at the guest house, a few minutes away. After all that driving, walking's a pleasure."

The real fire in the almost-empty pub was welcoming after the cold breeze. When she took her coat off, I saw that Amy was slim and long-limbed. She had an excellent complexion, her hair had been very nicely styled, and her clothing was good quality but understated. She wore little jewellery, only a necklace and two stud earrings, all gold. Her general style left me with the impression her family were comfortably off, but not ostentatious.

"Did you manage everything?" she asked. "It sounded like a rather hectic trip."

"Met the air-sea rescue team yesterday, the lifeboat crew this after-noon, and did a TV interview. A free day tomorrow, then a flying visit to my family down in Cornwall, and back for a few weeks of adminis-trative duties, exercise and physiotherapy."

"I'm sure your 'thank you' visits went down well."

I gestured at the menu folder on the table. "What's the food like here?"

"Not ideal for a healthy diet, but jolly tasty."

I slid the menu towards her. "My treat."

We talked easily for hours, starting to get to know each other. From the way our conversation flowed, I thought she was slowly lowering her guard as I opened up to her.

"Some of my patients tell me the strangest things," Amy said, conspiratorially. "I'm not a prude, but you wouldn't believe the intimate things they share. Some ask my advice about strange antics I'd never have thought one might find fulfilling."

I laughed. "Perhaps you could anonymously write a book about it?"

She pulled a face. "Certainly nothing for public consumption. I'd be too embarrassed if Mummy or Daddy found out, and they'd never let me live it down."

"What do your family do?"

"They manage a heritage attraction. Daddy's a retired diplomat, serves part-time on all sorts of committees, too."

I wondered about her accent. "Were you privately educated?"

"Daddy was posted abroad until I was in my teens, so I attended boarding schools. One of his job perks. When he retired, I attended the local school for four years." She glanced down at her glass, then looked up at me. "Your family?"

I felt she'd not told me something and wondered why. "My dad's a consulting engineer, and my brother's a software geek. His wife works for the county council. Their second child is due around Christmas."

"Your mother?"

"Breast cancer, nearly ten years ago."

She reached out and put her hand on my arm. "I'm so sorry," she said softly.

"Thanks. Dad remarried a couple of years ago, lovely woman."

I felt comfortable enough with her to be open about things I'd normally kept to myself, like my anxiety about not being passed fit to fly fast jets again. "It's physically very demanding, especially the tight turns at speed. I know I'll have to step down in a few years, one way or another, but I'd rather do it when I feel ready."

"I remember noting you were in good physical health," Amy said, with a wry smile. "Any reason you were so anxious to take your flying helmet off?"

"I'd was trapped under my parachute. It's something I've had a few nightmares about."

She looked shocked and put a hand on my arm. "How did you cope without panicking?"

"I nearly did, but I wasn't keen on dying." I shifted in my seat again, trying to find a more comfortable position.

"You've been moving around quite a lot, your back's giving you trouble, isn't it?"

"It is, but I spent a lot of time in my car yesterday. I find it helps if I keep moving. Any chance you can recommend a nice local walk I could do tomorrow?"

"I do, as it happens." She pursed her lips for a second. "It's my day off if you'd like some company."

I felt elated. "That would be great, thank you." I glanced at my watch. "It's getting on, I'm sure you've had a busy day, and I've taken up your whole evening. Can I see you home?"

I was treated to another lovely smile. "That would be lovely."

For the first time in years, I saw a lady home and was treated to a gentle kiss on the lips.

I almost forgot my aching back as I walked back to the guest house.

The next morning, I rang Amy's doorbell at the agreed time. I'd loitered for a while, arriving early because I was nervous. I'd really enjoyed our evening together and could all-too-easily fall for her. Perhaps today I might find out if she already had somebody special in her life.

Amy stepped out of her front door. "I've just seen your interview on the local TV. You came across rather well."

"Thanks. I appreciated the chance to publicly thank everyone and apologise if anyone felt scared."

Amy grinned. "You've been quite the conversation topic. It's 'hashtag ditched' on social media if you're curious."

We crossed the old stone bridge over the river, worked our way through the main car park, then dove into a nature reserve beside a subsidiary river. We walked side-by-side where the path was wide enough and chatted happily. The reserve was part of the woodland I'd noticed two weeks earlier, but this time I had time to really enjoy the view, admire the colours and get a few camera photos.

Amy asked why I'd chosen my career.

"I flew in a glider in my early teens and fell in love with it. I was lucky enough to be sponsored through university by the RAF. I love everything I do, but flying is the most amazing feeling."

She shuddered slightly. "I've always been one of hundreds of people crammed in together. We had bad turbulence on my first flight as a child, which scared me. Rather spoiled things, I suppose."

I wondered if I could arrange to take her up in a light aircraft some-time but changed the subject. "How did you end up being a GP here?"

The evenings are drawing in, and we don't want to be on the coastal path after dark. It'd be nice to amble and enjoy the views."

As we followed the path up a steep hill, Amy stopped to catch her breath. "I'm not as fit as you."

"Want a tow?"

She grinned and held her hand out. I took it, and we set off again, hand-in-hand. From time to time, we had to walk in line when the path narrowed, but she always took my hand when she could. After an hour or so, we stopped to sit on a wooden bench and enjoy the view and the antics of seabirds. She snuggled against me, I put an arm around her, and she looked up at me. I knew she wanted a kiss as much as I did. I turned towards her, and our lips met. It was slow and gentle at first as if we had all the time in the world. Then she turned towards me a little more, put a hand on my cheek, and our kiss became a lot deeper and more passionate.

"Thank you," I said when we had finished.

"Don't blame me, you started it."

"Should I apologise?"

"Only if you don't plan to do it again."

"Hmm, don't encourage me. It would be an easy habit to get into."

She rested her forehead against my chest and sighed. "Pity we live so far apart."

"That bugs me, too."

She looked up. "Any plans for an evening meal?"

I shrugged. "Happy to treat you anywhere you fancy."

"Are you willing to risk my culinary skills? I'm an ace with supermarket ready meals."

Amy may have told me the truth, but we had a delicious meal with locally-caught fresh fish. After we'd eaten, I insisted on helping with the washing-up, then we shared a bottle of wine as we cuddled and kissed on the sofa like two teenagers.

Tempted as I was to push my luck, I'd be off the next day and didn't want to leave her wondering if I'd turn up again. "I don't want things to go too fast," I murmured. "I'll definitely be back to see you again as soon as I can."

"Thank you," she murmured. "I know exactly what you mean, and I appreciate your thoughtfulness." She gave me a lovely smile, and we kissed a lot more, then just snuggled together. I held her while she dozed off in my arms.

After twenty minutes or so, she woke with a start. "I'm so sorry," she said. "Unspeakably rude of me."

"Showing you trust me isn't being rude." I stood. "You're clearly tired, so I'll leave you in peace."

She stood and leaned her head against my shoulder. "I'm so glad we met, even if under rather alarming circumstances. And it was lovely getting to know you a bit better."

"I'm glad too. I'd love to stay longer, but my family are really anxious to see me." I hugged her. "I'll be back to see you as soon as I can."

She smiled and kissed me gently. "Thank you, I'd love that, too."

"The surgery's just closed, Doctor Hesketh's taking a phone call," the receptionist told me. "She won't be long." She pulled on a warm jacket and smiled at me as she left.

We'd not seen each other for almost a month. I'd had a stint as duty officer, she'd worked one weekend, and had a few days away. I'd worried that our developing relationship had lost momentum, but Jennifer had given me another pep talk. "She's like you, an open book, what you see is what you get. Just relax and be yourself. You did okay last time, didn't you?"

I couldn't deny it and had felt encouraged by Amy's consistently open warmth and her insistence I use her spare room rather than book into a guest house for this visit.

Tired and stiff after my long car journey, I wandered around the waiting room, browsing the posters, notices and information leaflets. I looked up when the door swung open, and a man walked in. He was about my height and age, slim, with long, swept-back hair and a neatly trimmed beard. He wore an expensive-looking suit and good-quality leather shoes. He looked around as if there was a bad smell in the room, gave me an imperious glare, then strode confidently over to the door labelled 'consulting room' and pushed it open.

I heard Amy's voice. "Justin? What on Earth are you doing here?"

"We need to talk."

"I'm on the phone."

I was halfway across the waiting room when I heard a phone handset being slammed into the receiver. "We need to talk now," Justin said. "It's important."

"We've nothing to talk about." Amy sounded calm. "I thought I'd made that abundantly clear."

"You won't return my calls or emails, so this is my only option."

"I told you I don't want anything to do with you. Just go away."

When I reached the door, Amy was on her feet, pale and angry, facing Justin, who was clearly tense and on edge.

"I've had a fantastic offer," he said. "A top cosmetic place in Los Angeles. There are lots of opportunities for general practitioners. I want you to come with me."

"Why would I do anything so ludicrous?"

"We'd make a fortune in no time, and then set up our own place, a combined health spa and cosmetic clinic. I've planned it all."

"You're deluded to think I'd even consider it."

He stepped forward and took one of her arms. "With my reputation and your title, we'll be turning people away."

Amy tried to pull free from his grip. "I said no. Just go away." She glanced at me, and I saw fear flash across her face.

"Let go of her, please," I said, calmly and clearly.

Justin turned his head and sneered at me. "This is a private conversation."

"The doctor asked you to leave," I said, more forcefully.

She tugged harder and managed to pull her arm from his hand. She stepped back from him. "Justin, leave me alone. Now."

"Not until I've talked sense into you."

"You cheated on me and left me feeling utterly betrayed," she said. "You really think I'm going to trust you?"

Justin stepped towards Amy, and I moved closer to him.

"She's asked you to leave," I said.

Justin whirled towards me and threw a wild swing at my head. I saw it coming a mile

off, so stepped back to avoid the blow.

He advanced towards me, his fists raised like a boxer. From my martial arts training, I saw he had no idea about footwork and balance. I backed into the waiting room, drawing him out of Amy's office.

He tried a couple of jabs, which I easily blocked. "What's it to you?" he sneered. "Fancy your chances with her?"

"That's up to her." I kept as calm and relaxed as I could.

He tried to rush me, but I stepped aside and swept one of his feet from under him. He went down heavily, scattering plastic chairs as he sprawled.

"You're in trouble now," he shouted. "You assaulted me."

I pointed at the CCTV camera high on the wall. "Let's see what the police say when they see the recording."

He visibly deflated. He knew I'd acted in self-defence. He got to his feet. "Amy, last chance. Stay in this dump of a town, doling pills out to fat yokels, or have a fantastic life with me."

"I meant it when I ditched you, Justin. I want nothing to do with you ever again. You're a liar, a cheat and totally unscrupulous. Just go away." She turned and walked back into her office.

Justin looked at me and opened his mouth as if to speak.

I held up a hand. "You blew it, Justin. Go away."

He stormed out. I heard a car engine over-revving and tyres squealing as he left the car park. I hugged Amy until she stopped sobbing, then gave her tissues to dry her tears with.

"I can't believe it," she sniffed. "All those appeals to give him another chance, all because he wanted me to attract patients to his clinic."

"He said something about a title."

She looked embarrassed and flushed slightly. "My full name is Lady Samantha Amelia Hesketh-Seddon," she said quietly. "Daddy's a viscount, he inherited the title and a large estate from an uncle he hardly knew. That's why he took early retirement from the Diplomatic Service."

I tried not to look surprised. "I can see why he thought you'd be an asset to his ambitions."

"It came as a complete shock. The estate was running at a loss, and the bequest didn't make us rich by any stretch of the imagination. My parents worked hard and managed to turn the estate around financially. They've made the old house into a popular heritage attraction." She sighed. "Attending the local school wasn't easy, as some of the other pupils were really beastly. Not only did I have red hair, and a private school posh accent, I had a title."

She ran her hands through her hair. "I don't want to be thought of as a viscount's daughter and heir to some historic house and estate. I want to carry on being plain old me for as long as possible."

I stood and offered her my hand. "Doctor Amy Hesketh, may I take plain old you to the pub and ply you with alcoholic drinks until you feel better?"

She smiled. "I rather think I should treat you. It's only polite for a damsel in distress to thank the knight in shining armour who helps her."

An hour later, Amy had recovered her composure. She went into a reverie for a couple of minutes, slowly running her finger around the rim of her wine glass. "So, the title thing?" she murmured.

"It's certainly got a ring to it, but you'll always be Amy to me." The woman who had hurried to help me a few weeks before and stolen my breath away with my first glance.

She looked up at me, and I saw anxiety in her eyes. "You realise that I'll feel obliged to take over the estate when it gets too much for Mummy and Daddy? Along with a terrifying learning curve, huge responsibilities, endless bills, and headaches about business plans?"

"From what I've seen of you, I know you'll step up and do your absolute best, and that will probably be pretty damn good." I knew I wanted to be with her when that time came, but it was far too early to say so now.

She gave me a shy smile. "Not quite the evening I'd planned."

"Oh?"

She looked sheepish. "Some crazy idea about a nice romantic meal."

"Sounds lovely. Why don't we start our evening now?"

"No reason why not. Drink up."

A few hours later, we cuddled in her bed, talking quietly and swapping kisses. Amy's skin felt warm and soft against mine.

"I've a shocking temper," she said.

I shrugged. "I'll remember not to annoy you."

"When you see Mummy and Daddy's house, don't be impressed. It's a hand-me-down."

"But someday, it'll all be yours."

She giggled. "There's something else."

"Oh?"

"I can be awfully impulsive."

"Should I be alarmed?"

"Well..." she paused. "It was meant to be a nice surprise for this weekend. I've been offered a new job, starting in February, after my current contract ends."

I wondered how far apart we'd be then. "Congratulations. Anywhere nice?"

She snuggled up closer. "About twenty miles from where you live," she whispered. "And less than two hours' drive from my parents."

I turned towards her. "That's Olympic-standard impulsiveness."

"It's initially for twelve months."

I grinned. "Fantastic news." I had at least a year to win her heart. I'd give it my best shot.

My mind wandered to a possible future where Amy had agreed to marry me, and I wondered if we could talk Jennifer into being our bridesmaid. Knowing her, she'd want to act as my best man, just to be contrary. She hated feminine clothing, and only wore a skirt or dress when it was obligatory. Then I had a thought. "How did you find out about the job?"

"Oh, um, your chum Jennifer. She rang to say thanks and let me know how you were getting on. We've kept in touch. She's really sweet, isn't she?"

"Not a word I'd use in her hearing, but she's a really special friend." Bridesmaid, I decided. In an outrageously feminine outfit.

4

THE SWEET SCENT OF HOME

ANN SWANN

*T*he autumn leaves crunched underfoot as my Irish setter, Bordeaux, dashed down the crooked path ahead of me. The cool, sweet-scented air caressed my face and the back of my neck. I flipped my blonde ponytail up with one hand and reveled in the feel of my favorite season.

I'd arrived home from Ithaca—where I'd been working and attending college with my now-ex fiancé—just in time to help my parents decorate their bookshop, *Through the Pages*, for Halloween. I'd been gone four years and had only a few classes under my belt to show for it. This was not how I'd imagined my return, single and without even a degree for my efforts.

Bordie and I continued slowly down the path.

At the bookshop last night, my parents and I had decorated the large bay window with colorful fall leaves, rubber bats, and tissue ghosts. I also floated bits of cotton webbing in the corners for the plastic spiders. Dad contributed a large jack o' lantern lit by a small battery-operated light.

We'd completed the scene with some of our favorite scary books like *The Complete Works of Edgar Allan Poe*, Stephen King's *The Shining*, and Ray Bradbury's *Something Wicked this Way Comes*. When it was done, I'd pulled the dark curtains closed behind the display. That really made the spooky elements pop.

To their credit, my parents hadn't quizzed me too closely on what had gone wrong at school, or with Mitch. When I'd told them the wedding was off, Mom had simply hugged me, and Dad had patted my back. Then he'd said, "Rebel, I wish we had a small bale of hay for this display. Charlie always got us one. Really gave it an autumn feel."

Mom had added. "Charlie really loved this time of year." She'd given me another hug. "Remember that most of the shops on the square will stay open late tomorrow night so the kids can trick-or-treat."

"I can't wait," I'd replied. Halloween and Christmas had been two of my favorite times growing up in tiny Silo Springs.

"Don't forget the dance on the square afterward," Dad reminded.

I'd rolled my eyes. When I was a teen, those dances had seemed pretty lame. I doubted they had changed much over the last few years.

"Hey," Mom said. "Your dad and I have our costumes. Do you have anything?"

I thought about the closet in my old room. "Maybe I still have my witch's hat," I told her. "And I can pick up some green face paint at the drugstore."

Dad had laughed. "That sounds perfect. I'm going as The Mummy—"

"And I'll be a Gypsy fortune teller." Mom's eyes lit up. She and Dad had always been more like playmates for my brother Charlie and me. We had even jokingly called ourselves the four Musketeers.

As it turned out, that might not have been such a good thing. In one of our worst arguments, Mitch had called me a daddy's girl. Said I was too used to getting my own way. That my parents had spoiled me.

I blinked back a tear and tried to put Mitch's face out of my mind. That remark had scalded me. How could he take my precious relationship with my dad and try to turn it into something hurtful? Especially since I was the one working my tail off, taking a single night class here and there, killing myself so he could get all his basics and go on to law school after we married.

What an idiot I'd been.

With some effort, I pulled my thoughts back to the present.

I'd always loved this lane that paralleled the Oliver Apple Orchards. They were a small commercial grower owned by our neighbor Jinx Oliver and his son, Shane.

Shane Oliver. My brother's best friend, my first crush. I'd thought for a while that he had an interest in me, too, even though I was a couple years younger, but after everything that happened, it seemed it wasn't meant to be.

I inhaled deeply. In addition to row upon row of mature apple trees marching away in the distance, an ancient hand-hewn fence meandered along beside me like a guide to my past. The amazing fragrance of the orchard permeated the air. It made running even more pleasurable. It also smelled like my brother's cologne. I always wondered if he wore that particular scent because it reminded him of all the days he'd spent working and playing here with his best friend.

Bordie and I jogged on through the still morning air. Just like the old days, she tugged on her leash until I unclipped it and let her go. In moments, all I could see was the red frond of her tail disappearing into the tall roadside grass. It was sort of amazing how easily we'd fallen right back into our old routine.

Then Bordie did something completely out of character. She waited on me to catch up before darting through a gate I hadn't thought of since Charlie died. It was the gate he and Shane had used when they wanted a shortcut through the orchard or a quick way to ditch a pesky little sister.

After Charlie's death six years earlier, the gate had fallen into disrepair. In no time at all mother nature had hidden it with brush. Now it was clear and standing wide open again.

Suddenly, Bordeaux let out a string of short barks. A squirrel, I thought, hurrying to catch up. "Hey, Bordie. Come on, girl. Leave the wildlife alo—"

"Hello, beautiful," a voice said. "Where have you been hiding?"

I recognized that voice immediately. It belonged to Shane Oliver.

As I made my way through the gate, I saw him lean over and grasp my dog's head firmly between his palms.

Bordie's eyes never left his. I couldn't remember the last time I'd seen such a look of adoration on her face.

"Wildlife, huh?" He spoke toward me without taking his eyes off Bordeaux.

I was relieved to hear a smile in his voice. The last actual conversation I'd had with Shane had been at Charlie's funeral. And even though he seemed to think I blamed him for my brother's death, nothing could be further from the truth.

I'd told my parents long ago that they had obviously mixed up their children. Charlie should have been named Rebel, not me. There was nothing that boy wouldn't do, including Spring Break cliff diving.

"I should have stopped him, Rebbie," Shane had whispered in my ear at the funeral. "I knew it was a bad idea."

I'd wanted to tell him how he couldn't have stopped Charlie if he'd tried, but I couldn't say anything. My voice had been so clogged with emotion I hadn't been able to make a sound.

I think he mistook my silence for condemnation. At age sixteen, I'd been too young to understand that. It was nearly two years later that I got up the nerve to talk to someone about it. To tell someone how much I missed my brother and how much I missed our shared childhood friend.

Unfortunately, the someone I finally told had been Mitch, the boy who had been the assistant counselor at our senior-year leadership camp.

He hadn't been very sympathetic to my emotional trauma. Of course, being from the city, and an only child, he hadn't known my brother and our special bond.

At first, I'd thought he was a cold fish, but over the course of that summer camp, he'd somehow convinced me he was right, that I needed to grow up and leave the past behind. Now I realize I should have trusted my first instincts.

"I saw you in town last night." Shane straightened as he spoke. "In the window at the bookstore."

I laughed. I'd forgotten how tall he was, how deep-set his dark eyes. "We had fun decorating for Halloween."

Shane stuck his thumbs in his belt loops. "It's good to see you girls. What brings you home after all this time?"

I was saved from answering when my silly dog ran to his pickup and stood barking beside the cab.

Shane grinned crookedly. "Looks like someone is tired of jogging. Can I give you two a lift?"

Bordie sat by the truck as if I'd given her the order to stay. "Tell me the truth, have you been squiring my dog around town while I've been gone?"

In answer, he strode over, opened the door, picked the setter up, and lifted her into the seat.

I looked at him for an explanation.

He just shrugged. "She's getting up in years. Jumping is probably hard on those old joints."

My throat closed up. Once again, I couldn't make a sound. To think that this sweet, gentle man had cleared the brush from the gate so Bordie could come and go between our properties, and then to see how he lifted her into the truck because she was getting old... it boggled my mind.

Kindness like that had been sorely missing from my life the last few years.

I climbed in the passenger seat with a sudden inspiration. "Hey, would you guys happen to have a bit of hay we could use? My pop thinks we need it for our window display. You know, the way Charlie used to—"

"Sure," Shane started the engine. "Charlie always got a bale from the barn."

The apple barn. I remembered how sweet it smelled inside, not only due to the stored apples but also because of the ancient cider press that took up one entire corner. I also recalled how Shane and Charlie hid there for two days when Shane's mom and dad split up. He had been devastated when she moved back to the city.

"My dad should be at the barn by now," he said. "I think he's making cider for the dance tonight. We use the small bales of hay to decorate the cider booth you know."

I pictured Jinx Oliver in my mind. "How's he doing?"

"Dad's good." He smiled at Bordie sitting in the middle of the bench seat between us. Her tongue hung out one side of her mouth, and she appeared to be grinning.

Shane stuck his left elbow out the window. "It sure is good to see you, Rebel May Jerretson. It surely is."

I let my gaze travel to his square-jawed profile. How many times had I dreamed of that face when I was a girl? In my mind, he'd always been Mr. Perfect.

We started down a barely visible road alongside the first orchard. The trees in this grove were ready for harvesting. "This road still leads to the house," Shane said. "But I guess you know that."

"Haha. Very funny." I laughed. "Every time I tried to tag along, you and Charlie would chase me away so that you could go off exploring by yourselves."

He ducked his head, but not before I saw the shadow of a smile cross his face. "I didn't really want to chase you away, you know. That was all Charlie."

I studied him to see if he was serious, but he continued talking.

"Back then, it was Charlie and me against the world."

"I know." My voice came out soft. "Sometimes I envied your friendship with my big brother." I wanted to say more, but it didn't seem like the right time.

But Shane seemed ready to talk. "Remember that summer Dad made me visit my mother in the city?" He looked away. "It was Charlie who helped me deal with it." I saw his jaw muscles clench. "I didn't want anything to do with her and her new family."

"No," I said. "I didn't know about that."

Although we'd been friendly, we'd never been close the way he was with Charlie. Shane would teasingly call me Shortstuff and twitch the end of my ponytail every chance he got. I would melt and write his name on my notebooks in fancy script.

Charlie was a little more callus. When we were at home, he would say, "Hey Reb, I'm going downtown with your *boyfriend*... anything you want me to tell him?"

I would usually slug him and run off. But that was a long time ago, just kid stuff. Of course, I'd always hoped he would be my boyfriend someday, and as we grew I began to feel that he might, but then came that fateful Spring Break when the two of them went down to Mexico and Charlie came home in a hearse.

That was the end of our friendship. Shane had closed up and didn't come around anymore. By the time I graduated, he'd already gone away to college.

"We were drinking that day." His voice came out of the blue, almost as if he'd read my mind.

"I know..."

He swallowed hard, gripped the steering wheel even harder. "I just needed to tell you." We stopped in front of the barn. "I've had a long time to think about what happened," he continued. "To think about what we did."

I reached around Bordie and laid my palm on Shane's arm. "Charlie always did what he wanted. You couldn't have stopped him any more than you could stop the sun from rising."

Shane let go the steering wheel and grasped my fingers. "You don't understand, Rebel." He looked into my eyes. His were coffee brown, the irises ringed with black. If we'd lived a century earlier, he would've made a good bandit. One of those people wrote songs about.

"What?" I asked gently. "What is it I don't understand?"

He squeezed my fingers tighter. "I feel responsible. I always have."

"But you shouldn't—"

He closed his eyes. "It should have been me. I should've gone first, but I got to the edge of the cliff and hesitated. I'd had so many beers. So much tequila. My stomach was churning—"

"Shane—"

"Charlie pushed me aside," he blurted. "I still see him in my dreams. That smart-aleck smirk. The way he said, 'step aside bro, let me show you how it's done.'"

Bordie whined and placed a paw on his knee.

"Shane, you don't have to say this." A warm tear plopped onto my arm. I wiped it away without looking up. "No one blames you, least of all me. I was mad at Charlie. Furious with him for taking such a gamble. For drinking, for being so careless."

As if on cue, Bordie jumped down into the floorboard.

Shane drew me over into her warm vacated space.

All I once I found myself in the arms of the boy I'd once dreamed about, a boy who had become a man with a broken heart.

"Seeing you brings him back." He twitched the end of my ponytail. "You and your brother could have been twins." He touched my hair, my face, the corner of my mouth. "He was as much my brother as he was yours. At least I felt it was so..."

I smiled. "That would make me your sister."

He smiled, too. "Would I do this, if I thought of you as my sister?" He tilted my chin up and pressed his lips to mine.

It was a sweet kiss full of longing. Maybe it was only longing for the past, for the old days when Charlie was still here when we had "our" brother. Or maybe it was longing for something else entirely.

Bordie thrust her head between us as if to see what was going on.

"I'm sorry," Shane said. "I shouldn't have—"

"No, no, it's all right. I just—" Bordie smashed her muzzle into my cheek. "Bordie, stop!" I laughed.

She whined softly.

"Good grief, girl, what's gotten into you?"

"Look." Shane gazed out my window. "That's what she's trying to tell us."

Just inside the open barn door stood a tall man in an Oliver Orchards cap.

"Bordie must not recognize him," I said. "He's kind of in the shadows."

"Yeah," Shane said. "Or maybe she does." He chuckled under his breath as he opened the truck door.

"Maybe," I said. "We did often see him when we jogged by. But that's been a few years."

Shane stepped out and helped Bordie out, too. "Maybe not as long as you think."

As I opened the passenger door, I saw Mr. Oliver lean down in an

THE SWEET SCENT OF HOME | 73

eerie imitation of his son and grasp Bordie's face between his hands. "Why, Bordeaux, you good dog, what are doing with this lot?" He glanced up and caught my eye. I got the distinct impression he and my dog were fast friends.

"She comes across the pasture to visit me every now and then. Been doing it for a while now." He straightened and held his hand out. "Guess old dogs get lonely, too."

I tried not to let my astonishment show as I moved forward to take his outstretched hand. "Nice to see you, Mr. Oliver. I'm glad you're keeping an eye on her for me."

He chuckled. "Oh, it's the other way around. And it's not just me." He tilted his head toward Shane. "She keeps an eye on the both of us, isn't that right, son?"

The younger man looked away as if caught in a fib. "Yes, sir. That she does."

I recalled how the brush had been cleared from the gate. "Well, how about that? My dog has more of a social life than I do."

"It's good to see you home, Rebel." Mr. Oliver's voice was kind. "I hope you're here to stay."

"Thank you. It's good to be back."

Shane smiled, and I couldn't help noticing how one corner of his mouth turned up way more than the other. I couldn't stop thinking about how those lips had felt on mine. When I looked up, his dad was smiling, too.

"Guess I'd better get back to the house," I said. "I don't want Mom to worry. I only got home yesterday."

"I'll get that hay." Shane disappeared into the barn.

I'd already forgotten about the hay.

Mr. Oliver gave my dog one last pat. "You know after Shane finished his business degree, I gave him the reins to the orchards."

"No, sir. I didn't know. We've been completely out of touch since Charlie." I bit my lip and kept my eye on the darkened part of the barn in case Shane reappeared. "I can't believe he still blames himself. We all know it was just a tragic accident."

The tall man nodded. "I've tried to tell him that very thing, but Shane hangs onto his feelings. He still blames himself for his mother's departure all those years ago."

Wow. I guess if Mr. Perfect had a flaw, it was his inability to let things go. It gave me a whole new perspective on him. I just hoped that kiss hadn't been fueled by his inability to move on from our shared past. I couldn't stand the idea that it might have been based on guilt or regret.

Mr. Oliver seemed to notice my silence. "You okay, Rebel?" The concern in his voice was real. It made me wonder why such a kind, successful man had never remarried. Maybe he wasn't the only Oliver who had trouble letting things go.

I nodded. "It's just... being home, you know."

From the open doorway, the smell of hay mingled with the smell of apples.

Mr. Oliver said something I barely caught, "... home to stay, then? Like my Shane?"

I studied the ground. "I want to, but I need to finish my degree. I'm just not certain yet."

He cocked his head to one side. "So, the wedding is off?"

That got my attention. "You heard?"

"Small town."

A slight noise made me look up.

Shane stood behind his father. He held a miniature bale of hay. "This what you need?" His movements had stirred up a million dust motes. They danced in the golden rays slanting down through the barn slats.

I nodded, wondering what would happen if I did move back home. All my life I'd planned on being an elementary school teacher.

Shane shouldered the small bale. "I'll toss it in the truck."

I didn't meet his eye. I'd already been misled by one man—for four years—I couldn't let myself get sidetracked by another. No matter how sweet or spontaneous that kiss had been.

We bid goodbye to Mr. Oliver, and Shane helped Bordeaux into the seat like before. "I heard that part about the wedding." He started the engine.

I inhaled, not sure how much I should share. "Yeah. It's over."

"What happened?"

"It's kind of a long story."

He glanced at me across the top of Bordie's head. "I've got time."

Throwing caution to the wind, I plunged ahead. "I spent all my time working, only taking a class here and there while Mitch took a full course load." I realized that sounded selfish. "Don't get me wrong, that should've been fine. I didn't mind working while he got his basics out of the way. In fact, we'd had an agreement. First him, then me." I took another little breath.

"But when I went to register for my full course load after he graduated, Mitch said it still wasn't time. That it would cut into my work schedule." Unexpected anger burned within me as I told my story. "That's when I found out his wealthy parents had been offering to help all along." I clamped my lips together, but the words wouldn't be contained. "If he'd accepted their generosity, we would both have our degrees now."

Shane must've heard the change in my voice. "I don't understand. Why wouldn't he let them help so you could both go full time?"

I shrugged and wiped my eyes. "A matter of pride, he said. A way to control me, I say." I remembered the look in his eye when I told him we were through. "You can't leave me," he'd said. "You're nothing without me."

"Yet you were paying all the bills..."

"Yes, I was. But when I brought that to his attention, he called me a spoiled daddy's girl. Said I shouldn't mind putting my education on hold for the good of our relationship. Especially since I was only going to be a teacher and make a third of what he would make as an attorney."

Shane stopped the truck. "That's the stupidest thing I've ever heard. It sounds like he's way too full of himself—"

I couldn't argue with that.

"I felt used." I gritted my teeth. "I wasted four years already."

I glanced out the open passenger window in an effort to calm down. The tall yellow grasses swayed gently. Somewhere a cricket chirped.

"Give me five minutes," Shane growled. "Just five minutes alone with that guy. I'll show him how a real man is supposed to—"

I laughed in spite of myself. "Tough guy, huh?"

He flexed his bicep. "Ugh. Me Tarzan, you Jane."

"Oh, Shane... Tarzan? Just how old are you anyhow?"

He grinned and glanced at my dog. "Bordie and I watch old movies with Dad and Granddad almost every night." He tapped the steering wheel with his thumbs. "Granddad moved in a few months ago... after Grams lost her battle with Alzheimer's."

"That's awful. I can't believe you've been going through so much and here I am complaining about a selfish twit who shouldn't even be—"

"It's okay." He shook his head. "Bordie comes over each night. She's our therapy dog."

He smoothed the soft fur on top of her flat head. "She only stays long enough to get her supper handout, then she's off again." His hand traced her graying muzzle. "We all save a scrap or two off our dinner plates. It's become something of a ritual. I don't know where we'd be without her."

My sweet dog closed her eyes as Shane continued to pet her.

This news left me speechless. The fact that Mr. Perfect would come right out and admit that he'd been staying home every night, confiding in my old dog, taking care of her and looking after his father and his elderly grandfather... it made me look at him in a brand-new light. It wasn't that he had trouble letting go of the past; apparently, he simply knew how to step up and take care of the present.

"Hey," he said. "Even to myself, I sound like an old fogey." He shoved his cap back until a spiky tuft of dark hair peeked out. "Let's change that," he said. "The Halloween dance is tonight. Should we go?"

"Wait," I teased. "I thought you said you *didn't* want to sound like an old fogey."

"You've been away too long, Rebel. Have you forgotten mulled apple cider and waltzing on the courthouse lawn?"

I didn't know whether he was teasing or not. "Actually, I've never waltzed on the courthouse lawn. Never even been to one of those 'on the square' dances. I really did think they were for old fogies." I smiled to take the sting out. "Besides, I'm helping Mom and Dad with the trick-or-treaters at the shop, remember?"

"Oh, that's right! I saw you in the window." He grinned, then jerked his thumb over his shoulder. "Also, why I'm bringing the hay." He shifted into drive and headed back toward town. "Good thing the dance continues even after the shops close."

I laughed out loud. "In that case... I guess we should go. But I warn you; I haven't been dancing since the junior prom."

"I'll wear my boots. I won't even know when you step on my toes."

I felt a tiny flicker of excitement flare inside me. First the kiss, and now this. How long had it been since I'd felt excitement instead of resentment?

At my parents' shop, Mom hugged him and patted his back. "My goodness, we have missed you."

Shane removed his cap. "Ever since I took over the day-to-day at the orchards, I've discovered sun ups and sun downs and a whole lot of work in between."

Mom clucked her tongue. "Well, just don't work yourself into an old man before your time."

"No, ma'am, I won't. I hope you know I think of you guys every time I pass the shop on my way through town." Then he glanced toward me. "I sure am glad Mr. Jerretson sent Rebel for that hay."

Bordie barked, and I trailed my fingers through her wavy fur. Could Dad have had an ulterior motive when he'd mentioned Charlie and the hay?

I didn't have time to ask. Just then my father stepped in from the stock room and grabbed the younger man in a bear hug. "Shane! Where've you been keeping yourself?"

Shane leaned in and seemed content not to let go.

Dad pulled him even closer, hugged him hard, then stepped back.

"You were like a second son to us," Dad said. Something clicked in his throat, and he stopped talking and bent down to pick up the hay. "Let's go find a place for this."

From the corner of my eye, I caught a glimpse of a shadow moving over the books. I glanced at Mom to see if she'd noticed, but she was too busy patting away the moisture from her eyes.

Dad placed the hay at the back of the display and sat the jack o' lantern on top. Then he stacked the books in front of it.

"I'll go outside and see how it looks."

Shane followed me. "I've got to get back to the orchard, but I'll see you tonight." He scuffed the sole of his boot on the curb. "Rebbie..."

"Yes?"

He stopped his foot and shoved his hands down in his back pockets. I noticed how soft and worn his jeans were. When he stood like that, he looked just like the high school boy I had deemed Mr. Perfect.

"What is it, Shane? You already having second thoughts?"

He shook his head. "I just wanted you to know how much I missed you." He looked back at the shop as he spoke as if something had drawn his attention to the window.

I felt it, too, someone watching from the shop. It was probably only Dad, trying to get the display just right.

"I missed you, too," I murmured. "But to be honest... I never in a million years thought you would be thinking of me."

His eyes met mine.

Red and yellow leaves tumbled down the sidewalk ahead of an autumn breeze.

"I'd like to start over," Shane said. "Tonight. I don't want you to think of me as your brother's old friend anymore."

"Can *you* think of me as a person separate from Charlie?" I asked. "I mean, not just as Charlie's little sister?"

He rubbed the back of his neck. "I can't believe you didn't know this, but I'll tell you anyhow... I haven't thought of you as anyone's little sister in a long time. Not even before we lost your brother."

From the corner of my eye, I saw the dark drape behind the window display give a little twitch.

"Look." I nodded toward the display. "The hay made all the difference."

"It's perfect. Glad I could help."

I was about to say, "Perfect is right," but then I caught the reflection of a black Dodge Charger in the plate glass. The sight gave me a moment's pause. Mitch's parents had given him one just like it for graduation.

Nah, I thought. There must be a million black Chargers around. He wouldn't come here. I'd made my feelings very clear back in

Ithaca. I hadn't thrown the engagement ring at him, but it had been close.

Shane reached out as if to take my hand. At the last second, he pulled back so that only his thumb grazed my wrist. "I've got some work to take care of before I go home and clean up. But I'll be back soon." Then he stepped off the curb and climbed into the driver's seat of his truck.

Standing there waving, I felt myself grinning from ear to ear. The jack o' lantern in the window had nothing on me. As Shane drove away, I turned back toward the door of the shop.

Once again, I noticed the drapery twitch behind the bale of hay. Perhaps Dad wasn't satisfied with the placement of it after all.

But it wasn't Dad. When I looked closer, I could see him pricing books at the counter. My head swiveled back toward the display window. Mom?

Nope. There was Mom coming in from the stock room. I looked again just as a drift of spider webs floated to the floor of the window box. A white tissue ghost swayed as if someone had touched it.

A shiver crimped my skin into gooseflesh. Bordeaux stood facing the window. Her tail wagged hesitantly. I wanted to examine the scene further, but all around the square shop owners were coming out to decorate their storefronts for the trick-or-treaters.

I stuck my head inside the door. "We're getting behind."

Mom held up a box. "I've got everything we need right here."

"And I've got the rest," Dad joked.

Together we strung orange lights, hung a life-sized skeleton on the door, and set out an entire family of hand-carved jack o' lanterns which had been part of a pumpkin carving contest at the elementary school.

At last, we took turns going home to get changed.

By six o'clock, we were ready for the first wave of ghouls. Up and down the block we could hear the happy squeals of children dashing from store to store yelling, "Trick-or-Treat," at the tops of their lungs.

In the bookshop I handed out candy, relishing the astonished looks on the kids' faces when they saw my green skin and huge special effects chin wart. One little boy wouldn't take candy from my hand no matter what kind I offered.

Mom told silly fortunes behind the counter, and Dad lurched around as The Mummy, trailing toilet paper streamers all over the shop.

Around eight o'clock we began to run low on candy. "I can go over to the market," I volunteered.

"That won't be necessary."

I looked up to see a rugged cowboy with a huge lariat draped around his torso. He had on a black cowboy hat and wore his jeans tucked down into tall boots. A plastic grocery bag hung from his arm. It was full to the brim with candy bars and popcorn balls.

"Shane? Wow. You did go home and clean up."

He raised one booted foot. "I don't usually wear these outside the rodeo arena, but..."

Mom appeared and took the bag from his arm. "Did you buy this, or have you been trick-or-treating?"

"I'll never tell," Shane replied. "Just don't hand out that jumbo Payday." He rubbed his hands together greedily.

The bell over the door tinkled, and a trio of tiny fairies floated in. Shane reached into the bag that Mom had taken, pulled out two or three candies for each little girl, and waited until they said the magic words.

When each of them had chimed, "Trick-or-treat," he dropped the candy into their bags with a flourish.

"I hope you don't mind," he said. "I love handing out the treats." Mom took his arm and positioned him near the door.

"The job is now yours. At least until the dance begins."

Dear old Mom. She'd been thrilled when I told her Shane was taking me to the dance.

The next hour flew by, and when nine o'clock came, we were all ready to lock up. The four of us walked across the street to the courthouse lawn where a local country and western band was in full swing.

Mom and Dad immediately hit the dance floor. Mom's gypsy scarves and gold bangles lent a mysterious air to their dips and twirls, but they had a heck of a time trying to keep dad clothed in his wrappings.

We each enjoyed a warm mug of mulled cider from the booth manned by Mr. Oliver and a cadre of teens hired for the occasion. Overhead, a giant orange moon rose above us all.

Shane and I danced every dance. After an invigorating turn around the floor, he said, "There's only one more thing I want to ask you tonight."

"Just name it," I said.

The song ended, and we were standing in the middle of the floor. "Can we get rid of this?" He flicked my stick-on wart. "It sort of gives me the heebie-jeebies."

I laughed, peeled it off, and stuck it on the end of his nose. "How's that?"

He rolled his eyes and pulled me in close. And he was right. Looking at the faux growth gave me the heebie-jeebies, too. I pulled it off and stuck it in his shirt pocket with a laugh. We enjoyed a few more dances, and then Mom and Dad stopped by to say they were leaving.

Soon, Mr. Oliver closed up the cider stand, and we were on our own except for Bordeaux who was sleeping beneath our table.

Around midnight, the dancers had thinned out, and the band began to play that old Willie Nelson standard, "(*Turn Out The Lights) The Party's Over.*"

Shane propelled me onto the floor for one last dance. "I wish the night didn't have to end."

"I wish it didn't have to end either."

He pressed his hand into the middle of my back. His breath was warm against my cheek, and I turned my face to his. The kiss was sweet and wonderful and insistent. It was even more perfect than before.

"I lied," he murmured. "There's one more thing I need to ask you..."

I held my breath. "What?"

"Can you somehow finish your degree closer to home?"

I laughed. "You must be a mind reader. I was just wondering the same thing."

We lingered a moment longer until Brett Barque, one of Shane and Charlie's old friends, began pulling up the far corner of the snap-together oak floor.

"I've got to go help them dismantle," Shane said.

I saw Bordie work her way out from under our little table and stumble across the street. Her joints had obviously stiffened up lying on the cool autumn earth.

"I'd better go check on her. I'll be right back."

"No rush, it will take a few minutes to get the floor loaded on the trailer." He handed me his truck key. "Feel free to get in and start 'er up."

I nodded and took the key. Bordie had made a beeline for the bookshop. By the time I got there, she was standing under the streetlamp, tail once again wagging tentatively, staring into the eerily lit plate glass window.

I laid a hand on her back. "C'mon girl, let's—"

"Hey, Rebbie." The voice came from behind me.

I whirled around.

Mitch stepped out of the shadows.

Bordeaux turned, a growl building in her throat. I gripped her collar. "It's all right, Bordie. Everything's okay." But was it? Even from across the sidewalk I could smell a strong odor of alcohol. "Have you been drinking, Mitch?"

He uttered a harsh laugh. "Yeah. Pretty much all night. Waiting on you and Romeo to break it up." He took a step closer.

Bordie's growl intensified.

"Please, Mitch, I don't want a scene." I'd only seen him inebriated a few times, and it wasn't pretty.

"Please what?" He grinned, but it looked more like a rictus than a smile. "Please, Mitch, take me home? Please, Mitch, I'm sorry? Please, Mitch, forgive me, I know you're the best thing that ever happened to me?"

My scalp tingled. He wasn't making sense. I couldn't reason with someone who was too drunk to know what he was saying. "I *am* sorry, Mitch. Sorry you came all this way for nothing." I took a steadying breath. "You need to go on home now."

He started toward me again.

Bordie lunged out of my grasp.

He drew his foot back to kick her.

If he hurt my dog, I didn't know what I might do. I opened my mouth to tell him so, but as I did something heavy *whapped* the inside of the display window.

All three of us turned to look at the glass. It hadn't broken or even cracked, but we could see a large book lying open just below the sash. The fluttery pages reminded me of a strange bird. A sudden sweet scent saturated the air.

Bordie broke the spell. She turned back toward Mitch, who stood transfixed. I couldn't see anything else amiss, but the odor of fruit grew stronger and stronger. I could almost swear we'd gone back to the apple barn and the ancient cider press.

Shane appeared as if the scent had conjured him out of thin air. "What's going on?" He looked straight at Mitch. "Who are you?"

"This is my ex-fiancé," I said. "He was about to leave." I hesitated. "I'm just not sure if he's fit to drive."

I wanted him to go away, but I didn't want to see him splattered out on the highway in a drunken accident.

Shane shook his head. The look on his face was a mixture of pity and disdain. "Have you got a motel room?"

Mitch still appeared fixated on something inside the shop.

Shane grasped his shoulder and spun him around. "I said where is your motel?" Disgust coated his words. "I'll drive you there—"

"Did you see that?" Mitch's voice quivered. "Did you see that face in the glass?"

With a roll of his eyes, Shane ushered Mitch to the Charger, which was parked in the shadows. He turned back to me. "Can you and Bordie follow us in my pickup?"

I nodded. But before we left, I walked over to the window and looked down at the novel that had hit the inside of the glass. I gasped when I saw the title. It was fitting, but it wasn't one we had included in our original display.

Shane laid a hand on my shoulder, and I almost jumped out of my skin. "Mitch passed out in his car. Wanna tell me what's going on, and what is so darned interesting in that window?"

"He came to take me back to Ithaca." I shrugged. "I told him no, and then he started toward me, but Bordie intervened. When he acted like he was going to kick her something hit the glass from *inside* the shop." I pointed at the thick book. The title was *Ghost Story*, by Peter Straub.

The air around us grew thick. The dark drapery twitched.

"Do you smell something?" Shane asked. "It smells like the orchard—"

"Yes," I murmured. "Or like Charlie's old cologne." I inhaled deeply. "To me, it smells like the sweet scent of home."

Bordie whuffed and wagged her tail.

I'm pretty sure she agreed.

SANCTUARY

MELISSA GARDENER

*J*ulia Thomas has always lived a small life. Suburbia has its perks—one of them being able to live out her dreams without compromise.

But, what if by doing so, she ultimately gives up something else?

Relationships are hard to come by when you know everybody in town, and for Julia, who works at the local cat shelter, being known as "the cat lady" hasn't helped her love life one bit.

When his grandparents pass away and leave Connor Smyth with a parcel of land and a good chunk of change, Connor must decide if building a life in a town he's never lived in is what he wants to do.

Meadowbrook is small, and its community tight-knit, so when Julia sets her eyes on Connor, she is immediately intrigued.

Will the small town and the girl whose presence makes him feel as though he's come home, manage to keep Connor around, or will he end up selling the land and moving on?

. . . SANCTUARY . . .

Meadowbrook is small, and although it hasn't always been an easy place to live, I wouldn't want to live anywhere else.

When I finished high school and went off to college, I saw what city life was like, and decided it wasn't for me. With a certificate as a veterinary technician, I thought it would be easy to find a job locally. I was wrong. Our local vet has had the same staff for the past twenty years, and none of them is close to retiring. The perks of small-town life rearing their ugly head once again.

But I didn't lose hope.

Easy is a word I used to say a lot, but as I get older, I realize nothing I've done successfully has been easy. The paths were full of right and left turns that taught me wonderful life lessons, and led me to where I am. And I love it.

I turn on the light and breathe in. This place is my home away from home.

Odd smells and all.

The Meadow Cat Sanctuary has been under my care for the past three years. In that time, I've seen many staff and volunteers come and go, and have become familiar with all aspects of kitty care, which is where my education comes in handy.

I believe wholeheartedly I'm meant to do this with my life. Knowing I make a difference, even a minute one in this great big world, is what keeps me grounded.

Turning on the light to the first room, I smile witnessing some kitties stretch as they watch me come in.

"Good morning, Princess," I say to our resident bad girl as she yawns. The sound of her purring is loud enough for me to hear from ten feet away. Her bright green eyes meet mine, and I try to pet the soft tufts under her chin gently, but she rebuffs my caress with a swipe of her paw. It's a daily struggle.

I think she likes it.

"Not today, Satan," I tell her with a laugh, pulling my hand away quicker than she can put her claws into its skin. She's a nice girl, sadly only on her own terms, which makes her difficult to adopt out to a nice family.

I make the rounds quietly, assessing each cat I come across and greeting them by the name they were given upon their arrival. Mornings are quiet as we clean up the nightly litter messes and refill food and water bowls. It's cathartic walking around from room to room, the only noises coming from the radio playing softly in the background and my companions greeting me while I care for them.

There are usually two of us in here each morning to clean up, but Claire had a doctor's appointment and will only be in after lunch when we open to the public.

We have some cats in the quarantine area that need to be secluded from the others until they are well enough to be introduced to the rest of the residents. We also have a nursery with moms and their little ones. It has kittens of every age, making this room a favorite among visitors. And then there are our other rooms. Each is designed for optimum cat comfort. There are windows with wide ledges being warmed by the sun and catios for fresh air where felines can explore while staying safe.

Our sanctuary isn't just for cats; people like me find this place calming. Sometimes, I take a break and sit with the animals, enjoying the simplicity of kitty cuddles. I get elated whenever one of my babies is adopted, but it's also a bit sad because each one takes a tiny spot in my heart.

Sometimes, we get visits from different schools, so children can learn the importance of spaying and neutering their animals while seeing the many aspects of shelter life.

I wouldn't trade my job for anything.

Days turn into weeks that turn into months in this place. Each day is its own with different challenges. Summer is peak cat, adoption season, with a few slow patches here and there. Then the cooler months linger on forever, which means the kitties start looking for shelter from the harsh winter, and the cycle restarts.

Mornings are beginning to get chillier, and with the shelter at full capacity, I've been fielding call after call from people wanting to bring in strays. I simply have nowhere to put them, except on a waiting list until we can get more adoptions going.

It gets difficult saying no to people, and occasionally, we get some belligerent ones who don't understand we can only take in so many. Overcrowding breeds stress and disease, which is a very sad reality for us, and something I try to avoid.

I'm at the front desk, trying to crunch numbers to see if there is any way we can move a few of the ones from the quarantine into one of the cat rooms. I also make several calls to some foster families to gauge if any of them would be willing to take in new ones. Plus, I am fielding as many phone calls and appointments as I can before I must take one of our cats to the vet to be spayed.

The door dings, letting me know someone has come in, and my eyes shift from the computer monitor to the door and back.

And then I do a double take.

I've never seen the man standing awkwardly by the door. Judging by the way that he's looking around, I don't think he's at the right place. We don't get too many visitors this time of day.

"Are you lost?" I ask, because I can't read his face, and I don't have time to deal with anything non-cat-related.

My assistant and best friend, Allisson, is coming in later today to stay into the evening, and Gemma, who was supposed to come in this morning, called in sick.

He takes a couple of steps toward me, his eyes never leaving the collection of happy-cat adoption photos we have covering the wall by the entrance.

He clears his throat and takes another step toward me, finally meeting my eyes. "I'd like to visit with the cats if that's okay?" He seems shy, as if asking is the hardest thing he's had to do today. There is a slight sheen of sweat on his forehead, and his cheeks and ears are covered in a dark pink blush. It's cute.

I notice right away that his eyes are greener than Princess's, which makes me sit up straighter in my office chair.

This sudden interest in a stranger is a rare occurrence that makes me roll my eyes at myself.

I smile. "Of course." I stand and make my way around the counter to lead him down the hall to our first cat room. "We have five rooms you can visit freely. Don't go into the nursery unless an employee is with you," I instruct, pointing to a window where a mom and her babies are sleeping.

"Thank you," he says, and he walks into the first room.

I leave him be and go back to my computer. If I'm lucky, he'll fill out an application and adopt a couple of our babies. Wishful thinking, I suppose, but it's the kind of hope I feel every time people come by to visit. Sadly, not every visit turns into an adoption. Some people just like to cuddle my furry monsters without the responsibility, and that's okay since our residents need as much human interaction as possible.

I take a quick look at the security camera and smile to myself when I spot Mr. Green Eyes sitting on the floor with a toy mouse in his hand as he teases one of the friendlier cats, Frankie, while some of the shyer ones look on, readying themselves to pounce into the game.

"Anything new?" Allisson asks as soon as she walks in.

"Nah. A couple of people came in to buy food, and some guy spent an hour playing with Frankie and Peanut. Other than that, same old, same old."

I motion to my pile of paperwork.

"This stuff is finally getting done, though, so that's good." I give her a big smile and exhale a long breath. I don't elaborate about Mr. Green Eyes; there isn't much to tell. He slipped out of the shelter with a shy smile and a wave. I don't expect to see him again, though I do wonder who he is.

When I get home, Harlow and Phoebe, my fur-babies, greet me excitedly. Sitting with them on the couch, I enjoy a sandwich and some much-needed Netflix and chill. They're my solace in this quiet, quaint house. I know they'll be home, purring their little hearts out when they greet me at the end of what is sometimes an extremely trying day. Sisters that I bottle-fed when everyone else gave up and told me the tiny furry peanuts wouldn't make it. I proved them all wrong, and it was the catalyst to my education.

I can't save them all, and some decisions break my heart, but I believe everything happens for a reason.

It's Monday and raining. My mood is dire, at best, and I keep hearing one of my new arrivals sneeze while I try to concentrate on my paperwork. Ordering food and making sure my quotas are met after a busy adoption weekend, takes up my morning.

The bell over the door chimes, and on instinct, I look up.

I can't help the smile that crosses my face when Mr. Green Eyes walks over the threshold. For some reason, I sit straighter in my chair, my mood lifting.

"Can I visit the cats?" he asks. Today, he sounds more confident, and his eyes are instantly on me, and not the wall by the door.

"You know where to go." I give him a nod toward the hall and return his smile. His eyes sparkle, making this Monday not so bad after all.

Like a creeper, I watch him interact with the cats for a good five minutes, forgetting everything else on my to-do list. The way he plays and cuddles the cats is adorable. It's a rare occasion to have a grown man in here, let alone one who truly seems to enjoy my babies' company.

For a second, I contemplate going in and re-doing some of the cleaning. I could have a conversation with him about the benefits of adopting two at a time. We could discuss the weather. Anything to hear his voice, really.

My heart flutters for half a second, and then I remind myself I am still clueless as to who he is. My detective skills have not proven very fruitful. It seems I've been so busy I've neglected the usual daily gossip I have with the girls.

The cat-lady stigma is real, I remind myself with a somber shake of my head. Most of our adopters are either families with young children or women over forty. I'm not forty yet, but in no way am I a spring chicken.

It takes a ringing telephone to make me take my eyes off him and stop the delusions going on in my mind. By the time I hang up, Allisson lets me know he's gone.

"Well, he *was* tall, dark, and handsome. You should totally talk to him," she says as if I'm here to get a date instead of work. Somewhere deep inside, though, I know she's right.

Maybe next time.

"Some of us can focus on other things than the opposite sex," I tell her pointedly, but I don't believe it myself. I'm not desperate. I prefer to be alone than with the wrong person. I can't understand why that's so difficult to believe.

She giggles. "Sweetie, you're one cat away from cat-lady status."

I snort out a rather unattractive laugh. "Don't hate on my lifestyle. I've got another ten years before joining the Cat Ladies of America." I run a hand through my hair and fix my ponytail. "I'm okay with it. As should you be." I give her another pointed look, hoping this conversation ends.

It doesn't.

She rolls her eyes. "Honey, I am not hating on your lack of social skills. Though I would really hate for a cute little thing like yourself to miss out on life because you can't get the shelter out of your system. When's the last time you went out?" She doesn't give me time to answer and continues. "Heck, when's the last time you had a date? With a human?"

This time, I laugh out loud. Allisson and I have worked together for a couple of years. She knows me well, and I know she has my best interests at heart.

I try to think of a good reply but come up with nothing. She's right, though I can't tell her that. "I went to dinner with my mom last week."

She makes some sort of weird gagging noise in the back of her throat and squints at me. "You have dinner with your mom at least once a week, Julia. That doesn't count."

"It counts," I rebuff, fed up with the conversation. "Can we put a pin in this discussion?"

She rolls her eyes.

"Mika needs his boosters, by the way."

"Yes, ma'am." She salutes and turns, adding, "You're not getting any younger, you know."

Don't I know it.

I'm hanging out in the cat room, for the first time in forever, when I hear the sound of the bell over the front door. I can see from my vantage point that it's the same handsome man from the other day, aka, Mr. Green Eyes, and do a quick overview of myself. Pink scrub top with cats all over it and minimal actual cat hair—check. Unflattering gray work pants that make me look like I have no ass—check. Ponytail with sweaty wisps of hair all around my face—check. No makeup, dirty glasses, and chipped fingernails—check, check, and check. I'm a mess, and he's walking this way, so there's absolutely nothing I can do about it.

Not that I'd do anything about it anyway. I'm at work and have had a crazy, busy morning.

I pet Princess, talking to her and trying to look nonchalant. I'm sure I don't. Princess hates it, too.

"Hi," I greet, when he opens the door, bright green eyes meeting mine.

I laugh when Frankie runs right to Mr. Green Eyes and starts weaving his way around his ankles. "You've made a friend," I comment, laughing when Frankie's purring gets louder.

He nods and bends at the waist, picking up the small, furry kitten. "How old is he?"

"Eight months." I smile, watching him interact with my sweet Frankie. "You wouldn't believe how different he is now from when we first got him."

He grins, clearly enjoying how cuddly Frankie is. That cat gets right under your skin as if he's begging to go to his forever home. Sadly, nobody's put in an adoption application for him. I may need to bring him home with me. He wasn't one of those tiny ones I saved with patience and a plastic bottle, but he was so feral, Allisson thought we'd have to put him down. I persuaded her to give me time. And within that time, Frankie became a cuddle bug with the sweetest personality.

The air is heavy in the room. It's hot, but that's not the kind of heavy I feel. I want to talk. I want to ask him his name. I want to tell him to take Frankie with him. I want so many things. But nothing comes out of my mouth.

I look over at him, and he seems unaffected. He's here for the cats, I remind myself. Instead of trying my hand at conversation, I look at my watch and leave the room, pretending I have other things to do, which, I suppose, I do.

My mother's voice, along with Allisson's earlier comment, echoes in my mind.

If you don't try, nothing will change, Julia.

Do I really want change?

The sound of Harlow meowing in the kitchen wakes me from a deep slumber. I stretch, and with bleary eyes, go check on her. Her food bowl appears to have no kibbles in the center, a clear sign the apocalypse is coming, and we must ration. Her distress is palpable. Phoebe is unperturbed, sleeping peacefully on her perch next to the window.

Sleepily, I reach for the bowl, and she head-butts my hand, purring loudly. "Yes, yes, I know you're starving."

She follows me and watches as I pour kibble into her bowl and place it back on the floor. Yawning, I make it back to my bed, grumbling when I notice my alarm is set to go off in less than ten minutes.

There's no use going back to bed, but I do wish I could teach my cats how to tell time.

I get ready for my day and grab a coffee on my way to work. The morning ritual is the same, except I have three adoptions scheduled for the afternoon and a coffee date tonight with Claire. She's been on vacation all week and wants to catch up over coffee before coming back to work in a few days.

Allison is early, something she only does when she knows we are busy. Together, we make sure we've done the paperwork, and everything is ready for three of my darlings to go on and join their furrever family.

When my day is finally finished, I go home knowing three cats are now well placed and sleeping in a loving home tonight. The joy written on the faces of the children when they hold their new pet is always my favorite part of adoptions. Thoughts like those are what make my job fulfilling.

I take a much-needed shower before meeting Claire, hoping I don't look as haggard as I feel.

The coffee shop is quiet, and I order a coffee. The day is catching up to me, and I yawn and cover my mouth, hoping it won't be something I spend the entire evening doing.

Fifteen minutes after I arrive, she calls and tells me something came up, and she can't make it. We agree to meet later in the weekend, and I hang up the phone, disappointed I've made an effort and dolled myself up only to go back home to...my cats.

I rifle through my purse to keep my hands busy, social anxiety showing its ugly head. I contemplate whether to finish my coffee sitting alone, or take it home and drink it, while binge-watching *Shameless* curled up on the couch petting Phoebe.

"Julia, right?"

I recognize the voice immediately and look up, my cheeks warming. "Hi." I smile because Mr. Green Eyes knows my name. "I don't know your name," I say honestly, extending my hand and feeling as though I'm having an out of body experience.

This beats Netflix, hands down.

He takes my hand in his, the tips of his ears darkening to a shade of pink, probably mirroring my cheeks, and his face breaks out in a huge grin. "Connor. Connor Smyth."

The name rings a bell, and I can't fathom how I didn't put two and two together before.

"Right. You live out at Harold's old place." I nod, remembering the old man and how he'd handed the land down to his grandson. His incredibly attractive grandson. "He...he was a nice gentleman."

Looking away, I get a pang in my chest.

Harold was a kind, old man who still held a candle for his deceased wife. He talked about her any chance he got. Occasionally, he brought us cats that were dropped off at his place. His property is out several miles away from town, and some irresponsible pet owners use the woods around that area to get rid of their unwanted pets.

"He was my grandfather." Connor pulls out a chair across from me and takes his seat, placing his coffee on the table. "I...we, my family, I mean, nobody else wanted the property, and I used to love coming here as a kid," he explains, matter-of-fact. He seems just as nervous as I feel, which oddly helps me feel more grounded.

I can do this social thing Allisson is always talking about.

"I don't remember seeing you back then." I grimace. "I'm sorry, that's none of my business."

He looks to be around my age or a little older, though I'm horrible at guessing those kinds of things. I could end up being a cougar if this goes anywhere. Internally, I cringe and roll my eyes.

He gives me a warm smile. "That's because I stayed at the house. I loved it there. That property was mine to explore, and I enjoyed every moment. Mom and Grandpa came to town, but I always stayed back."

"That explains it. Though I have to ask: what's so great about it?" I take a sip of coffee, enjoying where this is going.

Adult conversation with someone I feel an instant connection to is strange. It's not a feeling I'm used to, but I can feel him everywhere around me, and it's so peculiar. I've never felt this way in the presence of another person. It's like the way the air felt around us at the shelter—heavy, yet comfortable.

I wish I could have spoken to him sooner, but here we are.

He visibly relaxes, his eyes meeting mine. "It wasn't the house as much as the land itself. There are trails in the woods that lead to a small cabin Grandpa helped me make, and I used to go fishing in the pond near the lake."

I imagine a younger version of him, walking in the woods with a fishing rod. "You must have been adorable."

His cheeks do that thing where they darken, and his lips quirk up in the corners. "Mom always says I was."

He *is* adorable.

Green meets blue, and my whole-body flushes warm, my cheeks matching his. "Are the trails still there?" I ask, completely ignoring the fact that he's just flirted with me.

Allisson's voice echoes in my head, telling me what to say, but I'm so curious about him that instead, I make myself look almost uninterested and not coy as I've seen other girls pull off.

I've never been that kind of girl. Coy is not even in my vocabulary.

"I've had to cut my way through a lot of them. I've been staying busy at the house, but it gets lonely." He shrugs. "That's why I visit the shelter."

That makes sense. "You know you could bring home a couple of them, right?"

He laughs. "I have some favorites. I just want things more settled before I bring them home. I don't want them to be alone in the house all the time. I'm almost done clearing out a trail all the way to the lake."

"You know cats are super independent? Like, they won't care that you're not home. Heck, some of them like it better when they're alone." I want to mention Princess, but I don't.

I feel like one of those used car salesmen trying to pawn off my kitties.

He laughs even harder. "I know. That's why I prefer them to dogs."

I swallow hard. A fellow cat lover. *Could it be?*

"Wait, so you like cats more than dogs?"

Am I dreaming?

He nods. "Always have. Grandpa was too allergic to keep any at the house, but I always thrilled when I found one on the property. One summer, he even let me care for a little gray tabby I found wandering the trails at the end of the road leading to a wooded area by the garage. I kept it in my cabin for the summer, but he brought it to the shelter once I went back home. I knew that was going to happen, but that cat was my best friend that summer. I will never forget it."

I sigh. "That's the cutest story I've ever heard."

We're quiet for a minute.

"I...I also went to the shelter to see you." He says these words carefully, quietly.

I frown.

"You did? But, I look awful most of the time. Heck, I'm pretty sure I have poop on me every day."

He laughs. "That's the appeal." He sips his coffee, his eyes on mine. "A woman after my own heart. You don't seem phased by your job, and you truly care for these animals as if they were yours."

"They are mine," I say, then add, "Until they have a forever home, I'm their family. We—the staff—are all these creatures know. They have to trust that we will do everything to make them feel at home."

"My hat is off to you. I couldn't do what you do." He drains his coffee cup.

"What do you do? Or did you do, I guess, before moving here?"

Curiosity gets me again, but this time I want to get more out of him.

"I used to be in sales. Right now, I don't know." He shrugs. "I'm getting settled, but job prospects are sparse."

I nod. "This town is smaller than you're used to, huh?"

He sighs. "I forgot about that part. I mean, it was great as a kid, but there are about twenty thousand fewer people here to deal with than where I lived."

"And where was that?" I empty the remnants of my own mug, surprised at how easy this is. It feels like I've known him all my life. Minus these idle details, of course.

"Bozeman, Montana. Real big for the artsy and college crowds." He looks away, frowning. "I needed a change."

I don't ask why. Even I know when to stop snooping. I figure he'll tell me on his own time.

"Never heard of it," I say with a laugh, lightening the mood.

"Big and sort of boring. Mom still lives there with my stepfather. She's happy the house is staying in the family," he says, then adds, "and even happier she's not the one to take it over."

"The trails must be gorgeous this time of year," I say.

He's told me about the cabin that's still standing and looking good, even after more than a dozen years without anyone touching it.

Our conversation flows easily with more back and forth questions. It feels like a date as I see the sunset in the large picture window behind him, the illuminating sky orange like the changing leaves. No more am I staring at him because his eyes are so bewitchingly green. I'm simply in awe that he's so easy to talk to and interesting.

The lights flicker overhead, and I spot the barista staring at us from across the room. The café is closing, and here we are deep in conversation, oblivious to everything around us.

Heading outside, we walk slowly and silently to my car.

"I guess I'll see you this week sometime?" I ask, hopeful.

He balances himself on the balls of his feet, and I notice how tall he is. His hands are in his pockets, and his bottom lip sucked in between his teeth. "I will come for a visit. I promised Frankie."

I laugh. "Yes, well you wouldn't want to disappoint him."

He nods, his eyes all squinty yet sparkling under the darkening sky. "There's also this girl I wouldn't mind seeing again."

My heart leaps and my breath catches in my throat. I don't know what to say to that, and I know he's flirting. I mean, even I'm not that oblivious. "I think I'd like that."

He backs away, nodding. "I'll see you soon, then?"

I open the car door, laughing, and say, "I hope so."

I hear his deep laughter echoing back, and head home wondering if this whole evening even happened.

Once at home, I'm excited and filled with a nervous energy I haven't felt in years. Sleep doesn't come easy, but the smile on my lips remains.

The weekend goes by quickly, and Monday comes too soon. I'm more alert than usual for a Monday, and I wonder if maybe it's because I may get a gentleman caller to visit me. The thought makes me smile.

"I see you had a nice weekend," Allisson says, picking up Princess and attempting to cuddle her.

I give her all the gritty details. Well, as gritty as having coffee in a coffee shop can get.

"Well, look at you, Miss Social Butterfly," she comments, for the third time in as many minutes.

I can tell she's giddy and happy for me. She always is. Having a friend like her on my side has gotten me through some tough times. Working together is just a bonus.

In the afternoon, I'm doing paperwork when the telltale bell over the door chimes, and I instinctively look up.

My eyes grow wide, and my lips turn up instantly. "Well hello, Sir."

Connor laughs. "Hello, Ma'am. May I visit your cats?"

I make my way around the counter, loving our banter. "Of course. Follow me."

I can feel his eyes on me all the way down the hall.

"How was your weekend?" He picks up Frankie and laughs when the young cat cuddles himself right into Connor's neck.

I cuddle some of the other cats while we talk about what we did. He tells me he cleared out more branches around the property while I caught up on some housework. I don't have time to chitchat too much as the bell chimes, and I must leave him to go take care of customers.

Sadly, I'm filling out adoption paperwork with a family when he waves from beside the door. His smile is enough to keep me giddy for the rest of the day.

I see him again twice during the week. It's easy. Too easy. He's friendly with Allisson and Claire, and with other visitors. I watch him interact with a little girl, and my heart melts as he helps her pick up one of the bigger cats so that she can kiss its forehead.

On Friday, he comes twenty minutes before we are due to close. This time, he doesn't ask to see the cats.

"Can I talk to you privately for a minute?" he whispers, getting Claire's attention.

"I can take over here, Julia." She winks, smiling like the cat that got the canary. I won't live this down.

I roll my eyes at her and tell him to follow me into the employee lounge area.

"What's up?" I'm nervous. I don't want to assume anything bad, and by the look on his face, I don't think this is going to be a negative conversation.

"I...I want you to come over for dinner tomorrow." He balances himself on his heels, something I notice he does when he's nervous.

"You want me to come over?" I smile, shivering with excitement, and happy we are in a private room with no cameras. Allisson and Claire are going to have a field day with this one.

He steps forward and leans in, his forehead close to mine, but not touching. "Julia, I would love...I would love for you to come have dinner with me. Please?"

I nod slightly. "I'd love that. Thank you for the invite."

He leans in closer and places the softest kiss to my forehead. "I'll see you at six?"

"Six," I repeat, deliriously happy.

We both exit the room, bantering about the benefits of living in a small town since there are never any traffic jams.

I call Allisson as soon as I get home. Today's her day off, and I can't wait to gossip.

"I'm seeing him again tomorrow night. Dinner at his place." I fidget nervously with a thread on the hem of my sweater. "I don't even know what to wear."

"Just don't wear scrubs and you'll be fine." She laughs.

I roll my eyes. "You think? Man, and all this because Claire couldn't make it for coffee."

"It was fate." She sighs. "So romantic."

"Oh, shut up!" I roll my eyes and giggle. I can't help it.

When we hang up the phone, I sigh and flop back on my bed wondering whose life I've stepped into.

The weather is beautiful. Leaves are changing color, and their crunch can be heard as we walk down the sidewalk, heading over to the trails he's promised to show me.

"Your grandmother was one of those tiny old ladies who always had candy in her purse," I recount when he tells me his grandfather never remarried. "She was so funny too. He loved her deeply."

"Grandpa was a nice man. I haven't heard anyone speak ill of him. The house was well kept, but a little dusty," he says, guiding me through some rough terrain.

When I drove up and parked in front of the house, Connor was already outside waiting for me. He gave me a quick tour of the home, telling me what he was going to paint and where he planned to put things.

I was in sales, and I think I can still do that here, as far as work is concerned. He shrugs as he shows me his office. The internet is a wonderful thing.

You don't seem like you're cooking anything, Connor, I say, as we pass through the kitchen and make our way to the living room.

He laughs. All in good time, my fair lady.

And maybe he was wooing me.

Or maybe he was going to skin me alive in the woods.

But maybe, just maybe, his plans were to sweep me off my feet.

He touches my arm to make sure I don't become tangled in a branch overhead, and I'm not sure what to do with the tingles shooting through me. I can feel them all the way down to my fingertips and at the ends of my toes.

He doesn't know it and probably doesn't realize it, but that small fraction of an action makes me feel more human. As though, I'd been missing those little vibrations my whole life. I could get addicted to the feel of them; I'm sure of it. I don't know how he manages it. Magic, maybe?

I've taken care of hundreds of lively furry things, and in all that time, nobody's taken care of me. I wonder what that would feel like. Is that what those tingles are?

He makes that magic happen with one single, insignificant touch to my shoulder, of all places.

I have been concentrating so much on taking care of animals that somewhere along the way I've forgotten I'm a girl. A grown woman. I haven't had a boyfriend in years. And now here he is. Connor Smyth. He's all I can think about. Every time I close my eyes, all I can see are his looking back at me.

I feel ridiculous.

A crush. I have an actual crush. Me—a grown woman—has a crush. And I think—hope—he does too.

Heading down the colorful trail, all I can think about is how isolated we are getting the farther into the woods we go.

"The cabin is close."

He takes my hand in his and threads our fingers together. That tingle intensifies.

I feel ridiculously overwhelmed. And quiet. So quiet, it's weird. I don't want to fill the silence with anything, as I take in the beauty around us.

"This place is magical, Connor." I'm awed at the small clearing surrounding the cabin that is perched upon a large tree.

He smiles. "Follow me."

And I will.

Inside the cabin is a small table set for two, a simple battery-operated light between the two place settings illuminating it perfectly. "This is beautiful."

Looking closer, I notice he's installed a bunch of those battery-operated flickering candles, which add to the overall ambience.

"Very fire-safe, I see." I turn to him and smile.

He's standing near the door, watching me take in every detail. The cabin is tiny. There are the table and two chairs near the door and a recliner with a coffee table in a corner. Two windows on the walls perpendicular to where the door is helping to let in light. The walls are bare wood, with a couple of posters adorning them.

Taking containers out of a cooler next to the table, he says, "I hope you like sandwiches and pasta salad."

"That sounds perfect." I pull out a chair and have a seat, while he opens containers and organizes our meal.

We talk about everything and anything while eating. It's quiet and peaceful; only the sounds from the birds chirping outside can be heard through the thin walls and windows.

I can see the appeal of this place and tell him as much. It reminds me of the shelter, as its removed from the real world and few can truly appreciate it.

Once we are done eating and have emptied a bottle of wine between the two of us, he invites me for a walk. The sun is setting, and a cool breeze settles around us. Ahead, a clearing can be seen.

"What's over there?"

"Let's go see."

He takes my hand, and we walk silently toward the clearing. I feel safe with him, something I would never have imagined with someone I've just met.

Had Allisson or Claire come to me with a story about a date like this —deep in the woods with a virtual stranger—I would have been leery in wondering what they were thinking, yet here I am.

We stand at the edge of the clearing looking over the lake in all its wondrous beauty. A mountain stands on the other side, trees of all sorts of colors bloom in front of us. It's like looking at a vibrant painting. One of those big ones full of oranges, reds, and greens.

"I think I'm going to build a house here," he says. His fingers thread through mine, his thumb softly caressing my hand.

"What about your grandfather's house?" I've always been practical and nosey. It appeared to be a decent house when he gave me the tour. He shrugs.

"I'll rent it out. Or sell it. It's sort of apart from this area anyway," he explains.

"You've thought about this, huh?" I smile, looking up at him.

He turns toward me and brings his other hand to my shoulder.

"I've always wanted to live out here. This is where I was meant to be. Last week, I wasn't so sure. I had some bad news about my job, and everything was a mess." He sighs. "But then, I thought, you know, these woods are part of me, and if I don't grasp this opportunity, it won't happen for me. Besides, Grandpa had a trust, and I was his only grand-kid." He says all of this earnestly, his eyes on mine, and his voice soft, open.

I lick my lips, wondering how soft his lips are because he's so close and I want them on mine. "That's true. Live for the moment, you know?"

His hand that's on my shoulder moves to my jaw, and he bends his knees, bringing his face closer to mine.

"Taking life by the moment meant finally speaking to you at the café. I would have never done that living out in the city."

"You mean speaking to a random woman you've only met a few times?" I whisper the words, unable to find my full voice, tingling all over once again. And I realize I talk way too much for someone who just wants this man to kiss her.

He smirks. "You're so beautiful. I went to the shelter to see the cats. I kept going to see you. You intrigued me. I don't know what it is…I just want to get to know you. It's like…this pull," he murmurs. "I am trying to figure out who I want to adopt, though, don't get me wrong, but seeing you there, being so caring…it…it's made me want to know who you are, everything about you."

"Me?"

It's all I can say before his lips are on mine, soft pecks that take my breath away, making me feel like I'm flying. And then, a swipe of his tongue, open-mouthed kisses, and hands pulling each other closer.

His kiss is as magical as the forest we're in, and if I could have anything in the world, it would be for this kiss never to end, but sadly, it does. As all good kisses do.

My grin is huge, and my lips swollen and tingly when we part. He leans his forehead against mine. "I'm really happy I met you, Julia. You make me feel like I'm home."

I sigh and kiss his lips reverently. "Connor Smyth, the pleasure is all mine."

The ups and downs of life bring forth so many different decisions and scenarios. I can't help but wonder if maybe the universe was smiling at me when Claire canceled our coffee date.

Sometimes, I wonder how things would have turned out had Connor not had the courage to sit with me that day. But then, he did, and I'd rather be where we are now, three years later; happy in our little sanctuary by the lake with Phoebe, Harlow, Frankie, Peanut, and of course, Princess.

The End

SWEET TALKING MAN

PEGGY PERRY

*L*ike a rock in the river of humanity, unmoving and silent, Nick held his place as people slipped around him up and down the stock show arena fence in front of the bleachers. The sound of their voices rose and fell around him like water sliding past the riverbanks at his favorite fishing spot.

He scowled as he stared out across the ring where riders were exercising their horses before the show began. If he hadn't promised to watch several clients show the horses he trained for them, he could have stayed home and enjoyed some hot coffee and his dog's company instead. It would sure beat being alone in this crowd.

He wished he had someone to talk with. He wished he *could* talk with someone. He recalled the last date he'd had, though he couldn't remember the woman's name. His friends set him up with a pretty girl who seemed nice. But the date ended abruptly after he overheard her speaking with a friend outside the restaurant where they dined. They didn't see him come out the door behind them.

"Sure, he looks like Matthew McConaughey, he's polite, and he's employed, but he's so quiet I can't help thinking he's wondering if I'll fit in his barbecue pit!"

The two women had giggled together until he pretended to have just arrived behind them. He hadn't had to pretend to look sick when he clutched his stomach without saying a word. Her friend had offered to take her home, so he didn't have to keep acting polite.

After that night he refused any more offers of introductions to women. He was lonely, but it was better than listening to remarks like that. But she had only been the latest in a long line of disappointing dates in his short thirty years. His friends had even tried setting him up with a deaf woman, but he didn't know sign language, and she couldn't read his lips if he rarely said anything. No, it was better to suffer in silence.

"Look! Over here!" An excited squeal almost in his ear made him jerk his head around. A young woman with short, curly blonde leaped onto the fence beside him. Her slim body was covered by a light tee-shirt covered with cartoon flowers and snug jeans. She waved wildly with one arm and whooped. "Marian! Marian! Go get 'em, Marian! Woohoo!" Several of the passing riders laughed and waved back.

"For heaven's sake, Cathy! They're only exercising before the show starts. There's no need to make a spectacle of yourself like that. Now calm down and stop embarrassing me!"

Nick raised his eyebrows. This guy was a real charmer.

"No, look, see? It's my niece. I promised I'd cheer for her at the show! Hey, Marian! Here I am! Just like I promised!" The young woman waved wildly again and whistled, ignoring her companion's attempts to tug her away from the fence. "Bring home that trophy! You're number one!"

People around them and in the arena were beginning to laugh. Some cheered for Cathy. "You tell 'em, girl!" Others started cheering and yelling for their favorites.

Nick watched the man step back and throw his hands in the air. "That's it! I've had enough!" He glared at the woman. "They warned me you were called 'Chatty Cathy,' but they didn't tell me you enjoyed making a fool of yourself—and me—in public! I don't have to put up with this!" He stomped off, muttering.

Nick looked back at the woman beside him. Please don't cry, please don't cry! Instead, she peered after the angry man from around Nick's sheltering bulk. When the man vanished in the moving crowd, she blew out her breath and wiped nonexistent sweat from her forehead.

"I thought I would NEVER get rid of him! Honestly, what were my friends thinking, trying to fix me up with that drip?" She shook her head. "Do you have friends like that? The ones used as the illustration for the saying about 'the road to hell'?"

Nick was startled into a laugh. Relief warmed him to find this cheerful person was not connected in any way with such an unpleasant man. He wished he could tell her that, but he settled for nodding, and managing to utter "Rude!" He tilted his head in the direction of the stranger, hoping she would understand he meant him.

She nodded. "He was like that from the moment he met me here this morning. Thank goodness I drove myself. I've learned my lesson about that! The first thing he said to me after 'hello' was 'Don't you watch the weather? You're dressed all wrong!' Can you imagine? Would you say that to a stranger?"

Nick shook his head. He searched for a response and decided on "Raised better."

"Yes! Exactly! Why, my momma would bust my butt if I ever talked like that!"

Nick laughed again. This gal was a firecracker! He hadn't been this amused in years. Feeling the wind shove against his back, he braced his hands on the fence. He saw her shiver and rub her arms. She caught his raised eyebrows.

"Chip the Drip was right, though," she admitted with a twist of her lips. "I did forget to watch the weather, so I didn't bring my coat." She leaned back and looked him up and down. "That wind is coming from behind you. Would you be offended if I used you as a windbreak? I want to watch the show, but I'm really cold!"

Nick stepped back and waved a hand at the spot in front of him. He was cheered that she hadn't found his silence awkward and left as well. Instead, she tucked herself between him and the fence and wrapped her arms around herself. "Oh, that's much better!" she exclaimed. She looked over her shoulder with a sudden grin and offered a hand. "Since I'm using you, I should introduce myself, I guess. Cathy Thompson."

He took her hand and shook it gently. "Nick. Williams." There. He'd managed to introduce himself without problems, at least. He hoped she wouldn't try to get to know him and discover his conversational skills were hopeless, like all the other women he'd met. But she didn't. She turned back around and chattered on about the horse show, her niece, and anything else that seemed to dart across her mind.

He noticed she still shivered as the wind gusted, though. He started to offer her his coat, but she was so much smaller than him the coat might be too heavy for her. He unbuttoned it and held the sides out around her. He only meant to provide a windbreak, but she surprised him again.

"You don't mind sharing? This is wonderful! Oh, wow, it's lined with sheepskin and already so warm!" She wrapped the lapels of the coat around her and leaned back against him. "This is great! You're like an electric blanket!"

Nick blinked. She sure was a trusting little lady. He could be a pervert for all she knew. But he shrugged and decided to make them both more comfortable. Taking the lapels from her hands, he rebuttoned his coat until her face peeked out. Instead of tensing and acting trapped, she giggled like a little girl. He could feel her tucking her hands up in her armpits and risked a word again.

"Pockets," he pointed out and patted them from the outside. The pockets inside were separated from the outside pockets by a thin cloth lining, and when she tucked her hands in he put his in the outside pockets and closed his fingers over hers.

"Now this is perfect! Mmm, and you smell good, too! What is that aftershave you're wearing?"

Nick stared, amazed, at the wild curls on the top of her head. He had never met anyone who got so personal so fast. "Polo," he managed. He was glad he didn't wear Versace, or Stetson, or one of those fancy named scents like Dolce and Gabbana. Even his dad's favorite Old Spice would have been a nightmare. He had a lot of trouble with the letter 's'. He didn't want to spit on her. She just nodded under his chin and took another deep sniff before going off on another subject.

As she talked on about whatever crossed her mind, he waited for her to get impatient with his occasional one-word replies and grunts when he couldn't figure out how to reply safely. But she seemed content, and he relaxed and enjoyed her chatter. Unlike most other women he had met, she never said anything mean, at least no worse than 'Chip the Drip,' and he figured Chip deserved it.

She was funny and sweet and talked about her family and friends with humor and fondness. When the show classes began, he knew he didn't want her to move on. He suggested, "Sit?" in her ear. Whew! No spitting. The single word remarks were working.

"Oh, yes, we'd better sit before everybody starts yelling 'Down in front'!" she said with a laugh, then laughed harder when she started to turn and was reminded she was buttoned into his coat. He grinned, too, and unbuttoned his coat. Touching her elbow, he guided her up the steps to the open row of seats halfway up. The crowd was not big yet, and there was nobody behind them to block the wind.

At first, she sat beside him, and he put his arm and coat around her shoulders. But the wind got stronger and colder, and before he knew it, he had a lap full of lavender scented woman who didn't seem to mind at all when he buttoned his coat up again over them both.

Cathy's stream of commentary interested and distracted him for a while, but the feel of a warm, soft female pressed up against him had an inevitable reaction. He shifted cautiously. But she moved too and felt the very thing he had tried to keep from her attention. She froze, her head down.

Nick clenched his jaw and reached for the lapels of his coat to open it. He didn't want her to panic and start fighting to get away. But she didn't move. When she spoke, her voice was very soft and…ashamed?

"Uh-oh. I guess you want me to leave now. I'm so sorry, but I forgot again. I keep telling myself to remember, but I never do! I'm sorry! I never meant to—I've got to go now." She sniffed and started to push at his coat.

Bewildered, he tightened his arms around her and lifted her chin with a gentle finger so he could see her face. "What?" was all he could manage. She was crying! "No, no," he crooned. "No t-t-tears." He winced. Now she knew.

Cathy didn't seem to notice. "You guys always get so mad at me," she mumbled. "I never get a second date because I always forget not to do it."

Nick cradled her face in his palm and swiped at the tears with his thumb. "F-f-forget what?"

She blinked and sniffed again. He reached into his coat pocket and pulled out a large white handkerchief. Holding it to her nose, he ordered, "Blow."

She did automatically, then gave him a watery smile. "Wow. A cloth handkerchief. I didn't know they still made them."

"Forget what?" Nick asked with a raised eyebrow. She wasn't going to distract him.

Cathy dropped her eyes again. "You know," she whispered. Her chin twitched just a little. "That!"

He still couldn't follow her. He could understand she was talking about, well, *that*, but not why she was blaming herself or why he should be angry. "What ab-b-bout it? Why cry?"

She sat up straight and glared at him. She poked his raised eyebrow. "Don't you raise your eyebrow at me! You think I don't know why everybody calls me C. T.? I know it's not my initials they're talking about! I know I'm not supposed to cuddle with guys and sit on their laps! My parents explained it to me! But it's their fault, darn it! I grew up watching them cuddle, and I got so used to it, I keep forgetting and now when I get comfortable with a guy like I have with you I forget and—and—!"

Nick stopped her rant with his hand over her mouth. He saw a dim light through the fog. "Call you what? Who d-d-does?"

Cathy pulled his hand down and scowled. "You know what C. T. stands for! And like I said, everybody! Even my friends! They told me to stop, too, like I could! I can't, or I would! But they act like I do it deliberately and I don't! I swear I don't! I just forget!" She huffed and started to push away from him again, and again he pulled her back.

"Not your fault," he told her. He tapped her nose with his finger. "S-s-sit still."

She stared wide-eyed. "You don't mind? Doesn't it, well, hurt? That's what some guys said."

Nick rolled his eyes. "Guilting you," he tried to explain.

"What do you mean 'guilting me'…wait a minute! You mean they expected me to—they pretended to—just to get me to—some of those guys were from my church! How dare they? I ought to tell their mommas!" She sagged against him. "But they'd probably say the same thing as my friends. 'You shouldn't lead them on! Only bad girls do that!" She continued to mutter half audibly. She didn't seem to notice she had tucked her head under his chin and slid her arm under his shoulder.

Nick couldn't stop smiling over her head as he caught a phrase here and there. As he heard things like "tell my daddy" he wondered just how old she was. He nudged her chin up again. "Hey," he said softly. He tried not to laugh at her pout. "How old ar-r-re you?"

She blinked, and her pout vanished. "Me? I'm twenty-three. Why? How old are you?" She sat upright as a horrified expression swept over her face. "Oh my gosh, I never asked you about the things my mamma always told me to find out about a man before I got too friendly with him! She'll kill me!" She thumped her forehead with her free hand.

Her eyes widened as greater alarm filled them. "If you answer wrong my daddy will kill YOU! Oh my gosh!"

Nick did his best to look serious and concerned and not start laughing. "Questions?"

Cathy held her hands to her cheeks and stared away from him. "It'll be fine, I'm sure. Maybe I just won't tell them. No, they'll guess as soon as they see my face!"

Nick jogged her elbow with his arm to get her attention. When she looked at him again, he repeated, "Questions?"

"Oh! Oh, yes, what I was supposed to find out!" She cleared her throat and didn't look at him. What Nick could see of her face made him think she looked at notes on a blackboard. "How old are you?"

"Thirty," Nick managed. He jerked back as her head whipped around.

"Thirty? I knew you were older than most of the guys I've dated! You just seem so, well, more mature than them."

"Boys," Nick sneered.

Cathy smiled. "Gosh, you sounded just like my dad, there." She laughed when he scowled. "You only sounded like him, okay?" Then she leaned forward, almost nose to nose with him as she peered into his eyes. "Now, the most important question—especially since I'm sitting in your lap—are you married?"

He had to apply iron self-control to stop the impulse to kiss her. She was adorable! He tried to sound serious. "Never. Raised right. D-d-d-don't fool around."

"Whew!" She relaxed. Then she tensed again. "Children?"

"Want some," Nick said with a nod. His lips began to curl into a smile again.

"Oh, good, I mean—wait, that wasn't what I meant…oh, never mind." She looked flustered. "Do you go to church? I mean, I'm a Baptist, I was just wondering…" She subsided again while a blush crept over her cheeks.

"Baptist deacon." He stopped hiding his smile. "Ridgeview. North of t-t-t-town."

"Really? I go to First Baptist here in town. I'm surprised I haven't seen you at any of the association meetings."

They both forgot about the show as they began to learn about each other. Cathy had been home-schooled by her mother and grew up in a sheltered family life. Nick figured that was why she seemed so young. He had to control his grin again when she explained.

"They said I talked too much at school! Can you believe that?" she huffed.

She learned he was a horse trainer. "Ooh, I just knew you were a cowboy! I work in a flower shop. I love flowers! They smell so good!" She leaned forward and sniffed his neck. "Not as good as you. But they are prettier!" She giggled when he pretended to growl.

Their stomachs reminded them to get something to eat at lunch. As he released her from his coat and she hopped up from his lap, he was reminded of the one question he had forgotten to ask her. He took her hand and tugged it gently. When she looked down at him, her brows raised in silent query, he stared at their joined hands. "You mind? Ab-b-b-out me?"

Cathy tilted her head and a wrinkle formed between her eyebrows. "Mind about you what?"

He scowled and jerked a thumb to his lips. She couldn't be that oblivious.

Her frown deepened, then cleared. "You mean your stutter? Do I mind? Why should I? You talk fine." She turned and pulled him along behind her. "Besides," she tossed over a shoulder. "My dad's is much worse. He usually just writes stuff down." Nick followed her down the steps in stunned silence.

Nick read about his clients and their events in the newspaper later that week. With his whole attention focused on his companion that day, he completely forgot the show. Since she didn't mind his stutter, he relaxed and said more to her than he did to his best friends. She still cuddled, too, which he enjoyed. He had never realized what he was missing. His pants felt tight at times, but it was worth it.

As the show closed and they realized they needed to leave, they strolled toward the parking lot. He debated with himself about how soon he should ask her out on a regular date. Come to think of it, it was the first time he had asked for a date. All his other dates had been arranged by his friends. That was pathetic, he thought with disgust.

"Are you mad about something, Nick?"

His attention snapped back to Cathy. She peered up at him in the dim light, a wrinkle between her eyebrows. "No," he denied, then shrugged. "Myself."

"You're mad at yourself? Why?"

He threw up his hands in frustration. There was no way he could explain it. He stared at her. Why couldn't he talk like her? She stared back at him, then smiled. He frowned. Did she think it was funny?

She patted his arm. "Where's your phone?"

He blinked but pulled it out of his pocket and showed it to her.

"Oh, good, it's the same as mine!" She took it from him and put her phone number and address in his contacts list. She handed it back to him and ordered, "Now send me a text and tell me what's wrong." She pulled her phone out and waved it at him.

Nick stared at the phone. Was she serious? After a moment's thought, though, he realized it was practical. He sighed and tapped a message into his phone. "Want to ask you for a date but not sure how," he typed and sent.

Her mouth dropped open. "Not sure how? What, haven't you ever asked anyone out before? Haven't you been on dates before?"

"Friends set up blind dates," he admitted, his lips pressed together as he sent it with a forceful tap of his thumb.

Her eyes opened wide. "Ooh, you have friends like mine, don't you?"

Nick laughed. Cathy had a gift for finding the humor in an embarrassing subject. He nodded and started typing again. "I enjoyed today. I want to see you again." They had reached her small truck by now.

She slipped out of the coat he had wrapped around her as they left the arena and handed it to him. He opened the door for her and watched her start the engine and turn the heater up. Then she surprised him by grabbing his face and pressing a quick kiss to his nose. "I had a wonderful time! When can we see each other again? What do you want to do next time?"

It wasn't hard for the two of them to spend time together. Neither of them was interested in spending time with other people in public. She shared an apartment with a couple of women, so they often wound up at his ranch when she didn't have to work. When he had time off from the horse training, they went on long drives through the countryside just talking. Much to his delight, the more he relaxed, the more his stutter eased off, and he was able to speak in longer sentences, but the texting still got a workout.

A few weeks later, Nick watched Cathy and her mom clear away the family's Thanksgiving leftovers. Cathy took after her mother, who smiled all the time and liked Nick immediately. Laura Thompson had welcomed him with a hug and a delighted squeal. "Oh, you look perfect together! Don't they look perfect, Mac?"

Her husband, Mac Thompson, was nothing like her or Cathy. Tall and muscled even more than Nick, he wore a grim expression all the time except when his eyes were on his wife and daughter. He stared at Nick and grunted. The grunt sounded doubtful.

Nick put his hand out and stared the man in the eye. "G-g-glad to m-m-meet you, s-sir."

Mac grunted again, but he shook Nick's hand. Nick felt optimistic when he let go and could still feel his fingers. He and Nick had no trouble communicating afterward, though both rarely spoke. Their body language and occasional grunts worked fine for them.

Nick understood what Cathy had been talking about when she complained about how it was their fault she cuddled without thinking. As soon as the two women walked out of the kitchen, they plopped themselves into their men's laps and made themselves comfortable. If Cathy saw her parents do this every night, it was no wonder she did it herself out of habit.

"It was so funny, Mom! I wish you had been there. There was Nick trying to explain something, and this old lady scolded him about ignoring me for his phone. The look on poor Nick's face!"

He looked away from Cathy's chuckles and caught the look from her father. Nick raised his eyebrows in mute question. The older man held his eyes, cocked his head, and raised his left hand, wiggling his ring finger. The question was clear to Nick. Was he going to propose?

Nick frowned at the other man. Of course, he was, but he didn't need to be prodded. He had a very romantic night planned, and he didn't need any help. Then he felt Cathy stiffen and looked up to see her glare at her dad. He sighed. This was not good.

"What do you think you're doing? You leave Nick alone. We've only known each other a few weeks," she snapped at her father.

Her mother spotted her husband's gesture before he dropped his hand. "Mac Thompson, how dare you ask Nick his intentions already? They barely know each other. Give them some time."

Mac just raised his eyebrows and looked back at the younger couple.

He ran his gaze up and down his daughter in Nick's lap. Cathy scowled again. Her mother did, too, and poked her husband in the eyebrow. Nick hid a grin. So that's where Cathy picked up that habit.

"Don't you raise your eyebrows at them." Cathy's mom scolded. "They have a right to get to know each other better without you prodding him with a shotgun."

Mac looked at his ring finger and waggled it in his wife's face. "No gun."

She swatted him but started chuckling. "Just because you sweet-talked me into marriage after only two weeks doesn't mean anybody else decides that fast."

Nick's eyebrows went up as well as he raised two fingers. Mac nodded and waggled his ring finger at the younger man again. Great, a pushy in-law in his future. Nick scowled, but Mac wouldn't back down.

"Whatever," Cathy grumbled. "But stop pushing Nick. Our relationship is our business, right, Nick? Nick!" She squealed as he stood with her in his arms.

He marched to the front door. Mac made it there just before them and swung it open with a bland smile. Nick glared at him. "Ruined my p-p-plans!" He strode out the door and ignored Cathy's sputters. He glanced back before stepping off the porch and saw Laura on the couch, her hands over her mouth and a gleam in her eyes. Mac just waved and shut the door.

Nick headed for his truck, glad the erratic Texas autumn weather had produced a cool Thanksgiving evening warmer than the October day they had met. He didn't mind keeping Cathy warm with his body heat, but he didn't want the distraction of goose bumps right now.

"Nick? What's wrong? What are you doing? Nick, answer me!"

He grumbled under his breath the whole way to his truck. He ignored Cathy's questions until she tugged hard on his ear. He tossed her over his shoulder and swatted her bottom. "Be still!" he snapped and stomped over to his truck's passenger door. Opening it, he dumped her sideways in the seat with her legs hanging out. Tugging her knees apart, he stepped between her legs. Pulling her tight, he planted a hard kiss on her lips and silenced her outrage.

When he leaned back so they could both catch their breath, he examined her dazed expression with satisfaction. He wouldn't use his fingers to stop her rants often in the future. Kisses were much better. He leaned past her and opened the glove compartment.

Cathy blinked her eyes as he straightened and dropped a softer kiss on her mouth. "What are you doing, why…" she started. Then her voice died away as she stared at the hand he held up in front of her face. Her eyes focused on the open ring box.

"That—th-th-that's a," she stammered, staring from it to him and back again.

"It's a r-r-ring," Nick said with a smile. He tugged her forward with his free arm around her until her feet hit the ground, then he dropped to one knee before her. "And this is a p-p-p-proposal." He took her shaking hand and kissed it while he held the ring up higher. "Love you. Want to marry you. Had plans, d-d-darn your dad."

Cathy sagged down to her knees before him and took his face in her hands. "You were going to propose already? Daddy didn't force you into this. You were going to do it anyway?"

He scowled. "Had p-p-p-plans," he repeated through tight lips. "Roses, c-c-candles, dinner. Could p-p-punch him."

Cathy's laughter rang out, and she threw her arms around his neck. "Oh, Nick, we don't have to have a romantic dinner. I'd love one, but this is perfect. I love your proposal, and I love you. I want to marry you and have your children and cuddle with you every day. Love you, love you, love you!" She dropped kisses all over his face until he captured her mouth and pinned her in place.

They sat back after a few minutes. "L-l-love you," Nick started.

Laura's voice came from the front door. "I don't see them anywhere. Did they leave? But his truck is still here. Did they go for a walk?"

Cathy buried her giggles in Nick's shoulder as he sighed. "I guess we'd better go back before they come looking for us and we'll all be wandering around in the dark," she suggested through her laughter.

He nodded, resigned, but he held her in place until he placed the ring on her finger and kissed her again. They helped each other up and went back to the house.

It wasn't until Nick saw Mac's raised eyebrows and the direction of his stare that he realized both he and Cathy were dusty from the knees down. He was grateful she had decided to wear jeans for Thanksgiving dinner like him. He bent down and dusted both their legs, hiding his blush.

Cathy's mother was more interested in the ring Cathy waved in her face. She grabbed them both by the elbows and pulled them into the house. "Oh my gosh, Nick, it's beautiful! Mac didn't pressure you into this, did he?" she asked with sudden alarm.

Cathy shook her head. "He was going to take me to a romantic dinner. I told him we could still go, but he already planned to ask me. Isn't it wonderful?" She spun around and hugged Nick hard. "You're wonderful! I love you so much! I'm so happy right now!"

Mac folded his arms. "When?"

His wife rolled her eyes. "They can go to dinner anytime, silly. Who cares? They're engaged now, so leave them alone."

Nick and Mac both shook their heads and sighed.

Mac tapped his wife's bottom to get her attention off Cathy's ring, which both women were admiring again. "Wedding!" he corrected.

Cathy scowled at her father. "Since you ruined Nick's plans for a proposal, he gets to pick the date!"

Nick blinked as the Thompson family stared at him. No pressure, right. His eye caught the flashing lights on the Christmas tree he had helped decorate that afternoon. "Christmas." He didn't want to see his future father-in-law give him that grim stare every time they met.

"Next Christmas? Well, we'd certainly be able to arrange a nice wedding by then," Laura said, disappointment clear on her face.

"Next Christmas!" Cathy exclaimed. "Why do you want to wait a whole year?"

Mac and Nick locked eyes for a moment over the women's heads, then rolled their eyes, dropped their heads back to stare at the ceiling, and said, "Gah!"

Laura tapped her husband's chest with the back of her hand. "Just what is that supposed to mean?"

Cathy put her hands on her hips. "Exactly what I want to know!"

Nick threw his hands in the air, snatched her up, and tossed her over his shoulder again. He strode to the big calendar that hung just inside the kitchen doorway and dropped her to her feet.

"Nick Williams, if you ever pull that stunt again, I'm going to—!"

He stopped her threats with another hard kiss. Yep, kisses were the best way to shut her up. He took her chin as she took a breath and turned her face to the calendar. The two-month display had November and December together on it. He thrust his forefinger at the date marked with a Christmas tree. "Christmas!" he repeated with emphasis.

Cathy's mouth dropped open. "You mean this Christmas? But that's so soon! Why not Valentine's Day or another day? It will be hard to get everything done by Christmas."

Nick clenched his jaw. He glared at the doorway as Mac bent over with silent laughter and Laura swatted her husband with a dishcloth. He marched over to the door and closed it in their faces. Then, returning to Cathy, he lifted her up to sit on the counter and held her hips as he fought to speak the words he wanted so badly to say.

Cathy touched his cheek gently. "Nick, it's okay. We can do it by Christmas."

Nick shook his head. "N-n-need to t-t-tell you. Want t-t-to t-t-tell you!"

She smiled. "Then whip out your phone and text it. It will be fine."

He shook his head. "Not for t-t-typing. Must s-s-say it. You d-d-deserve it!"

Cathy opened her mouth to speak again, but he kissed her quickly. He shook his head and held his hands up to signal her to wait. Shoving away from her, he began to pace back and forth in front of her. He tugged at his hair as he struggled with his mouth.

"L-l-love you. Want you. N-need you." He jerked to a stop in front of her and waved his hands. "You—you light my w-world. S-s-sunlight. Can s-s-see colors I never c-could. M-make me want to smile. Make m-me happy. W-want that every d-day. Want it n-now!"

He wrapped his arms around her as he saw her cry. "No, not t-tears!"

She shook her head and hugged him until he could barely breathe.

"Happy tears, silly man! Oh, Nick, that speech makes me want to run off to Vegas right now! Who needs to wait until Christmas!"

Both their heads jerked around as a wail arose on the other side of the door. "No! Darn you, Nick Williams, you may be a sweet talker like her daddy, but don't you dare cheat me out of my only daughter's wedding! We're going to have a fancy church wedding with her in my wedding dress and a real preacher! Don't you dare run off to Vegas! What—you put me down this instant, Mac Thompson!"

The younger couple opened the door in time to see Cathy's daddy walking away with her mother over his shoulder. "N-no Vegas," Mac said, warning clear in his tone and the look over his shoulder at the two in the kitchen doorway.

Cathy rolled her eyes and heaved a sigh, but Nick laughed. "No Vegas," he agreed. "W-want to s-see her dressed fancy and s-show everybody m-my good taste."

Cathy slapped his chest but smiled. "I want to see you—and my daddy—in a tuxedo, then."

Mac stopped dead and dropped his beaming wife to her feet as he swung around to share a look of horror with Nick. Tuxedos? Fittings? They both grimaced. Cathy and her mom shared a look of triumph. Nick opened his mouth, but Cathy used his own method, kissing him to shut him up.

"Don't bother arguing," Cathy told him. "You may be a sweet-talking man, but I'm stubborn! Besides, I want all the women who walked away from you to see what I was smart enough to keep! They'll kick themselves all the way home."

Nick could only laugh at the glee on her face. He thanked God again for the cold day He had brought warmth into his lonely life.

The End

A VERY BRITISH AUTUMN

MORGEN BAILEY

"*I*t's all very romantic, isn't it?"

Iris looked over at her colleague, Carrie, who was staring out of their office window, down onto the English city of Cambridge, and more specifically their university's nearest courtyard where its yearly late-October 'Great Court Run' was about to take place. "Sorry?"

"This vista. Very romantic. All the old architecture nestled among the new."

It was the first race in Carrie's lifetime at Trinity College, so it was understandable that she'd find it exciting. Given that this was Iris' seventeenth, the novelty had waned years earlier, but a small spark of passion had ignited when Carrie had spoken of romance. Although love seemed as far away as the sea from where they were, Iris was ever hopeful of an 'autumn adventure'.

Iris smiled as Carrie giggled. "There's a guy here in a penguin suit. Ooh, and a girl with huge white hands and a red outfit, just like Minnie Mouse."

"Very sensible. They'll be nice and snug. It's biting out there."

Carrie then turned to face Iris. "Are you coming to watch?"

Iris shook her head. "Tom wants these reports by three." She tapped the top file as if there had been any doubt as to what she was talking about. She looked at the clock. Eleven forty. No wonder there was such a buzz below them, not least because the run was taking place on a Friday rather than the usual Saturday. No reason had been given, but with a protest against global warming hitting the city the following day, Iris thought the switch eminently sensible.

"Twenty minutes," Carrie proclaimed, lifting her left wrist, around which was her pedometer watch.

"You go. I'll take any calls. It's nearly lunchtime anyway."

They always took it in turns to have their breaks; Carrie half-past twelve to half-past one then Iris had the next hour. No one would notice if Carrie had a bit longer. She'd put in enough overtime over the previous few weeks and claimed none of it.

Had Iris and Bob had children, she would have wanted a daughter exactly like Carrie. She couldn't have wished for a better colleague. They needed to get on as they were the only two in the small square office but then Iris gelled with most people—taking some under her wing—the exception being only those who didn't get on with anyone else, but her relationship with Carrie had felt natural from day one.

Carrie too was single, and Iris's brain had whirred into action as soon as Carrie had let slip that she had enrolled on a dating site shortly after moving to Cambridge from Wales to take up the assistant position. Iris had fallen for the girl's soft accent, and both had been happy to talk while they worked until anyone came in.

Iris had quickly written off trying to play cupid between Tom, their boss, and Carrie. Apart from him being older than her, and too young for Iris, he was far too stuffy, a typical old-school academic, although Aaron, who had joined the team the day before Carrie, was a possible suitor being no more than five years her senior... and much more fun.

"Suitor." Iris laughed when she thought of the pairing. How old-fashioned she felt despite being the right side of sixty-five.

"Huh?" Carrie said, still looking out of the window.

"Nothing. You'd better get going, or you'll miss the start."

Carrie looked at her watch again. "Ooh. Yes. Thanks, Iris. I'll make it up to you."

Iris shook her head. "No need."

Carrie blew her a kiss before heading downstairs.

It was true. Tom did need the reports, but Iris knew that the race itself would be over in less than a minute. Being eleven years since the record of 42.7 seconds had been set, it was unlikely that anyone would break it. Even Olympians Sebastian Coe and Steve Cram had only managed 46.0 and 46.3 seconds respectively in 1988. Dating back to the 1920s, the event had been replicated in the classic 1981 movie *Chariots of Fire*, although it hadn't actually been filmed at Trinity.

"The course is approximately 370 metres long. Depending upon the state of winding, the clock takes between about 43 and 44½ seconds," Iris said to herself, quoting the college's page, although she knew the weather could also be a contributing factor. She wondered how many people, having seen the film, would play the iconic music in their heads while doing the run. She thought they'd probably be too busy concentrating, and anyway, it had seemed slower because of the music. No. That had been the run on the beach, not the courtyard. Iris shook her head and frowned at her grey cells' unreliability.

A high-pitched squeal made Iris rush to the window. How she'd heard the sound above the hubbub, she'd never know, but it had been there. She couldn't be sure who had made it, but Iris spotted Carrie jumping up and down and hugging a man Iris had never seen before. He was suited and booted so likely a new lecturer from another area of the campus—Iris knew all the long-term professors—or perhaps from one of the other colleges, but how Carrie knew him baffled Iris. But she'd knew she'd find out. Carrie wouldn't be able to keep it to herself when she returned to the office. Was he why she'd made such a brave move across the country? A five-hour trip every time she wanted to go home.

Aaron was also there, standing the other side of Carrie. They were colleagues, nothing unusual about that until Iris spotted Aaron slipping his hand into Carrie's and squeezing. Was that what he was doing? Iris was actually a little too far to see for sure, but she liked to think that nice things happened to other people, even if they rarely did—when it came to affairs of the heart—to Iris.

So, Iris stayed at the window.

With two minutes to go, the noise ceased, and Iris looked back at her desk wondering whether she had any pins she could drop. *Silly woman*, she thought and smiled.

Everyone waited for the first chime, and the air seemed to crackle with anticipation.

She pictured the scene from the film. The two men running then, the dozens now. How times had changed. Here there were... Iris started counting but simply too many. Like the number of words on a page, she counted heads across and how many rows there might be. Two, three hundred runners in total? Many more than the two in *Chariots of Fire*, that was for sure.

Finally, Iris mouthed four 'bong bings' in time with the introductory chimes as they primed the racers for the 'off'.

A loud cheer went up at the first strike of twelve, and the competitors were off, lunging forward. The noise over the next minute was deafening, with shouts varying from names to "go on", "yeah!", and Iris was sure there was a "faster" thrown in more than once.

Despite always having had a 'thing' for Nigel Havers, Iris didn't mind that he hadn't won in the film version. She couldn't remember who the other actor was—Jeremy Irons, she thought, someone with dark hair—but she'd check when she got back to her desk.

With it soon all over, a very serious-looking young man in a tracksuit was hailed as the hero, and rather than being proud, he seemed disappointed. Perhaps he'd not made his personal best, or not beaten the second placed by enough, Iris didn't know, but she tut-tutted at how competitive everything had become but then...

Minnie Mouse and the penguin were among the last but didn't seem at all bothered as they gave each other a hug that lasted longer than friendship and certainly more than strangers. They didn't kiss before pulling away, but both looked somewhat embarrassed.

Iris couldn't see Carrie nor the older man she'd seemed so pleased to greet, but Iris would get all the gory details after lunch.

Returning to her desk, Iris googled 'chariots of fire courtyard race' and clicked on the YouTube video link.

A man with a stripy cap was drawing a chalk line on the stone slabs before asking the crowd blocking the path to move away. Announcing the sole runner, who Iris didn't recognise—he wasn't Jeremy Irons, she'd check later—Nigel appeared through the crowd, throwing his hat not into the ring, courtyard, but to a friend, followed by a bottle of what looked like champagne. Then his scarf went, and he was ready.

Iris paid little attention to the conversation as she was too intrigued by a man resembling the actor Peter Davidson in the background looking baffled by the events. She guessed she'd have to watch the film in its entirety to find out who he was and why he was reacting thus, but the camera then panned to the two participants, and Iris again mouthed the bong bings before cheering along with the crowd, clapping slightly then bringing her fingers to her nose, palms together in a prayer-like action.

She lowered her middle fingers either side of each other and then twisted her palms and wiggled her middle fingers, giggling like a four-year-old. Spring was long gone, and the next seemed far too distant, but there was definitely something in the air.

With the reports done and a couple of minutes to spare before the lunchtime changeover, Iris drank the last of her summer fruits flavoured water and washed the glass in the tiny sink in the corner of their office. The drying rack clattered as Iris knocked the bottom of the glass against it. The work surface was really too small as the rack competed for space with a microwave and table top fridge, but it wasn't in Iris' brain at that moment.

When Carrie returned, Aaron appeared with her, alongside the older man Iris had seen them with earlier. She didn't say anything when they crossed the small office but waited for Carrie to explain. She didn't disappoint.

"Dad, Iris, Iris, my father. Dr. Robert Foster." Carrie beamed, seeming happier than ever. Iris couldn't blame her.

Carrie's father stepped forward. "Robert Foster. Very pleased to meet you, Iris. Carrie's told me so much about you. I feel I know you already." His accent, as if Iris should be surprised, replicated Carrie's exactly.

Iris wanted to say the same but couldn't. Carrie had never mentioned her father. She'd always skirted around the topic of her parents whenever Iris had brought it up. It also meant that Iris didn't know whether there was a Mrs. Foster. Not that it mattered. Carrie's father lived in Wales. A well-known five-hour commute. "Lovely to meet you," was all Iris said and shook the proffered hand.

She'd almost expected him to kiss her hand as he lifted it but instead just said a simple, "Enchanté."

Iris felt heat rising from her neck and put one hand to it as if to disguise any outward evidence. She knew she could get blotchy at the hint of embarrassment and it was not the time for that.

"Dad and I have just been to The Senate for lunch... with Aaron of course."

"Of course," Iris said and hoped that hadn't come across as snippy. She was pleased for them, really, she was, just surprised. She'd had no inkling that the two of them had done anything more than chatted about work. Iris certainly hadn't spotted any flirting or... what was the word? Banter?

"I'm stuffed," Carrie continued, putting a hand on her almost-flat stomach. "Do you have any plans for lunch, Iris?"

Iris hadn't, beyond the usual removing of her salad and bottle of flavoured water from the fridge and sitting on one of the benches in the grounds, reading another chapter of her latest book—currently Simon Hall's *The TV Detective*. She was enjoying it, especially given that the author was local, although this book was set in Devon, where Iris had contemplated retiring to in a few years' time. She gave a weak no.

"Great!" Carrie looked at her father, who shrugged, then at Aaron.

"Dr Foster's my guest for the afternoon, Iris, but I have things I can be doing for an hour..." Without waiting for an answer, Aaron headed to his office, leaving Iris somewhat confused.

Dr Foster clapped. "Okay, then. If you really don't mind a chaperone..."

"Erm... If you don't mind watching me eat." Iris blushed.

"Not at all."

"That's settled then," Carrie concluded, sitting down at her desk.

Iris gave a weak smile and went to the fridge to retrieve her lunch. With her handbag looped over her shoulder, the new pair left the room.

As they crossed the courtyard to one of only two benches in the sun, Iris imagined Carrie's eyes boring down on her. Iris didn't know if she was looking and wasn't going to turn around to check. Anyway, she was too engrossed in what Robert was saying to think about it any further.

"Yes, just here for a few days. When Carrie told me where she was moving to, I admit I wasn't surprised. She was born in Cambridge, I went to school here, met her mother in the city, so it's natural that Carrie would want to return. She'd been rather restless since her mother died."

"I'm sorry," Iris said instinctively.

Robert simply nodded.

"So, you're familiar with the Great Run," Iris continued.

Robert shook his head. "That's the crazy thing. Although I went to school here, it wasn't Trinity, so I never got to see the run. I could have come later, but we moved back to Wales when Carrie was five—"

"Back?"

"I'm a Glasbury baby, not to be confused with Glastonbury, and not a million miles from Hay on Wye, hence the accent—our accent—and our love of books."

"A beautiful part of the country, kingdom, United Kingdom. Stop waffling, Iris."

Robert smiled. "Please don't be nervous. Are you nervous? There's no need to be."

Iris wasn't sure, but yes, she felt something. Was it nerves? It had to be.

"No, no need at all." Robert looked around the courtyard. "So, is this what you do with your lunch breaks?"

"Watch crazy people run about in costumes?"

Robert laughed. "Something like that."

"No, although I did look from above." She pointed to her office window.

"Lovely vista."

"Just what Carrie said, or something similar anyway."

"Like father, like daughter."

"Very."

"Have you worked here long, Iris?"

Iris blew out a breath. "Seventeen years. Eighteen in January."

Robert whistled. "That's good going. Although it strikes me as the kind of place where you either move on quickly or stay forever."

Iris laughed. "I guess I'm the latter."

"Do you have any plans?"

"What do you mean?"

"Work. Play. What you want to do with your life?"

"Like a bucket list?"

"Yes, something like that."

"Retire by the sea, have a dog, a camper van perhaps. It depends."

"Upon?"

Iris didn't want to say anymore. Although it was clear that they were both single, she didn't want to take anything for granted. She hadn't wanted their status to be a reason for something to happen. It couldn't anyway. The five-hour gap would see to that.

They sat in companionable silence while Iris ate her salad. She wasn't particularly hungry which was just as well as she'd forgotten to bring the cheese, which she had dutifully wrapped in cellophane to stop it getting soggy... then left it by the toaster, and she'd run out of beef tomatoes—her favourites—so there was no real substance to it.

Robert shook his head to Iris' offer of sharing her drink. "But thank you. I had a Wyld Woods with my lunch. Boy, was it wild!"

Iris crinkled her face. "Wild woods?"

"Oh, cider. Not quite scrumpy as I know it. Kicks like a mule."

They laughed, and Iris felt any tension seeping away. They'd been thrown together, she'd had no choice but to say yes to his company, but she had no regrets.

Talking all the way back to the office about something and everything, they'd covered their life histories in less than ten minutes.

Iris noticed Carrie sit up straighter as Iris and Robert walked into the office. Aaron must have heard them as he joined them a few seconds later.

"Hey," Carrie said, and the two men smiled.

A subtle look passed between them, though not subtle enough for

Iris to have missed it and she wondered whether they had met before, that Carrie and Aaron had been a 'thing' for longer than a day, a week, a month. Iris hoped so.

"Ready for your tour?" Aaron asked Robert.

"Absolutely. Looking forward to it." Robert then turned to Iris. "Thank you so much, young lady, for your company. It's been a pleasure."

"Never a chore," Iris blurted before slapping her hand over her mouth.

"Her favourite line from *Maybe Baby*," Carrie explained. "Hugh Laurie to Joely Richardson after they've had sex on Primrose Hill."

Iris flushed and wanted the ground to open and swallow her whole, but Robert just laughed.

"I remember. Fabulous film. Carrie made me sit through it, oh, at least a dozen times. Altogether. Not one after the other. There was at least…" He turned to Carrie then back to Iris. "A day in between?"

Iris smiled.

Robert continued. "I'm more of a Notting Hill fan myself. Prefer babies when they're this…" He pointed to Carrie. "Age."

It was Carrie's turn to flush and looked at Aaron. "The tour?"

"Yes. Robert?"

Robert was still looking at Iris. "Again, a pleasure. I hope to see you upon our return?"

Iris nodded, said nothing.

Peering at her keyboard, Carrie said, "Later, Dad."

It took less than a minute for Carrie to jabber about her father and the reason for his visit—although he'd already told Iris, Carrie wasn't to know that.

Iris hardly got a word in, but she didn't mind. The filing cabinet between the ends of the women's desks was positioned so Iris could still face Carrie even when returning seemingly endless files. It was a job both women had been putting off, but the pile had threatened to collapse on the floor, and with the weekend looming, Iris wanted to leave a tidy office.

The afternoon sped by, chat interspersed with the women taking it in turns to make hot drinks, and Iris looking at the doorway far too often in the hope that the men would return. Tom was conspicuous by his absence, but Iris knew he had a board meeting on Monday and it was more than her job was worth to disturb him. He had his own coffee machine, with plenty of supplies, so other than nature breaks, no one would have known he was there.

The college clock struck four as the office door opened. Iris hadn't noticed it close since the last time she'd looked at it but then had remembered Carrie had gone to the ladies a few minutes earlier. Iris had been printing some address labels for Tom's official Christmas cards, tutting at the festivities being planned so early. *August in the shops*, she reminded herself so perhaps eight weeks before wasn't so bad.

"I've cleared it with Tom that we can all leave," Aaron announced as he and Robert entered the room. Aaron raised an eyebrow at Iris then winked at Carrie. "Everyone taking part in the run... and their families and so on... went to the pub straight after so we'd be late to the party, but it would be a shame not to get the ambience..."

"Great!" Carrie beamed, logging off from her computer.

"You ready?" Aaron asked, retrieving Carrie's coat from a nearby stand and holding the coat for her to slip into it.

Carrie nodded furiously then whispered something to her father.

As Iris put on her coat, he approached her desk and picked up her handbag, holding it for her until she was ready. *Suits you*, Iris had been tempted to say but felt silly, unsure of his sense of humour.

"Just my colour, don't you think?" Robert said, placing Iris' bag against his hip.

The four friends burst out laughing.

Aaron winked at Iris as a blush spread across her face. He slipped his hand into Carrie's and led her out of the office. Robert offered Iris his hand, and she felt her heart thump as her skin touched his.

The End

8

A SEASON FOR A SECOND CHANCE

RENEE MARSKI

*T*he ink smudged as he signed his name with a flourish. "So glad that's over," he muttered, shoving the document away from him.

His lawyer picked up the packet and handed it to the lawyer across the table. He attempted a smile, but it didn't quite reach his grey eyes. It had been a long process, getting these two to come to an agreement over the dissolution of their marriage.

His lawyer grasped his hand tightly. "Glad I could be of service, Jack."

Jack nodded, barely looking at him. In fact, only one person in the room held his attention. She sat across the table, her hands clasped firmly in her lap. Her dark brown hair fell about her shoulders in waves. Her mouth was a thin line of pink. He searched her hazel eyes like a man drowning.

"I can't change your mind, can I?"

She stood, ignoring him. Shaking her lawyer's hand, she sighed with relief, then quickly walked out of the room. Her lawyer smiled sadly at him. The older gentleman had seen divorces like this—one party trying to reach the other through the gap that had been built. In his experience, it had never ended well. He ran a hand through his grey hair, regretting that he hadn't gotten it cut before the meeting.

"Until next time, Tom," he said, nodding at Jack's lawyer.

"Frank. Pleasure as always." They shook hands, both glancing at Jack. "You think he'll be OK?"

Tom shrugged. "I think so. It'll take time."

Frank eyed Tom closely. The last six months had taken their toll. His black hair had more grey than when they'd started, and more lines had appeared on his craggy face. Jack's haggard appearance worried everyone. He hadn't shaved in three weeks, and his sandy hair brushed the collar of his blue button-up.

"Hey, Jack, why don't we go to dinner?"

Jack slowly looked away from the door. His shoulders slumped, and he quickly brushed a tear from his green eyes. "Yeah, a meal sounds good."

The lawyers nodded at each other. Tom clapped Jack's shoulder as he led him out of the room.

Over dinner, Jack lamented the end of his marriage. "She just stopped talking to me, Tom. I couldn't get her to respond to anything I said. You can't fix a marriage when one person won't participate."

Tom nodded, taking a bite of his burger. Jack's third beer glistened in the light of the bar. "Any idea what happened?"

Popping a fry in his mouth, Jack shrugged. "Who knows? One day she was fine, the next it was over. Guess I'll never know." He finished his beer in one swig and slammed down the glass. "Better get home." He shook Tom's hand one last time. "I really hope I never have to use your services again." Tom nodded as Jack rushed into the night, pulling his coat tightly closed.

"Me too, buddy, me too."

Hannah leaned back in her chair, rubbing her eyes. Staring at a computer screen all day really did a number on the brain. Glancing at the clock, she sighed. She had managed to work past 8pm again. Staying late for the third night that week had taken its toll on her personal life.

While her boyfriend loved her work ethic, he wished she would take more time for herself. In the six months since her divorce, she had immersed herself in work. It helped distract her from the pain that still managed to creep up.

The beeping of her phone pulled her out of her reverie. "Hello?"

"Babe, where are you?"

She smiled, her eyes crinkling. "I'm at work. Where else would I be?"

A sigh escaped before he could stop it. "At dinner with me, remember?" Champagne Lounge, 8:30?"

She leaned her forehead on her desk. "Ugh, Danny, I'm sorry. I'll leave now."

"I'll save a place for you."

He hung up, leaving her staring at her phone. She gathered her things and shut down her computer. She hurried out of the office, pulling her dark hair back from her face. In the three months since she'd been dating Danny, she'd been late to every single date. It seemed he almost expected it of her.

As she sat, he kissed her cheek. His slicked-back hair and clean-shaven face gave him a youthful look. His youthful smile hid his four-year seniority over her. "Busy day?"

She nodded, taking a sip of the wine he had ordered for her. "Same as usual."

He nodded, looking down at his menu. His manner unnerved her. His quietness worried her. She looked at the menu without seeing it, slowly chewing on her bottom lip.

"Hannah…"

She looked up. Worry creased her brow as she mentally prepared herself. They'd had a good run, but she knew he could take only so much before admitting they didn't work as a couple.

"Maybe you aren't ready yet."

"What?"

"Maybe it's too soon for you to be dating. You seem more likely to forget me than anything else. And you really don't let me in. I think we're jumping in too fast. You need time to get over him."

"Danny, don't be ridiculous. I promise I'm over Jack."

He took her hand. "No, you aren't. You run from intimacy like it's going to burn you. That's normal. If you remember, I was like that after my divorce. I'm not going anywhere. I'll be here when you're ready."

Tears sprang to her eyes. "He begged me not to. I still hear him in the back of my mind."

Danny nodded. "Again, normal. You'll be fine. Let's just take it slow."

She nodded, feeling her whole body relax. Taking another sip of her wine, she smiled.

Dinner ended three hours later when the restaurant kicked them out. They laughed as they walked to their cars. He held her door open for her, then kissed her cheek as she climbed in. She giggled, smiling up at him.

As he leaned down for a deeper kiss, her phone beeped. "Ignore it," he breathed against her cheek. She shook her head, blindly pulling her phone out of her purse.

Flipping it open, she scrunched her eyebrows, then bit her lip, clasping the phone to her ear. After a few seconds, it fell from her shaking hands with a clatter.

Danny grabbed her hand, turning her to him. The light from the street lamps illuminated her pale face.

"It's Jack. He's, um, he's…" She bit her fist, closing her eyes.

"Talk to me, Hannah. What's wrong with Jack?"

Tears glistened in her eyes as she looked at him. "There's been an accident. He's in the hospital."

"Why did they contact you?"

She shook her head, reaching for her keys. "I don't know, but I have to go. He must not have changed his emergency contact." Starting her car, she looked up at him. "I'll call you once I know more."

He nodded, closing her car door. She sped off into the night, unsure what she'd find.

A doctor looked up as Hannah rushed into the room, her hair a tangle around her shoulders, her eyes searching frantically. As they rested on Jack's serene face, she sighed and slumped into a chair.

"You must be Mrs. Tannen."

She shook her head. "Connor. I went back to my maiden name." She took a deep breath. "How is he?"

"Sleeping. We gave him a sedative. He was pretty out of it when he got out of surgery."

She nodded, reaching for Jack's hand. Its warmth reassured her. "He'll recover?"

The doctor nodded. His brown hair fell into his dark eyes as he looked at her. "There's one problem, though. It seems he has some amnesia. He hit his head pretty hard. He woke up asking for you. We aren't sure how extensive it is yet, but it seems he may not remember the accident or a period before it."

"How long of a period?"

The doctor shook his head, his broad shoulders moving slightly. "Like I said, we don't know yet."

She nodded, sitting back in the chair. "He may not know we're divorced."

The doctor leaned closer. "It's probably best if you don't mention that yet. Let's get him out of the hospital first."

"So, what should I do? Play wife?" She crossed her arms, hunching over in the chair.

"Only for a day or two. Hopefully, the memories will come back on their own, and you won't have to pretend for long."

Clenching her jaw, she glared up at him. "Easy for you to say."

"Suit yourself. The shock alone won't be good for him." The doctor marched out of the room, not looking back.

Hannah curled up further into herself, wrapping her arms around her knees. She looked at Jack's face, noting the hard lines around his mouth. Not a lot to smile about in the last year. She rubbed her forehead and stretched out on the couch, unsure what to do.

"Hannah?"

Her head popped up at the sound of his voice. She looked to the bed to find him still asleep, calling her name. She wiped her eyes, amazed she had slept so well. She stood and paced the room, rolling her shoulders as she went.

"Sore neck," he whispered.

She spun quickly to find him staring at her. His eyes softened, and he reached out his hand. She took it, unsure what to say. "Are you, uh, thirsty?"

He nodded, glancing at the bedside table. She grabbed a cup and poured his water, handing it shakily to him. His fingers brushed hers as he took it, sending a chill up her spine. It had been over a year since he'd touched her. She turned away quickly, clutching her fingers like they burned.

"How long have I been here? What happened?"

She turned back, plastering a smile on her face. "They brought you in last night. There was a car accident. You hit your head badly. The doctor says you may have forgotten some things but that they'll return in time."

Jack scratched his cheek and looked up at the ceiling. "Let's see...I remember who I am and my job. Best of all, I remember you, my lovely wife." He grinned from ear to ear, the biggest smile she had seen in a while.

She nodded slowly, looking down at her hands. "Yes, but he said you may not remember the accident or the events leading up to it." She grabbed her purse and pulled out a business card. "I have to go home, get ready for work. Call me if you need anything."

He eyed the card, his eyebrows wrinkling. "Why do I need your card to do that?"

She spun around with a smile. "I've changed my number recently. I wasn't sure you'd remember the new one."

He eyed the number and sighed, placing the card on his bedside table. "You're right, I don't remember it. Good thinking, babe."

He looked at her expectantly. She realized he wanted a kiss. Hannah held her breath, pecking him quickly on the cheek.

"I'll call at lunch to check on you." She strode from the room as quickly as she could without running.

———

That evening, his doctor told her he would be able to go home the following day. "We would prefer he didn't go alone. Someone should stay with him."

She sighed, rubbing her temples. "So now you expect me to stay with him? I haven't lived with him in over a year. None of my stuff is there."

The doctor shrugged. "Just a suggestion." He moved away, stopping a nurse to discuss the chart in his hand.

She leaned against the pillar next to the nurses' station, fighting back the tears. Life just didn't seem fair. Her phone vibrated, pulling her out of her self-pity. "Hello?"

"Hannah, is everything okay? How's Jack?" Danny's voice soothed her frayed nerves.

"Oh, Danny, it's horrible. He can't remember the accident or this last year. He thinks we're still married and now the doctor expects me to go home with him."

"Why? They do know you're divorced, right?"

"Yes, but they fear the shock will hurt him more. They want him to gain the memories back slowly. I don't want to hurt him, but I don't want to live with him, either."

"How long would it be?"

"They don't know." A nurse waved at her, and she sighed. "I have to go. I'll call you later."

She walked into the room, bracing herself. Jack shoveled food into himself, stopping only to take a swig of coffee. He looked up with a smile—the same smile he'd bestowed on her at the beginning of their marriage. "The food isn't half bad, but I'm really looking forward to your cooking."

She sat next to the bed, gripping her hands in her lap. "They say you can go home tomorrow."

He nodded.

She picked up his applesauce, taking a bite.

"It'll be nice to sleep in our bed instead of here."

She looked at the floor, gathering her thoughts. "There are some things you should know before we go home. There have been, um, changes. We moved, or rather are in the process of moving. Most of my stuff is still at our old place. I haven't had a chance to move it all yet." She wiped her sweaty hands on her pants before continuing. "It's a little smaller than our old place. We decided to save money so that we could eventually get a house."

He sat back, crossing his arms. "I finally gave in, huh? After all that arguing. What convinced me?"

She gulped, thinking quickly. "I can be persuasive when I need to be."

He laughed, a deep, throaty sound that shook his body. "Don't I know it."

She stood, gripping her purse tightly. "I have to go get things ready for you to come home. I'll see you tomorrow." She quickly kissed his cheek, then pulled away before he could stop her. His eyebrows knit together as she scurried from the room.

———

Hannah finished folding and placing her clothes in the tall oaken dresser. Thankfully, Jack had kept most of their furniture. Pressing her hands to the small of her back, she examined her handiwork. She had put up framed photos—including their wedding photo—that she'd found in the closet. She was amazed that he still had it.

She glanced at the clock wearily. The time to get him had come quicker than she'd anticipated.

He sat waiting for her at the front of the hospital. The eager look on his face made her smile. The Jack sitting in front of her reminded Hannah of the Jack he'd been when they first got married. The thought gave her pause until she remembered that his memory would one day come back, and he'd revert to being the man he'd become.

With a smile, he slid into the seat next to her. "Can we get food on the way? I'm starving."

Putting the car into drive, she smiled. "I'm making dinner like you asked, remember?"

He nodded. "I did, didn't I?"

She drove quickly, feeling trapped in the car with him. She prayed the amnesia wouldn't last too long. The longer she spent with this version of him, the more she remembered what had attracted her in the first place. "I got your favorite beer, too," she muttered.

He smiled. "Good. I called Danny this morning and invited him over tonight. I hope that's okay?"

Her breath came in short gasps. Danny had advised her that they not tell Jack of their relationship until after the divorce was finalized. The fact that they were best friends had always made Danny pause. He hadn't wanted to hurt Jack with news of their relationship. Hannah had agreed. Now, with the accident, they were trapped.

"That should be fine. I have enough food for all of us."

Jack leaned back and crossed his hands behind his head. Hannah glanced at him out of the corner of her eye. He seemed so relaxed, so calm. If only he'd stayed like this, she never would've left him. She shook the thoughts from her head. What ifs wouldn't do her any good.

As Jack settled himself, Hannah began cooking. Tonight, she would make chicken parmesan, Jack's favorite. She planned to play the part of the dutiful wife. The doctor ordered that Jack rest, so Hannah made him comfortable on the couch. He looked around the room, making note of the decorations. "It's small but homey. How much are we saving?"

She hesitated, biting her lip. She'd looked up the rent for this place, but it still hurt lying to him. "We save $400 a month here."

"And how long do we have to live here for?"

She closed her eyes, gathering her thoughts. "A year, two at the most."

He nodded, settling back into the couch cushions. With the flat screen in front of him, it really looked like a bachelor pad if you ignored the pictures.

A knock at the door brought her out of her reverie. Jack got to the door before she could move. Danny pulled him into a firm hug, patting his back. "Jack! It's so good to see you're up and moving." He looked over at Hannah and winked. "I see our cook is hard at work."

Jack laughed, slapping Danny on the back and pulling him towards the couch. "The best cook we could ask for."

Hannah brought Danny a beer, avoiding his eyes. She hunched her shoulders, quickly pulling her hand away from his. Then she set the table, blocking out his and Jack's conversation. When she called them to eat, Jack surprised her with a hug and a kiss. The warmth that spread from her toes to the top of her head made her quiver. Danny noticed the tremble in her hand and reached over to gently squeeze it. Hannah quickly pulled her hand away, turning from him. "Eat slowly, it's hot."

Both men nodded, blowing gently on their food. Jack kept smiling at Hannah, talking about all the things he wanted to do once the doctor gave him the okay. "Having a near-death experience really does that to you." He clasped Hannah's hand tightly. "I want to take you on that trip to Europe you've been asking for. And I was thinking we could start talking children."

Hannah coughed, choking on her wine. She poured herself another glass, taking a huge gulp. "A child? You always said you didn't want them."

He shook his head. "That was before. I've reexamined my priorities. I want a family with you, a future. I'm sorry I put you off for so long."

Hannah looked at Danny before turning back to Jack. "I don't know what to say; it's what I've always wanted." Her voice cracked, and she stood, grabbing her empty plate. Danny stood too, picking up his and Jack's plates.

"I'll help you with the dishes. Jack, put your feet up, buddy."

Jack headed to the couch while Danny followed Hannah into the kitchen. As soon as she set down her plate, he took her hands. "What are you thinking? You can't think this will work."

"I don't know what you're talking about."

He grabbed her face, forcing her to look at him. "You're falling for him. Everything he says is what you've been wanting to hear for years. This isn't him, Hannah. Soon, he'll remember, and it'll all be over."

She looked down, pulling away from him. "I know that. Let me enjoy the man he used to be; for just one night."

It sounded silly, even to her own ears. The man he used to be could disappear at any moment, and she wanted to enjoy him while she could.

Danny turned away. "Have it your way."

He left the kitchen, giving Jack a hug on his way out. Hannah scrubbed the plates, drinking more wine. She knew they could have only one night, and she wanted it to be a good one.

She jumped when she felt Jack's fingers trailing down her back. She turned into his embrace, kissing him for real this time. It felt so familiar, so like home. His hands explored her body, and she opened up to him, feeling free for the first time in ages. His hands on her felt right. She deepened her kiss, pulling him closer. She reached for his shirt, but he grabbed her hands, stopping her. She looked into his eyes, only to stop. His forehead crinkled as he searched her face.

"Hannah, why?"

She stepped back, wiping her mouth. "Why what?"

"Why did you leave me?"

She stumbled back, her hands covering her mouth. "You-you remember? Since when?"

He stepped toward her, brushing the hair from her face. "Since the second morning in the hospital."

Her eyes flashed in anger. "And you didn't tell me? I went through all this, and you lied to me?"

"Well, technically you were lying to me, but that's not the point. Be honest with me. Just this once, please tell me why."

She bit her lip, looking down. "For everything you were willing to give tonight. Children, the house of our dreams, everything. The more I asked, the more you pulled away until I was in the marriage alone. You were so selfish, you couldn't see what I needed. It broke my heart to do it, but you wouldn't listen to me. What else could I do?"

He touched her face gently. "I meant what I said tonight. About the trip and children. Spending the last few days with you has been amazing. I want to prove I can be the man you deserve and give you the life you want if you'll take me back. Please let me show you."

She enfolded his hand in hers, kissing the palm. "But we're divorced."

"We can fix that. We can turn our trip to Europe into another honeymoon."

"Do you really mean that?"

He pulled her close, pressing his lips to hers. "I do."

"Looks like we have another wedding to plan."

He laughed, picking her up and spinning her around. "Everyone will think we're crazy."

"I'm pretty sure we are."

"I now pronounce you husband and wife. You may kiss the bride."

Jack leaned in, pulling up Hannah's lace veil. She smiled at him, the grin spreading from ear to ear. Their kiss lasted for a full minute, stopping only when the pastor cleared his throat. Hannah pulled away with a giggle.

"Sorry, Brother Hank. Couldn't help ourselves."

He shook his head and pointed at the wedding guests. "If we could head to the reception, we can get your marriage license signed, and the party started."

The guests cheered, jumping up to follow the couple out.

Danny stood behind Jack as he signed. "It better stick this time, man. She isn't the kind of girl you let go of twice."

Jack looked up at him, frowning. "Because someone will steal her?" He slid the license over to Danny, who signed the witness spot.

"She's worth it. But in the end, she didn't love me the way she loves you. She wasn't willing to plan a life with me. To be honest, the biggest issue was that I wasn't you."

Jack shook Danny's hand, then pulled the license back towards him. "I know. I don't intend to mess up this time."

Danny grinned. "Hannah will make sure of it."

Jack looked over at his beautiful bride, her happiness blocking everything else. She batted her eyelashes, then dipped her head. She reached for Jack's hand, pulling him close.

"Ready to start this journey?" he asked.

Hannah nodded, pulling him through the door and into their new life.

The End

9

HARVEST ON THE MOUNTAIN

MICHELLE PRESLEY

CHAPTER ONE

A voice boomed over the walkie-talkie. "Randy, can you come to the gift shop?"

Randy stopped walking to answer the call. This day was not an easy day for him, as a matter of fact, the entire week had been rough. So, he had decided to take a walk through the many vines that made up Livingston Vineyard and Winery. The peace that the vines brought him always helped to get him moving again. Randy left his quiet sanctuary to see what was going on.

As he walked across the field through the many rows of perfectly lined grapes, he started thinking about what he would have to do to get ready for this year's harvest. His train of thought was broken when he walked into the gift shop.

Courtney, the girl his family hired to manage the gift shop walked up to him with another lady and a child. Randy was taken aback. There was something about this lady. He just couldn't take his eyes off her.

"Randy, this customer would like to know if we do tours of the vineyard. I told her that I didn't think we did. She asked to speak to you."

"Thanks, Courtney, I can take it from here."

With that, she left them to go back to the counter.

"So, what exactly can I help you with?" Randy asked.

"My son and I were wondering if you do tours? I have been telling him stories about the vineyard my grandparents and great-grandparents owned in Italy before World War Two. He's been curious ever since. I saw your vineyard as we were coming into town, I thought since we were going to be here for a few days that maybe you would let him look around."

Randy knelt down to the little boy's level. He couldn't be more than six years old. "Hello, I'm Randy. What's your name?"

The little boy smiled back and said his name was Steven. Randy was correct about his age; he was six years old. He had to be the cutest little boy Randy had seen in a while. Steven had chestnut hair, green eyes and a dimple in his left cheek. He was also wearing an Indians baseball cap sideways.

"Well, Steven, we don't usually do tours. However, given what your mom has told me, I think we can make an exception this one time so that you can see some of the things your grandparents would have done with their vineyard."

Steven was so excited he started jumping up and down. Randy stood back up to talk to
the boy's mother.

"Why don't you bring him back tomorrow evening after we close. That way we can take our time. He will be able to see everything that way."

"Thank you."

"By the way, I'm Randy." He smiled, offering his hand.

"I'm Diana," she responded, reaching out to shake the hand he offered.

When their hands touched, it sent a shock through Randy that nearly knocked him off his feet. He definitely wasn't expecting to react that way. When he looked up at her, he thought he saw something flicker in her eyes. Maybe he wasn't imagining it. Maybe, it wasn't just him. He knew she felt it, too.

When they let go, Diana stepped back, thanked him again and walked out the door with her son. As he watched her leave, Brad, one of the guys who worked at the tasting bar walked over.

"Hey, boss, are you okay?"

"Huh, um, yea," Randy answered.

He turned and walked out through the storage room to his office.

Good lord, what just happened?

In his head, he replayed the last five minutes. He couldn't remember ever feeling that way with any other woman, including his wife. Melissa passed away eight months earlier from injuries sustained in a car accident.

CHAPTER TWO

After a night of not sleeping well, Diana decided to take Steven to the restaurant next door to eat.

"Hey, Momma," Steven yelled while hitting the table.

Diana was also playing back everything that had happened the day before. This was the cause of her not sleeping.

"Yes, baby. What do you need?"

"Food. I'm hungry."

Diana couldn't help but smile. She loved her little man more than anything. After ordering Steven's breakfast, Diana's mind wandered back to what happened with Randy. She couldn't help herself. There was something about him that just twisted her up in knots. Not to mention he was easy on the eyes. But was she ready to jump into another relationship after what Steven's father did to her?

Steven hit the table again. Diana really needed to set what happened with Randy aside for now.

"Okay, honey, I'm sorry. What would you like to do after breakfast?"

Steven sat there for a minute fidgeting with his plate before answering.

"Can we go see the bears?" he asked anxiously.

Helen was known as an alpine style town. There were so many things that drew people to the area. Everything from the bears, the castle, the trolls, carriage rides, and Oktoberfest.

Diana had to come to town to meet a client and decided to arrive early to make it a holiday for her son as well.

"Baby, we can go see the bears."

While Diana and Steven were off seeing the sites, Randy was at the winery setting up for an event. These were the last three they had on the books before the harvest. Everyone was doing their best to make sure their guests enjoyed their visit to the winery.

Randy had people dusting shelves and putting out gift ideas while others polished and stocked the antique bar his great-grandfather hand-crafted almost a hundred years ago. All hands were setting up tables for a buffet lined with food specifically paired with the wines the guests would be tasting.

"Hey, boss, are you all right?" Jake asked as he walked by with a tray of food for the buffet.

"Yea, I'm okay."

Randy had been thinking about Diana and lost his train of thought. He was beginning to feel guilty about being attracted to her. The wedding party would be arriving soon. He had to shake it off. He needed to get through these last three events.

His family always shut the winery down every season for three weeks to bring the harvest in.

CHAPTER THREE

"Mom! Come on, I'm hungry, and I want to go see the vineyard."

Steven was so wound up that he was literally dragging his mother across the parking lot of the pizza parlor where they were going to have dinner.

"Hold on, honey, we have plenty of time. I promise the vineyard will still be there after you eat."

Diana couldn't help but smile at her son. Bringing him along turned out better than

she thought it would. She was surprised that he wasn't completely exhausted. It made her heart burst to see how happy he was.

Steven took it extremely hard when his dad left. Ever since that time, Diana tried to do what she could to make sure he was okay. While they enjoyed their dinner, Diana's client came in. Connie Abrams walked over to where they were sitting.

"Hello, Mrs. Abrams," Diana called to her client.

"Hello, I'm glad I ran into you."

"Is there anything wrong?" Diana asked.

She didn't think there was a problem. They had already planned everything for Connie's new boarding house over the phone and the internet. This was just a meeting to finalize everything they had already discussed.

"No, not at all. I just wanted to let you know that I was here early."

"Oh, okay. Where are you staying?"

"I got lucky. The Castle had an opening, so I snagged it."

"Did you come alone?" Diana asked.

"Yes, I figured it would be easier to get work done that way."

"Sounds good. I have Steven signed up for day camp at the Castle tomorrow so that we can work." Diana replied.

Connie smiled at Steven who was busy eating his pizza.

"How about we meet at the hotel restaurant for brunch around ten. That way I have time to get Steven where he needs to be. Working there we won't need to stop to go get anything."

"That'll work. I will see you then. Enjoy your evening."

Connie turned and walked to the counter to place her order.

Diana noticed that Steven was fidgeting again.

"All right, little man. Are you ready to go?"

Steven jumped up out of the booth so fast Diana thought her son had grown wings on his feet.

Randy was finishing up his last event of the summer season; it was for the Silver Ladies

Of Michigan. One of the ladies heard about the winery from her daughter, so they agreed to visit there.

"Mr. Livingston, can I have a moment please?"

"Absolutely, Miss Beverly. What can I do for you?"

Randy gestured for her to take the seat across from him.

"I just wanted to say thank you for everything you have done for us. We have really enjoyed ourselves. Your winery is beautiful, and the wine is some of the best I have ever tasted."

"Thank you, ma'am. We pride ourselves on making the experience just as good as the wine." He smiled.

"We have already booked to come back next year. We will also be telling all of our friends."

Randy couldn't help but smile. He motioned for Courtney, one of the servers, to come over.

"Miss Beverly, how did you travel here?"

"By bus."

"Courtney, would you please put together a box of the wines they tasted for them to take home with them; on me."

Courtney smiled and walked to the back of the tasting room and disappeared through the door.

"That is very kind of you, Mr. Livingston. We will definitely hold our own tasting when we get back home so everyone can sample your wonderful wines."

"I appreciate that Miss Beverly. I'm glad you lovely ladies enjoyed your visit with us."

Randy stood up to shake her hand. As he was sending Miss Beverly and her group off, he spotted her. She looked even more beautiful than she did yesterday; if that was even possible. After he shook loose of the memories of yesterday, he walked up to her.

"Welcome back. If you would like you can take a seat while I finish up." Randy gestured towards the tables they used for today's events.

Diana and her son walked over to one of the tables at the back of the room and sat down. She enjoyed watching everyone buzzing around, cleaning up and putting everything back in the
proper order.

It didn't take much time at all for him to finish up the last of the event paperwork. Randy was looking forward to showing this little boy and his mother around the winery. He was proud of the business his family has built over the past hundred plus years. He did have a moment of regret before leaving his office.

Diana looked up and saw Randy approaching. She nudged Steven.

"Hey, sorry it took so long. It's the end of the season. Wrapping everything up takes a bit of time."

"It's no problem. We didn't mind waiting... did we Steven?"

Diana had to nudge her son again to get his attention. She, however, did notice that he was busy taking in everything around him.

"Well, then let's get started."

Randy led them out the front door. They walked over to the huge metal building that stood to the left of the gift shop.

"This is where we process all the grapes we grow."

Randy proceeded to show them everything from where they are brought in and sorted to where they juice them, mix and barrel the wine to age. He couldn't believe how excited Steven was at seeing all of these things. Randy had always taken the winery for granted; it has always been there. Steven's excitement was causing him to see it in a new light. He wasn't sure where it would lead, but he would figure it out.

"Mr. Livingston, this is great. Can we go out and see the grapes?" Steven asked, interrupting Randy's thoughts.

Randy got on his walkie-talkie to tell Jake they were ready.

"Follow me."

He led them outside to where Jake was waiting with a golf cart. This wasn't just any old golf cart. This cart had all terrain tires on it. It sat up higher than most golf carts. It also had a cool paint job with the winery logo on it.

Randy had arraigned for Jake to do the driving, so instead of sitting on the front seat, he sat on the same one with Diana and Steven. As Jake drove across the field to the vineyard, Randy

put his arm across the back of the seat behind Steven. He turned to face both of them so that he could point out the different types of grapes.

There were grapes for the Zinfandel wines, grapes for Chardonnay wines and

lots more. Jake stopped next to the start of the Merlot grapes. Randy helped Steven and Diana get out. He walked them over to the vines and knelt next to Stephen.

"Well, Steven, what do you think?"

"Can I taste one?"

"I don't think that's a good idea, honey. They grow these for wine," Diana responded.

"It won't hurt anything," Randy countered.

He pulled a few grapes off the bundle in front of him. He handed a few to Steven then turned to Diana and handed her a couple, too.

"These are the grapes we use to make our merlots. They are a deep red with hints of cherry and raspberry. It's one of our best sellers."

Just as they were about to go around the corner to see another type of grape, Diana almost fell. Luckily for her, Randy was close enough to her to keep her from falling. He reached out and quickly grabbed her around the waist to prevent her from tumbling to the ground.

"Are you okay?"

"Yes, I think I just stepped the wrong way and lost my balance," Diana admitted.

The last thing she wanted to do was fall face first in front of him. Randy reached up to brush her hair out of her eyes. His touch was so lite that Diana almost shivered from the tingle it sent through her. She didn't know if she wanted to run away or if she wanted him to kiss her.

Randy was feeling the same inner turmoil for different reasons. He wanted to kiss her, but he didn't know if he would be able to live with himself if he did. Fortunately, the choice was made for them when Steven came running up to them.

"Are you coming?" he asked.

Randy dropped his hold on Diana.

"Sweetheart, I think it's about time we go. I think we have taken up enough of this nice man's time."

Randy cut in to tell her everything was okay. She cut him off, said thank you and then turned to Jake to ask him to take them back.

They rode back to the gift shop in silence.

CHAPTER FOUR

What on earth was I thinking? I can't possibly do this to Steven. What if we got involved and he gets close to my little man then leaves. I can't have Steven going through that pain again. No, it can't happen. I will just stay away from him until we leave. Besides, I have work to do.

Diana continued to pace the hotel room. She was struggling with the fact that this guy she had just met has this crazy hold on her. She was so caught up in her own thoughts that she didn't hear her son get up.

"Mommy, what are you doing?"

"I'm sorry, sweetheart. Mommy has a lot to think about. I also have a business meeting later, so we better get you some breakfast."

Steven was all for that. He went to grab his shoes and handed them to his mom for help.

"Ok sweet boy, where would you like to get breakfast?"

"Where can we get pancakes?"

"Is that what you want?"

Steven shook his head yes. Diana finished getting him ready, and they left for the pancake house across the street from the hotel.

Randy was busy driving himself crazy over Diana. He was fighting his attraction for her and his guilt for his wife. Was eight months long enough to mourn the loss of your spouse? Was he really ready to jump into a new relationship? Could his heart take it again? How would he know if he was ready to start over?

While Randy was busy wearing a hole in the office carpet, Jake was looking for him. He finally called over the walkie-talkie trying to get his boss's attention. Hearing his name, Randy finally came back to the present.

"Yea, Jake. What's up?"

"It's time to organize so we can get these grapes in. Should I just go ahead without you or are you coming to help?"

"I'm coming, I'm coming."

Randy set the walkie down. He grabbed his clipboard and keys and hooked the walkie back on his belt. By the time he got out to the staging area, Jake already had the crates ready to go. People were headed to the rows where they would be working.

"About time, boss," Jake smiled.

"Yea, yea, I'm here."

Randy really wasn't in the mood to deal with any of this. He's rather be talking to Diana

about what happened. Unfortunately, that would have to wait. Work had to come first.

Diana was feeling the same as Randy. However, she had to get her son to his day camp and then get ready for her meeting in the hotel restaurant.

"Steven, you need to quit messing around. It's almost time for camp."

Steven was playing with his breakfast instead of eating.

"Okay, Mom," Steven answered as he took another bite.

A few minutes later Steven wiped his mouth and told his mother he was ready to go. She left a tip on the table, and they walked out, heading across the street to the hotel. Diana asked at the front desk to find out where they were holding the camp. The receptionist pointed them in the right direction. They managed to get Steven in and settled with a few minutes to spare. Now, Diana needed to run back up to their room to get her files and laptop for her meeting.

Diana walked into the tavern and chose a table in the back corner. They would need a little bit of quiet to get the designs settled for Mrs. Abrams bed and breakfast.

The tavern was known for its ambience and its Reuben sandwich. Diana figured that's what she would have for lunch. However, for now, it would just be coffee. While Diana waited for her coffee, Connie Abrams came in and walked over to the table.

"Good morning, Diana."

"Good morning. How was your night?"

"Actually, my night was lovely. I ordered a bottle of wine from the local winery, turned on some music and took a long bubble bath. It's been a long time since I've had even a few hours to myself."

Diana could not help but smile. She understood about wanting time to herself. Luckily, she had an aunt who enjoyed spending time with Steven, so she got me time pretty regularly.

"I'm glad to hear you are enjoying yourself."

Connie waved at the waitress.

"Can I help you, ma'am?"

"Yes, can I get some coffee and a bagel?"

While Connie ate her bagel, Diana set up her laptop and pulled out her files.

"So, do you have a diagram of what the B&B will look like when it's finished?"

"Actually, I have a full digital model for you to look at. This way if you want any changes we can make them now before I start on the actual job," Diana said as she turned her laptop around to show Connie a three-dimensional view of the outside of the building.

"Wow, Diana, this looks amazing. Even the landscaping looks right."

"I'm glad you like it so far. It was easy to make the outside look good. You picked a beautiful house to transform."

"It was hard to decide on just one. There are so many beautiful old homes in this area that just need a little love to be made right again."

"I couldn't agree more. I've only been up here a couple of times. I think I may be visiting more often," Diana stated.

She moved the diagram from the exterior of the building to the first floor of the interior.

"This floor was easy to design. The house was well kept. I want to refinish the floors in all the rooms. I was thinking hardwood throughout the house except for bathrooms, kitchen and mud room. Tile would be better in those. We should keep the rustic style cabinets in the kitchen, just refinish them. However, I do want to update the appliances and put a big farm sink in."

"Diana, this is amazing. It must have taken you days to put this together."

Just as Diana was about to respond, Jake walked up to their table.

"Miss Blakely, may I speak to you for a minute?"

"Excuse me for a minute, Connie."

Connie nodded her head in agreement.

Diana got up and walked away from the table with Jake.

"What's this about?"

"Ma'am, I'm sorry I interrupted, but I needed to talk to you about Randy."

"What about him?"

"Well, he seems to be really taken with you…."

"What? I'm not sure I follow. I just met him a couple of days ago. How can that even be possible?"

Diana's mind was racing. How could this be happening? She was not ready to dive headlong into another relationship, though she had an idea of how Randy felt. She was struggling, too.

"I know y'all just met. There is another issue. He's struggling with this more than he should be because his wife passed only eight months ago. So, you see, he has some guilt playing on him as well."

"Oh, I had no clue. The way he was with Steven and I the other day, you would never know."

Jake shrugged.

"Yea, over the past few months he's gotten pretty good at burying it."

"So, what does this have to do with me?"

"I saw the way you looked at him while you were at the winery. You can't tell me you don't feel something for him."

Diana blushed. She couldn't help it.

"I want to know if there is a chance you could make a relationship work with him or not. Either way, he needs to know so that he will quit beating himself up over this."

Diana was stunned. She never expected anyone to confront her about how she felt about anyone much less a man she just met.

"Honestly, I'm don't know. My background is tainted. My first husband took off and left Steven and me to fend for ourselves. I will admit there is something there but, is it worth the risk of getting hurt again?"

"Only you know what's in your heart. Think about what I said."

Jake tipped his hat to Diana and walked off.

"What was that all about?" Connie asked when Diana got back to the table.

"Have you ever met someone and just knew that there was something between you. I mean the pull between you is so strong that you have to find out what it is."

"Diana, what are you talking about?"

Connie looked completely confused.

"The other day I took Steven over to the winery so that he could get an idea of what his great-grandparents did in Italy before World War Two. Anyway, I met the owner, and it was like being struck with a lightning bolt. Every part of me just knew there was something special about him."

"Was that him you were talking to?"

"No, that was one of the guys who works at the winery. My guess is he is a close friend."

Connie was grinning.

"I think I will stay in town a couple more days just to see what happens."

Diana and Connie finished up looking over the designs.

CHAPTER FIVE

Diana spent another night pacing. Could she set aside what her ex did in order to be happy again?

Thankfully, Steven had another day of camp. Diana needed to get him up. She needed to know what he thought about the possibility of a new man coming around.

"Steven, wake up. Momma needs to talk to you."

"What about?" he asked, rubbing his eyes.

"I need to see how you feel about momma possibly dating again."

"You gonna replace Dad?"

"Maybe."

Stevens comment made Diana nervous. She didn't want him thinking that he wasn't allowed to care about his father anymore, even though he had not seen him since they divorced.

"Okay, Mom."

Steven smiled, jumped out of bed and ran to the bathroom. Diana could almost breathe a sigh of relief, but she wanted to make sure she was right about his comment.

Diana took Steven down to the hotel camp. Connie met her in the lobby on her way out.

"Thanks for meeting me," Diana said, walking up to Connie.

"Not a problem. What's going on?"

"Would you mind going over to the winery with me? I need to talk to Jake."

"Absolutely, let's go."

They left the hotel and headed up the street to the winery.

"Have you made a decision on your issue?"

"Surprisingly, I think I have."

Diana felt pretty good about her decision even though she was extremely nervous about the outcome. When they got to the winery, Jake was the first person they saw.

"I was hoping I would see you."

Jake smiled walking towards Diana and Connie.

"I was up all night thinking about this."

"Ok, do you want to tell me first or him?"

"If you don't mind I'd like to tell him."

"No problem. He's out helping with the harvest.:"

"Is there any way I can surprise him?"

"Yea, actually there is. Come on. I can get you up there without him seeing you."

Jake walked with Diana and Connie up to the beautiful full rows of grapes. Jake knelt down to look under the vines to see if he could tell where Randy was.

"Randy is two rows over. Stay here. Connie, I have a golf cart at the end of the next row. Would you like to wait there?"

"That sounds good," she said as she turned to Diana.

"You're going to be just fine. Just speak from the heart."

Connie hugged Diana and walked off with Jake.

"I need you to wait right here. I need to get him over there."

Jake left Connie at the golf cart so that he could send Randy over to where Diana was waiting.

Jake saw Randy move a row closer to where Diana was.

"Hey boss, can you bring some of those crates over here? I have people in this row working."

Jake couldn't help but grin. He knew Randy might get mad, but it was worth the risk.

"Yea, give me a sec."

Randy set more crates by the workers at the end of the row he was on. Picking up more crates he walked to the row Jake was referring to.

"Set them down, boss. There's someone down there who wants to talk to you."

"Who?" Randy was confused.

"Just go see. You won't be sorry."

"All right."

He set the crates down and walked around the vines to go down the specified row, but he stopped.

"What's wrong?" Jake asked.

"It's Diana. Is she the one who wants to talk to me?"

"Yea, go on."

After what happened before Randy couldn't imagine why she would want to talk to him.

Just as he reached Diana, she looked up at him and smiled.

Well, maybe she's here for a good reason.

"What are you doing here?"

"I need to talk to you about something."

"Ok, what is it?" Randy was nervous.

"I know you felt the same thing I did when we first met. It literally scared the crap out of me. You see, Steven's dad walked out and never looked back. No reason, no excuse and he hasn't seen Steven since. I was afraid to open up again as that was a truly painful time. Well, between Jake and Steven, I think they're very well could be a chance that this could be something good."

Randy didn't say anything. He reached up to brush a hair out of her face and he kissed her. It was a kiss both of healing and desperation. They were both desperate to be loved again.

When they finally tore themselves apart neither could barely stand much less breath.

"I want you and your son in my life."

Randy couldn't help but kiss her again.

"Then, we will see what comes next," Diana responded.

10

THE UGLY PUMPKIN

BETH BAYLEY

*T*he pumpkin sat waiting outside the storefront. It was the last one. Nobody wanted a damaged and ugly pumpkin, not even for soup. Its thick orange skin was torn and pockmarked in all the wrong places to use as a lantern. All the best had gone to warm homes where young children and their parents were carving out grotesque faces and pulling all the innards out. In a way, the damaged pumpkin was lucky even if it was lonely.

"Mom, look there's one left. Can we have it? Purrleease, Mom. I promise I'll be good and do my chores," said the little boy.

"You know we can't afford…"

"You can use my chore money, Mom." He tugged her hand, dragging her towards the store where a warm glow from the lights inside beckoned them into the warmth.

"We can't, Tommy."

"B-but… Mom," his lip trembled, a tear fell over his cold rosy cheeks when the store door opened, and a man stepped out.

"You can have it for a quarter." He smiled, having heard their voices.

Honey's eyes left her sons face, slowly traveling up the man's body until their eyes met. His dark cacao brown eyes twinkled at her, making her blush.

"I-I can't do that, sir," she murmured. "Tisn't right."

"A-are you sure, sir?"

"Aye. The names Rick," he held out his large rough hand. Honey placed her small delicate on in his with a slight smile. His warmth radiated through her making her draw back her hand in shock.

"Thank you, Rick.

"Yay," shouted Tommy, jumping up and down. "Thank you, Rick."

"Tommy," she scolded. "Show some respect."

"What do I call you, sir?" he looked up, his eyes imploring.

"Rick's fine. What are you and your mom's name?" he crouched down so he was at the same level as the boy.

"I'm Thomas Caldive, and my mom's called Honey coz of her hair."

"Tommy, you know that's not true." He giggled, making Rick smile.

"A beautiful name for a beautiful woman. Come on inside and get warm. I've got coffee, and I'm sure I can find some sweet hot chocolate for you, son."

"Are you my dad?"

Honey flushed. "Tommy, it's a term some people use when talking to young children—like you."

Rick ushered them both inside with a huge grin and a sweep of his arm. "I've not seen you around here?" he said to Honey.

"We just moved. We're over by the river."

"Orchard Place. It's nice," Tommy shouted as he ran inside. "Where's the hot chocolate?"

"Sit on the stool by the counter while I make you some."

"Thank you, Rick." He climbed on the stool, kneeling on the seat and holding tight to the dark wooden counter.

"You take the stool beside him, and I'll be right back," he disappeared into the back of his shop.

"This place has everything you can imagine," Tommy looked round in awe at the mixture of merchandise. "Look at the hobbyhorses! I wish I had one."

"Perhaps Santa will bring you one for Christmas this year. Meanwhile, sit on your butt so you don't fall off." The stool wobbled as he stood up on it so that he could sit down properly. "Careful."

The stool toppled, Tommy grabbed the counter with a squeal, feeling himself starting to fall when two large hands hauled him back against a hard, warm chest.

"You're good," he sat Tommy on the countertop.

"Thank you, Rick," he giggled, throwing his arms around his neck. "I like you. You are kind."

"We'd best go before he breaks something," Honey tugged her son towards her, holding his hand tightly.

"Hey, don't worry about it. I've got your drinks, too," he picked up the tray, placing it on the counter. "Come drink, and then you can collect the pumpkin to take home."

"Thank you, Rick," Honey smiled.

Ricks' eyes widened as her whole face lit up. He saw a splattering of freckles across her pixie nose, her rich deep-sea blue eyes shining bright, with rosy cheeks.

"We appreciate all you've done for us. Thank you for your kindness."

"This town is full of kind folks, Honey."

"I do hope you're right. It's time we settled in one spot, and I need a job and schooling for Tommy."

"You'll need to talk with Mrs. Gregory about schools, she's on the school board and runs the haberdashery further along the street. As for a job, what sort of experience do you have? Can you do financials?"

"I was a whizz on a computer and at maths, though I've never trained in anything or gone to university due to Tommy. My husband expected a stay at home mom," she shrugged. "Which of course is detrimental to our lives since…"

"Daddy died," Tommy's lip trembled, he leaned over climbing on his mother's knees to hug her.

"I'm sorry about your loss," Rick murmured.

"It's been two years. Tommy didn't really know him due to the long hours he worked to support us."

"So, you've little employable experience?"

"Yeah," she shook her head.

"Well…I need someone to help me with my accounts and budgets. Do you…"

"You've been so kind to us, Rick, I'm not sure I should..."

"Listen, Honey. If you don't like the work you can stop, it's just I'm struggling due to my dyslexia."

"I thought dyslexia was with words and writing."

"Yeah, it is, though no one has heard of Dyscalculia which is the real name of the condition I have."

"I can see your point. In that case, I'll help. It isn't a problem, though I'll need to learn how to use your computer and the financial program it uses."

"I can show you now," he stood up, placing his empty cup on the tray and started to walk to the office.

"Actually, we have to go. I need to make dinner and get Tommy into bed," she looked down at him. "He's already asleep. Can you put the pumpkin to one side for me? I'll have to pick it up tomorrow."

"I'll drop you both off if you give me your address."

"I prefer to walk."

"He'll get heavy, Honey."

"Used to it." She slid off the stool to her feet, Tommy clung harder, snuggling his face into her neck. "I'll see you tomorrow, what time should I pop in?"

"How about ten in the morning?" he smiled, walking them to the door. The bell tinkled as he opened it.

"Thank you for the drink and the pumpkin, Rick. I'll see you tomorrow."

"Welcome to Farndon Fayre. I'll see you in the morning."

Walking away down the street, Honey turned and waved before disappearing down a side street. Rick sighed as he watched, his heart thrumming faster seeing her walk away, her hips swaying, showing off her curves before she disappeared with her son.

"Wow," he whispered looking down at the ugly pumpkin. "You, Mr. Pumpkin, are one lucky fellow to be going home with the lush Ms. Caldive," he grinned, picking up the pumpkin. Closing and locking the shop door, he moved swiftly to the office. Frowning at the mess, he shrugged. He placed the ugly pumpkin beside the computer, switched off the light and put on the alarm. He exited the back door making sure he locked it.

Hurrying down the side street, Honey shifted Tommy to her other shoulder wishing she'd accepted the lift from Rick. She hated being outside in the twilight. Entering her street, the street lights blinked on as she progressed, making her smile.

She hurried up to number fifteen, struggling to get her keys out of her purse, cussing when she dropped them. Kneeling down, she went to grab them when another hand covered them. Honey blinked, slowly looking up into hazel eyes and a scarred face.

The young man shook his head, handing her the keys and scurried away like a scared rabbit. Hands shaking, Honey managed to push the key into the lock. Twisting it, the door swung open and she stepped inside with Tommy—still asleep on her shoulder.

Closing the door behind her, the lock snicked into place. Glad she'd left a lamp on, she made her way upstairs, placing Tommy into his bed, tucking the covers around him and kissing his forehead.

"Too late for romance," she sighed, standing up washing her cup in her tiny kitchen. "Tommy comes first, men later."

Stretching her arms over her head, her back arching, she stared out of the window and nearly screamed at the scarred face at her window. She dashed over opening it, startling her young man.

"Who are you? What do you want?"

"Sorry," he muttered, melting into the darkness.

Honey slammed the window shut, her body shaking. Taking five deep breaths, she locked up, closed the curtains and pulled out the sofa-bed. Undressing quickly, she tugged on her nightgown, turned off the lights before stumbling into her lumpy bed praying for sleep.

In another part of town, Rick stood on his doorstep looking up at the hills, snow still icing the top like ice cream. His young twins wrapped their arms around his sturdy legs waiting with him. Finally, he looked up to the stars, placing a hand on each of their heads.

"Can you see your mother tonight?"

"There," said Toby pointing at the biggest shining star.

"Can you find her sweet pea," he lifted his mute daughter into his arms.

Smiling she pointed to the same star her brother had.

"I told you she knows dad."

"You sure did, son. Let's get inside, and I'll make dinner while you tell me all about school and what you did today."

"It was cool. We're getting ready for All Hallow's Eve," he scrunched up his nose making his dad laugh.

"What?"

"I thought it was called Halloween!"

"Well it is, though there is more to the celebration than Trick or Treats and Pumpkin Lanterns," he ruffled his son's hair as they stepped inside closing and locking the door for the night.

"Can you tell us about it?"

"Sounds like you'll be learning at school. How about you entertain your sister while I make pizza for dinner."

"Go play or do your chores and I'll call you when the pizza is ready."

"Gone."

Grabbing his twin's hand, they smiled at each other, rushing off to their playroom. Sighing Rick moved into the kitchen looking at the dirty dishes from their late morning. Opening the dishwasher, he filled it and turned it on. Wiping the counters down he took out the ingredients needed and proceeded to make the pizza base and chop up the cheese and meats for the top.

His mind wandered back to Honey and their reaction to each other. Though he'd dated since his wife died, none had affected him like Honey had. Honey seemed sad and lonely, though her personality had shown through. When she'd smiled, his heart had sped up in shock. Though she was tiny—only coming up to his shoulder, she had curves to end all curves.

"Ouch, hell and damnation," he stuck his finger in his mouth, stopping the blood from getting all over the food. "Concentrate," he muttered, finding the first aid kit and placing a plaster over his damaged finger.

"Stupid idiot."

"Who's a stupid idiot," said his son from behind him.

"Oh…" he jumped and bit his lip to stop swearing again. "Jaison, please don't scare me like that."

"Sorry. Is dinner ready?"

"I said I'd call you when it was. Now go keep your sister company."

"She's boring and wants to play with her dolls."

"Either go play in the playroom or go bring your sister in here and you can do your homework at the table while I cook."

"Ok," he ran back down to the playroom. "Rebecca, Rebecca, come to the dining room, and we can do our homework."

He tugged her back down the hall, she pulled back finally releasing her hand and sitting on the floor her arms crossed frowning at Jaison.

"Becca!"

She shook her head, getting to her feet, wagging her finger at him and stormed off back to the playroom.

"Daddy, she won't come."

"Go sit with her or dinner will never get cooked at this rate." He brushed his fingers through his hair. Jaison giggled, and Rick groaned realizing he still had flour on his hands.

"You look old."

"Thanks. Now scamper before…" Jaison ran down the hall laughing.

Rick rolled out the bread base, spreading pasta sauce and cheese over it, adding ham, pineapple, and mushrooms on top. Shaking on Oregano, he put it in the oven closing the door as his phone rang.

"Now what?" He sighed. Washing his hands, he picked up his cell phone. "Hello, Rick speaking."

Leave the woman alone. You've been warned.

"Who the…" The phone went dead.

Rick scratched his head perplexed. Shrugging his shoulders, he called the twins in to wash their hands and eat.

"Can we come to the shop tomorrow, Daddy?"

"Well, I can't leave you here on your own, you're only six."

"We like spending time with you." Becca nodded her agreement.

"You can finish your homework, and perhaps we can go to the movies in the afternoon."

"Cool." He munched another slice of pizza. "Can we go to our favourite…"

"You know the rules," said his dad. "Finish all your homework, and then we can go to the restaurant."

"We can do that," he turned to look at Becca. "Can't we?"

She nodded her head and smiled.

"Right time for bed, go and get ready while I clear this away. I'll be up in fifteen minutes."

"Read us a story?"

"Always," he smiled. "Now get."

Rick and his children arrived at his shop at eight in the morning, bundled up in thick warm coats, hats and scarves they entered the back and straight into the office and kitchen area.

"What's this ugly pumpkin doing in here, Daddy?"

"It's for Honey and Tommy."

"Who are they? Surely they don't want something this ugly."

"It's the only pumpkin left in town. Now you two come in here and finish off your homework while I open the store."

"Can you put up the scary decorations?"

"Later. Honey and Tommy might like to help when they stop by to collect the ugly pumpkin."

"Who…"

"A young lady and her son. I think he's about three years old."

"Another boy to play with, awesome," Jaison grinned, dancing around in a circle.

"Don't forget about your sister."

"She can play, too. Let's do our homework while it's quiet," he pulled his sister to the table, they sat on chairs emptying their backpacks and began to work.

Smiling, Rick entered the shop walking to the entrance and stopped short. A stone had been thrown through the window on his door. He scowled, kneeling to inspect the stone.

Noting it was wrapped in paper and string, he pulled on his work gloves taking it to the counter, opening the string he spread the paper out to find a news clipping and three words.

YOU'VE BEEN WARNED

Rick began to read the cutting. It seemed a young woman had been accused of murdering her husband and disappearing. There was a warrant out for her arrest. He looked at her photo, his eyes widening when he recognized Honey Caldive.

Frowning, he took his phone out of his pocket ringing the police to let them know he'd a broken window. Now wasn't the time to report Honey, there was no way she was capable of murdering anyone. He needed to talk to her and find out what was going on. Folding the news clipping, he shoved it into his back pocket with his phone just as he saw a face at his door. Standing straight, he walked forward opening the door indicating the officer enter.

"You didn't take long, Gerry."

"Quiet morning, Rick. What happened?"

"Found the window smashed and this stone with a note wrapped around it."

Gerry read the note. "Who's warning you and what for?"

"No idea and no idea," he shrugged.

"Why would someone send you an un-associated warning? This is a quiet town, not much changes. I don't get it."

"Well, I didn't touch it, so perhaps you could get fingerprints. I need to finish opening the shop."

"Ok. I'll let you know if I find anything."

"Thanks."

Honey woke to Tommy climbing and sitting on her rather full bladder, and his fingers on her face trying to open her eyes.

"Tommy." She sighed. "Stop. I'll get you some breakfast soon."

"Wake up," he yelled and bounced.

She quickly put him on the floor, staggering up and heading for the bathroom. Relief was bliss. Splashing her face with cold water, she entered the kitchenette to find Tommy tucking into a slice of bread. There was a trail of milk on the floor where he'd tried to pour himself a cup of milk sloshing more on the lino than in the plastic cup.

"Tommy. You need to learn to wait."

"Sorry, Mom."

Honey mopped up the mess, sat Tommy on the couch while she made him some scrambled eggs with toast. Placing it on the table, Tommy grinned, hopping off the couch and climbed on the chair to eat.

"I'm going to get dressed, please behave. We have to collect the ugly pumpkin today and meet with…"

"Rick. I get to see Rick. Yay."

"Yeah. Now eat your food, and I'll be back shortly."

Picking up her hot coffee and some clothes out of her drawers, she ambled back to the bathroom for a quick shower, dressing in clean jeans and a t-shirt. Back in the lounge, she looked in the kitchenette as she folded the sofa-bed away.

"Tommy!"

"I'm here," he yelled.

Turning around she found him dressed in his winter coat with his shoes, hat, and gloves on waiting by the door.

"You in a hurry?"

"I want to see Rick."

Honey rolled her eyes. It was weird to see Tommy attach himself to a man he'd only just met. Mind he missed the father figure a lot. Finishing her task, she cleaned up the kitchenette, grabbed her coat and they set off into town.

"I can't wait to get the ugly pumpkin. What are we going to do with it?"

"Make soup with the innards and see if we can design something in the skin so we can make it glow with a candle."

"Cool. I love you, Mom."

"Loves you, too."

Tommy swung his mother's arm as they walked down the main street, stopping outside Ricks shop to find a piece of wood covering the window in the door.

"Wonder what happened!" she muttered, quickly looking around her before she opened the door and stepped inside with her son.

Rick looked up from the cash register.

"Good morning, Ms. Caldive," his eyes wandered down to her hands. "Hello,

Tommy. How are you today?"

"I'm good. We're here to get the ugly pumpkin."

"I left it out back. Come on I'll show you."

"Thanks."

Tommy took Rick's hand, and they walked down the back of the shop.

"Ms. Caldive, can you keep an eye on the shop please?" he smiled.

"Sure."

She sat down behind the counter watching the customers enter and leave when a screech of kid's voices had her standing up quickly. Before she could move, Ricks' head popped out of the office door.

"It's okay, Ms. Caldive. Tommy just met my twins."

"Oh, right." She settled back on the chair wondering why he'd not said he was married the previous night.

"Rick, what was it you wanted...oh, aren't they gorgeous children," she smiled as the twins ran out to say hello.

"Are you really taking the ugly pumpkin?"

"Yes. I'm going to make it beautiful. You have to remember beauty is in the eye of the beholder, what might look ugly on the outside may be the nicest on the inside."

"Really? How do you know that, Ms. Caldive?"

"Call me Honey. What are your names?"

"I'm Jaison, and this is my sister Becca. She doesn't speak."

"Hello Becca, it's nice to meet you."

Becca nodded and smiled, lifting her arms up to Honey. Honey looked at Rick who raised his eyebrows in surprise. Nodding once, Honey picked her up sitting her on her knees.

"How are you going to make the ugly pumpkin beautiful?"

"Well, if you ask your mom and dad, you could both come around to my house and help Tommy and me get the pumpkin ready.

"Our mom's dead. That's why Becca doesn't speak."

"Oh, I'm sorry," her eyes met Ricks who shrugged his shoulders.

"My daddy's dead," said Tommy.

"I wondered where you'd gotten to, Tommy," smiled Honey.

"I was building with some blocks in the kitchen."

"I need to get your father to show me his office so that I can look at his accounts and bring them up to date," Honey said to Becca.

"We're staying a while?" grinned Tommy.

"Yes. You need to be on your best behaviour."

"Of course, Mom, I promise."

Honey stood up, and Becca curled into her body. Honey followed Rick into his office and laughed looking at the mess.

"You really don't like office work do you, Rick?"

"My wife was in charge of the office," he sighed. "She was a financial genius."

"Remember I'm not. Though I'll try and sort this out for you, it may take about a month."

"That's fine."

"I can only do school hours, I've no one to look after Tommy…"

"My neighbour looks after the twins after school, I'm sure she won't mind one more child."

"I'd need to meet her."

"Sure. She's a grandma and adores kids."

"Thank you."

She looked at Becca. "Becca, I need to put you down now so that I can do some work." Becca held on tighter.

"You can stay with me if you'll be good, though you'll have to sit in another chair, okay?"

Nodding, she wriggled out of Honey's arms and sat on a chair in the corner, picking up a book to read.

"I've never seen her take to someone so fast," he smiled.

"I'm a bit shocked myself," she smiled. "Now, show me how to use the computer program and then go sell some of your goods."

"Yes, ma'am."

Becca giggled, getting a shocked look from her father. Honey glanced at his face, but Rick shook his head.

"Later," he muttered and walked around the desk to switch on the computer. "Let's get you started on those hated accounts."

Honey watched over his shoulder, her breath caressing his neck, Rick tried not to react when she leaned forward pointing to an error on the screen.

"This is out of whack."

All he could think of was her heat entering his body. Closing his eyes for a moment, he inhaled a deep breath and wished he hadn't. He could smell her, and her fragrance nearly made him groan.

"Are you listening," she said by his ear. He shuddered. "Rick?"

He turned his head looking up at her, their eyes met, heat exchanged making her gasp and stand back, her eyes wide.

"You're a beautiful woman, Honey." He whispered before turning back to the computer screen.

"Please don't. I really need this work." Taking another deep breath, she shut out the desire and concentrated on the financial records. "What system are you using?"

"I think it's something…"

"I'd advise you to buy a financial package for your computer. We can do that online and then I'll upload everything for you. From then on most of it will be automatic, however, if you don't have an electronic cash register then…"

"Damn it."

Honey stepped to the side as he shoved out the chair barely missing her legs.

"Sorry. You do what you need to get this working. I'm going to open the shop and keep an eye on the children."

He turned to his daughter.

"Are you staying here, Becca?"

She nodded her head with a smile and went back to her reading.

"You mean you'll look after the boys," she smiled.

Rick closed his eyes, turning away from Honey and leaving without another word.

"Damn," he muttered under his breath as he opened his shop door and turned the sign over. "Broken window, a lush woman and a bloody warning; what next?"

"What are you muttering at?" asked Maribel as she waltzed through the door banging it against the ledge. "And what on earth did you do to your door?"

"Morning, Maribel. How are you today?"

"Don't think you can get away from answering my questions, young man."

"How can I help you today?"

"It's how MAY I help you today, come now, your momma taught you better manners than that."

Rick walked behind the counter feeling safer. Maribel was a terror and nosey as anything. "How may I help you, Maribel?"

"Much better," she smiled. "I'd like a yard of the yellow checked fabric…"

"Rick can you come here a moment?" yelled out Honey, interrupting Maribel who glared.

"Who's the hussy…"

"Ms. Caldive is my new accounts clerk, Maribel. Please be nice."

"Caldive, can't say I've heard of her. Where's she…"

Rick had walked away to the office making Maribel wait. Maribel crossed her arms tapping her foot impatiently. Rick appeared five minutes later, smiling.

"About time. I hope you realize I have other things to do today, young man."

"Yes, Maribel. I'll cut the fabric for you and have it delivered."

"Good, that will make amends for your tardiness."

She turned and left, forgetting to pay.

"Is she for real?" asked Honey, walking out of the office with a collection of papers in her hands.

"Yes, Honey, she is."

"She didn't pay you."

"Put it on her credit line."

"You're going to have to cut some of your credit lines, or you'll end up losing your business. You need to send out invoices for payments. I've printed off the most urgent ones."

She handed him the sheaf of paperwork.

"Well damn, I'll lose customers doing that." He scowled.

"Actually, they'll probably give you a bit more respect, which you certainly deserve."

She stepped away, moving down the aisle, Rick watching her hips sway. Honey looked over her shoulder and glowered.

"If that woman calls me a hussy again, I'll wring her neck." She shut the office door.

"Well, it's about time someone put Maribel in her place," laughed Dean. "Now, what's this about no more credit?"

"Honey is doing my accounts," he sighed. "It seems I'm giving out too much credit, so I need folks to pay up."

"About bloody time you stopped letting people take advantage of you, Rick," he pulled out his wallet. How much do I owe you?"

"$179.82."

"Not so bad for me. Not so good for you. You should put a credit limit if you're going to keep running them."

"I heard that," shouted Honey. "Limit will be $25 and not a cent more."

"Good advice. I'd take it if I were you, Rick."

"What did you need today, Dean," he put the money through the cash register, handing him a receipt.

"I came in to see about your door. What happened?"

"Gerry's looking into it."

"It's unusual to get broken windows here."

"I honestly have no idea what's going on," he shrugged.

"I'll keep my eyes open," he left, pulling the door closed.

"Whatever... next," he muttered.

Honey walked behind the counter again.

"You need to charge a delivery fee for anyone more than five miles away."

"Right. You really have it in for Maribel, don't you," he chuckled.

"Hussy indeed," she muttered.

"You are a lovely young woman, Honey. I was wondering if you'd like to come to dinner tonight as a thank you for starting the financials at such short notice."

"I've got to put Tommy..."

"He's invited, too. In fact, he can sleep over if he wishes and you approve."

"I'll think about it."

"Mommy!" Tommy tore out of the kitchen screaming, tears flooding his eyes as he crashed into her body, wrapping his arms around her legs.

"I didn't do nothing," said Jaison, hanging his head as he ran after Tommy.

"Which means you did, and it was an accident," said Rick, crouching down in front of the boys. The scent of Honey's perfume invaded his senses, distracting him for a moment. "Tell us what happened, Jaison."

"He took my Lego tower and smashed it, so I kicked his..."

"My best starship," Tommy whimpered, rubbing his eyes with his fist.

Honey crouched down in front of her son. "You know you can rebuild it and make it even better. In fact, why don't you both build a bigger and better starship between you? I'm sure it'll be magnificent."

"Now, that's a great idea." The boys looked at each other, smiled and took off back to the kitchen. "Well, that solved the problem."

Rick turned to face Honey who promptly fell on her butt when Thomas released his hold on her. Rick moved closer.

Their eyes met, heat and desire flowed through their bodies, their faces inching closer, lips poised for a kiss when the door tinkled, and a customer entered. Rick leaped back, Honey flushed as he helped her up off the floor while the customer watched on with interest.

"Is everything ok?" said Germaine.

"Yes. A few issues with the children," said Rick. "May I introduce you to Honey, my accounts clerk. Her young son just needed some attention."

"Yes, I'm sure," Germaine smirked.

"What can I help you with today, Germaine?"

Honey brushed down her jeans and t-shirt before heading back to the office, without looking back.

"You still have the wool I use? I need at least six balls of it."

"What colour?"

"Blue and green, six of each one. Now, what happened to the window?"

"Read the local newspaper tomorrow, and you'll probably find out because I sure as hell don't know."

"Watch your language," she replied. "Put the price on my account, please."

Rick approached with the wool, placing it on the counter.

"I'm sorry, I can't do that unless you pay off your account."

Her jaw dropped, but he continued.

"I have a credit limit of $25 now."

"Well," she huffed. "I'll get my wool elsewhere then," she started to walk out when Rick spoke again.

"You can't. I'm the only store which sells it."

"Fine. I'll pay the account off tomorrow after the Halloween celebrations."

"Thank you, Germaine."

The day finally came to an end. It was early closing with all the celebrations starting at six o'clock. Escorting everyone out of the shop, he picked up the ugly pumpkin and locked the door. Shaking his head, he wondered what Honey would do to it to make it beautiful.

Holding his hand out to Becca, Honey held the hands of the boys, and they walked down the street until they arrived at Rick's home.

"Nice place you have, Rick," she smiled at the wraparound porch with the swing. "I love the blue shutters, it gives it charm."

"Mommy did them," said Jaison. "She liked decorating."

"She did a fab job."

"What are you going to do with the ugly pumpkin?"

"Make something beautiful, Jaison."

"Let's go inside, get a bite to eat and watch how something ugly can be turned into something beautiful," smiled Rick at the kids."

"Yay," said Tommy. "Can I really stay the night?" he whispered to his mom as they walked through the door.

"Perhaps. I've not decided yet."

"Please, Mommy."

"Take your coat off and go play with Jaison and Becca until your dinner is ready."

"We'll call you," said Rick, placing the pumpkin on the kitchen table. "Honey, I'd like to show you something if you'd come outside."

"Sure," she said, looking at him in puzzlement.

Taking her hand, he pulled her towards the French doors. Opening them, they walked out on the deck looking up at the clear sky.

"Each night we—the three of us, stand out here and the children point out their mother's star," he smiled. "I'd like to introduce you to her."

His left arm raised as he pointed to the brightest star in the sky. Honey smiled, enjoying the warmth of his hand as her eyes followed his arm up to the star.

"She's beautiful."

"Yes, she is. You're beautiful too, Honey, though in a different way."

He raised their clasped hands kissing her knuckles. Her eyes connected to his, heat flaring. His left hand moved to her waist as he stepped closer his eyes dropping to her lips. He leaned forward to press his lips to hers; he heard her breathing hitch.

"Daddy! Becca pinched me," wailed Jaison as he ran out of the door slamming into Ricks' legs causing Honey and Rick to leap apart.

Tommy came running after him, scowling. "You deserved it, Jaison.

You shouldn't…ouch," he cried out when Jaison pushed him, and he fell on his bottom.

"Jaison," growled his father. "You stop right now, or you'll end up in your room and no trick or treating."

"I'm sorry, Daddy," he muttered.

"Go apologize to your sister and Tommy."

Pouting, he turned away, scowling at Tommy as he helped him to his feet. They both ran back to the playroom.

Honey walked back inside with a sigh, wondering about her attraction to Rick. It hadn't happened before, not even with the ex-husband; evil bastard that he was.

Picking up the ugly scarred pumpkin she smiled knowing it was lovely inside. Rick opened a drawer passing her a sharp knife. Piercing the thick skin, she sliced the lid off, inside the deep orange flesh took her breath away. Placing the knife down she picked up the spoon and began to pull the soft flesh out of the pumpkin and into a dish.

"What are you going to do with the flesh?"

"Soup and perhaps some delicious muffins with cream cheese icing."

"How can I help?"

"Either sit down and watch the magic happen or make dinner."

"Holy hell," he mumbled, opening and closing cupboard doors leaving Honey to her magic.

"What are you mumbling at?"

"What to make for dinner."

"I'm sure you don't usually have this problem?"

"No…" he turned, resting against the counter. "I want to kiss you. I've no idea what… damn," he turned back to the cupboards.

"I want you to, too, Rick."

Rick stilled feeling the heat of her body behind his. Closing his eyes, he groaned, turning slowly, his hands automatically going to her lush hips tugging her forward. Honey licked her lips. Rick pushed her hair off her face.

"You're a beautiful woman. I'm not sure what's going on."

"Kiss me, you daft sod."

He drew her closer, Honey lifted to her toes, their lips meeting in a soft, gentle kiss. Rick cupped her head, his tongue swiping over her lips. She opened to him with a sigh; his tongue pushing inside her mouth and their tongues entwined. She slid her fingers up around his neck tangling with his hair. The ugly pumpkin lay forgotten.

If they'd looked through the window a negative force was waiting, his eyes glaring, the knife in his hand at his side twitching as he planned his next move.

11

THE BEST NEXT THING

KAROLINE BARRETT

CHAPTER ONE

*M*eg had just pulled a homemade blackberry pie out of her oven when someone rapped on the kitchen's wooden screen door. "One second!" she hollered over her shoulder.

She was used to people coming to her kitchen door. Living on the same upstate New York farm she grew up on had at least one advantage, she knew all the neighbors, and like them. She had no fears about leaving her doors unlocked and windows open whether she was home or not.

"Good morning! Is that blackberry pie I smell?" a man asked as she approached the door.

"It is."

He smiled widely. "I remember my grandmother's pies. She's a farm girl, too. In fact, she was raised not too far from here."

He seemed nice enough, was handsome in a well put together way, but she wasn't going to offer him a piece of pie. It was going to the Pullam County Autumn/Winter Festival later this afternoon. "Can I help you?"

He removed his sunglasses, revealing eyes that were somewhere between brilliant aqua and green. In any other situation Meg would acknowledge that they were eyes made to drown in, but for all she knew, he was a serial killer.

"Sorry," he threw her a sheepish grin. "I should have introduced myself right away. Nick, Nick Garrett. I'm with Garrett & McNeil. I'm looking for Meg Larson."

Meg recoiled then inhaled sharply as a shot of adrenaline boosted her heart rate. He may as well have announced he was carrying an infectious disease. "I'm Meg Larson. Look, Mr. Garrett, I am not now, or ever, selling Lemon Meadow Farm. Not to you, not to anyone. I've seen news reports about you and your so-called development company.

"I don't want to see all this beautiful land disappearing so that you and your ilk can make a bazillion dollars building ugly look-alike homes that sit on top of each other and bake in the sun. And please," she glared at him, "save me the made-up story about your grandmother."

To her disgust, his eyes crinkled in amusement, and he gave her a half-smile. Her heart did a little flip. What was that about?

"My *ilk*?" he asked. "My grandmother still lives on her farm. Would you care to call her?" His eyes held hers, the challenge in them clear.

"No, I would not care to call her. The farms around here have been in the same families for generations. Who do you think you are coming in here and destroying lives and crops?"

His amused look disappeared. "Ms. Larson, we don't want to destroy anyone or anything. We aren't forcing anyone to give up their land. That's not what Garrett & Mc Neil does. I'm from upstate New York myself. Lots of farmers, including some of your neighbors, approached us first. That's why we've decided to go out and talk to the rest of the community of farmers."

"Hah! Really? Who? None of my neighbors want to see a developer come in and take over all this land. We have nothing else to discuss. Please see yourself to your car."

"I'm afraid you'll regret not selling to me." His eyes, now looking rather stormy, drilled into hers.

Meg stared at him. "Is that a threat?"

He was obviously a man used to getting his own way, but threatening her was out of line, and this time, her stomach did a little flip.

"Not at all. I'm merely saying that when you see all your neighbors signing on, and the money they receive, you'll regret that you didn't." He slipped on his sunglasses. "Thanks for talking to me."

Meg stayed put until he got into his car and drove down the gravel path leading to the main road that eventually led back into town. Of all the nerve! She would never sell the farm. She didn't care how great looking he was, how rich he was, or how charming, or how *whatever*. She wasn't about to puddle at his feet as she suspected women were inclined to do, and hand over Lemon Meadow to him.

Meg groaned. "Are you sure your mother didn't have some kind of computer malfunction? Algorithm glitch?"

Shelby frowned back. "Of course not. What's wrong with him? He's gorgeous! Annnnd… he's looking to settle down. He loves sports—"

"Blah, blah, blah," Meg cut off her best friend. "Let me guess. And long walks on the beach and romantic dinners. So, cliché. Do men really think that's what all women want?"

Shelby peered at the computer screen again, then glanced back at Meg. "Why are you being so weird? Why don't you read about him yourself? No, it doesn't say anything about beaches or walks. He loves to travel, time with family, his dog, art museums, book clubs, and building his business. Like you, except substitute business for farm."

Meg leaned back on the couch and stared at her laptop. Shelby's mother had recently started a dating site called *Heart Connection*. So far, it had been phenomenally successful. A couple of weeks ago, Shelby had talked Meg into joining. She reluctantly had.

Now she stared at the man at the screen. Her match with this guy was four-and-a-half hearts. Five was the best. She sighed. She'd definitely be interested if the guy she was staring at wasn't the same man who appeared at her door yesterday trying to talk her into selling her precious farm.

"Meg? Meg!" Shelby's voice intruded on her thoughts. "Are you listening to me? Why are you making a face about him? What's wrong with him? Four-and-a-half hearts, Meg. That's a great match. It means you have a lot—"

"I know what it means." Meg interrupted again. She glanced at her friend. "Sorry, Shel. I'm being rude. I've met him."

Shelby's eyes grew round. "You have? Why didn't you tell me? How did it go? Where did you meet him?"

Meg held up a hand. "Stop! We didn't meet on a date. He came to my door yesterday. He's a developer and is buying up farmland to put houses on. He wants to buy Lemon Meadow, too. Over my dead body."

"Seriously?"

"Yes."

Shelby chewed on her lower lip. "At least he's not a hit man or something. I mean, he's obviously responsible, and smart if he has his own company."

"Yes, and he's trying to steal away our land."

"Okay. I get what you're saying, but isn't that what developers do? You can't blame him for having a business."

Meg threw her a pointed look. "You have a minuscule point, which I'm ignoring. But I can't stand the thought of the farms all disappearing. And what about the Amish who have settled here? Is he going to try and wrestle their land away, too?"

"I don't know," replied Shelby. "But look at it this way. It's a date. One date. You don't have to commit to him, you don't have to marry him. You have a lot in common. Never mind that he's the only one that popped up as a match for you. Right?"

"I'm not sure. He was the first one, so I stopped at him because I was in shock; am in shock. I haven't logged in before now. If he's so great, why does he have to resort to a dating site?"

"Maybe he's super busy and doesn't have time to find a suitable mate. Why did *you* join?"

"You forced me to."

Shelby glared at her. "I did not. But face it, when's the last time you were on a date?"

Meg had to admit Shelby was right. When was the last time she *had* been on a date? Had a real relationship? Isn't that really why she signed up at *Heart Connection*? One date with him. How bad could it be? "How about if you and Kevin come along?"

Shelby looked sideways at her. "A double date? We aren't in high school. Are you afraid of him? You know mom vets everyone within an inch of their lives."

"Yeah. I know," Meg pulled a face. "Even me and she's known me since I was in second grade. No, I'm not afraid of him."

Shelby leaned back. "You'll be fine with Nick. I'm sure of it."

"All right. I'll go alone.

"Megs, is this about Trace? You don't still have a thing for him, do you?"

CHAPTER TWO

And there was the one downside of having a best friend. They knew too much. Not that she'd trade Shelby for anyone, but the woman never forgot anything. Especially, it seemed, anything that Meg had ever said or done since they'd met in second grade. "There's nothing between Trace and me."

"Do you want there to be?" Shelby pressed. "I wouldn't fight him off myself, if I didn't already have the best husband in the world, that is."

Meg rolled her eyes. "You're such a cornball."

But Kevin was indeed a great guy, and Meg loved him. She had known Trace all her life; his father, grandfather, and great-grandfather had worked on Lemon Meadow Farm. The farm had been in her family forever. Now that her parents were gone, she ran it with him, and the men he was in charge of.

The days were long, which meant a meager social life, which was painfully obvious since she'd stooped to signing up for a dating site, but the farm was in her blood. The cows were like children to her, she'd named them all, and she loved wandering through the acres of apple trees, their branches loaded with juicy red and green fruit. They'd had a bountiful crop of them this autumn.

Her thoughts returned to Trace. They'd dated in high school briefly, and she'd fallen hard for him. She knew he'd liked her a lot, but he was more interested in dating around, and partying; things Meg hadn't been in to. There had never been anything romantic between them since then, but lately, she'd noticed a heightened awareness whenever they were together. Like a high-pitched hum that only the two of them could hear.

Or maybe she was reading too many romance books by the fire before she went to bed. The sun was still warm at times during the day, but the summer green had mostly surrendered to the gold of autumn and the nights had started getting chilly enough for one of her grandmother's homemade quilts as well as a toasty fire.

"Meg? You have a goofy look on your face. Do you want there to be something with Trace?"

Meg blinked and focused on Shelby. "Sometimes I think he has feelings for me, although he hasn't said anything. I'm not sure what I want with Trace, or if I want anything. I do feel something between us, though."

"Let's not talk about him. What happens with the land robber? Does he know we're a match? I still think it's weird. I mean, what are the chances?"

"Maybe it's meant to be. Hopefully, he's been notified that you two are a hit. He should be emailing you soon."

"Oh joy," Meg groused.

"Come on. Don't be such a grump. This guy could be the one."

Meg raised an eyebrow. "I doubt it. We're at odds. I love farms, he hates them."

"Despite that, obviously you have a lot in common. Think about that. Now stop complaining." Shelby pushed off the couch. "Listen, I've got to go. Check your emails, and if Nick hasn't contacted you, you contact him. Got it?"

"Got it."

"And you'll call me as soon as you finish talking to him?"

Meg put aside her laptop and got up. "Yes, I promise."

"Good girl."

***

Meg watched Trace from her kitchen window as she rinsed the last of her breakfast dishes. She hadn't checked her emails yet to see if Nick had contacted her. She wondered if he'd be as surprised as she was that they were a match. She still couldn't believe a man like him had to join a dating service. She couldn't deny he was great looking, but looks weren't everything. She turned as Trace came through the screen door, letting it slam behind him.

"Hey," she greeted him. "You want to sit for a few? Coffee?"

He lifted a cup in salute. "For a minute. I brought my own, thanks anyway." He scraped a kitchen chair across the faded yellow linoleum.

"Welcome." She sat across from him and tried not to study his chiseled jawline, neatly cropped dark facial hair, and deep brown eyes as she finished her coffee. It went without saying that the hard work he did kept him lean and muscled. "What's on your agenda today?"

"Aside from meeting with the nutritionist, nothing but the usual."

Meg nodded. People were always surprised to find out the cows had their own nutritionist. But Trace loved the girls, as they called them, as much as she did, and neither of them was about to scrimp on their care. "Done with your cup?"

Trace got up. "I got it. You done, too?"

She nodded. "Thanks." She watched him at the sink as he rinsed the cups and put them neatly in the dishwasher. It had been a long time since she'd had a man in her life. She liked Trace in her kitchen being all domestic. "You don't usually come by in the morning, what's up?"

He turned, wiping his hands on his faded jeans. "Did you hear about the DeLuca farm?"

"No, what happened?"

"They sold it to that developer who keeps coming around."

Meg sucked in a breath. "Oh no. That's too bad. I never thought they would ever sell. A guy named Nick Garret came by the other day about selling Lemon Meadow."

Nick's expression darkened like a thunder cloud. "Jeez. What the…" He paced. "What did you tell him? You should've called me. I'd have taken care of him. No way we are ever selling the farm. I can't believe he would come here."

"It's okay. I told him I have no intention of selling the farm. I think he got the message."

He grabbed her upper arms and almost shook her. "Meg, if he comes back, I want you to come get me. I'll take care of him. He won't show his face anywhere near here when I'm finished with him. I'll always take care of things here. You know that."

"I do. And thank you."

Meg briefly thought about telling him about joining a dating service, and that Nick was her first match, but he'd convince her not to pursue anything with him. And it wouldn't take much to convince her that a date with Nick Garrett was not a good idea.

"On another subject, I have something to ask you," Trace said.

"Sure, what is it?"

He ran his hand through his hair. "Look, I know this is coming out of left field, and believe me, if you say no, that's fine. I thought you and I could see a movie sometime. You aren't seeing anyone, are you? I'm definitely not."

Meg stared at him. Was he asking her out? He must feel something between them as well. Wait till Shelby heard about this. "No. I'm not seeing anyone. It sounds like a good idea, I'd like that."

He leaned back against the sink, folded his arms across his chest and relaxed. "Good. It won't be awkward? I mean because I work for you?"

She grinned "First, I've known you since we were in diapers. Second, you don't work *for* me, you work *with* me. Trace, I couldn't do all this without you. You know that. You're the only person I trust. So awkward? No."

He returned her grin and visibly relaxed. "Great. I'm glad. How about this Saturday? The new movie with James West and Grace Markum is out."

"Sounds fabulous. It's a date. You want to get dinner first? Maybe try the new seafood place on Route 525?"

"Sure. I'll pick you up around six, okay?"

"I'm looking forward to it."

"Me too," he replied, his voice husky. Then he leaned in and kissed her, his lips barely touching hers. Perfect and sweet. Like Trace.

CHAPTER THREE

Meg settled in bed, scooched under the fluffy comforter, and waited for her laptop to boot up. She couldn't believe she had a date with Trace and was matched to Nick Garrett on *Heart Connections*. She'd gone from no men to two men; sort of. She signed into her email, holding her breath. Why, she didn't know. It wasn't as if she were floating on air thinking of going on a date with a wealthy, good-looking man whose mind was set on gobbling up her farm, and any others he could get his mitts on. Yep, there it was. An email from NGarrett@GarrettMcNeil.com. She let go of the breath she'd been holding and clicked to open it.

I'm sure you are as surprised as I am that we're such a close match. Fate? What do you say? It looks like we have a lot in common, and we've already met. Neither of us appeared to be repulsed by the other. As a matter of fact, you seemed quite taken by me, haha! How about dinner at the Lakeside Inn? I promise not to talk about buying Lemon Meadow. You'll find my number below in my signature line. I'll leave this all up to you. No pressure! I do hope to hear from you soon, and maybe get a tour of your farm. Best wishes, Nick.

Why was she smiling like an idiot? Okay, the little smiley face emoji after he promised not to talk about buying Lemon Meadow was cute, and he did seem to have a sense of humor which she appreciated, but her smile was quickly replaced by a frown. Just because he promised not to talk about buying Lemon Meadow Farm, didn't mean he wasn't still going to pursue it.

Had he read her profile on *Heart Connection* and then made his to suit hers? Was he trying to get close so that he could convince her to sell?

She Googled Nick Garrett as well as his company. Yes, they had bought up a substantial number of farms in the area, which turned her stomach. She wondered about the quality of his houses; the pictures of them looked like they'd buckle under the first storm and wind. Why did people want to live on top of one another like that? Why were so many of the surrounding farmers willing to sell?

She kept reading. Nick Garrett also gave millions away to charity. Point in his favor. There was yet another article that caught her eye. It was only two paragraphs, but after reading it, her mind was made up. She hit reply and began typing.

"I had a great time, Meg," Trace told her. "I've been thinking about you a lot. I've always had a thing for you. I wasn't sure how you felt about me. I didn't want to ruin our friendship, and how close we've always been."

They were standing in Meg's kitchen after their date. The light from the hood above the stove pooled over them. "I was in love with you in high school."

His eyebrows shot up in surprise. "I had no idea. I wish I'd known." He brushed one of her cheeks with the knuckles of his right hand.

"You were a party guy, you weren't interested in anything serious."

"What if I am now?"

She answered by parting her lips in invitation. He responded by capturing them with his own.

She pulled away a few minutes later. From the look on his face, the kiss had affected Trace, too.

"That was nice, Meggy," he told her, using his childhood nickname for her. "You feel right in my arms."

"I had a wonderful time tonight, too."

He kissed her again, this time a peck on the forehead. "I better say goodnight, or I won't want to leave. I'll see you tomorrow."

"Good night, Trace."

She stood at the screen door as he disappeared into the night. He lived in a small two-bedroom cottage past the dairy barns. She knew he'd had women in his life, but no one that he had wanted to marry, apparently. She turned off the light on the hood and made her way upstairs to her bedroom.

She changed into her favorite Buffalo Bills football jersey and scooted under the covers. Something had happened tonight. Or rather, hadn't happened. Oh, she'd been affected by his kiss, but not in the same way he had been. She reached for her phone and called Shelby.

"What do you mean you didn't feel anything?" Shelby demanded after Meg told her about her date. "And what are you doing with Trace all of a sudden? What about Nick?"

"I mean he kissed me, and I didn't feel a spark. He's a great kisser, but I didn't want to—"

"Drag him upstairs to your bed, strip him, run your hands down that broad chest, and have—," Shelby supplied.

"Yes," Meg interrupted before Shelby could go any further. "That's exactly it. It was kind of a letdown. I've been thinking there's something between us for weeks and now that there might be, I don't think I want it. I think we're too familiar, if that makes sense. Maybe like siblings, or good friends rather than lovers."

"I think you're nuts. But if that's the way you feel, you'd better tell him that if he asks you out again."

"I will. I don't want to lead him on."

"Now. What about Nick? Did you agree to see him? Have you talked to him?"

"Yes. We have a date this coming Friday. He's taking me to the Lakeside Inn.

"Holy moly! Aren't you a lucky woman. I'm glad. I was afraid you would turn him down."

"I thought about it, but as you said, it's one date. I do need to get out more."

"I'm happy for you. I bet this is going to turn into something. I feel it."

Meg laughed. "I can't get involved with someone who wants to take away farmland."

"Why don't you ask him what his intentions are, and why these farmers decided to sell to him? Maybe you'll see things differently."

"I hate when you make sense." She yawned. "I've got to get some sleep. It'll be four a.m. before I know it."

"Sweet dreams."

The next morning, Meg had just finished her breakfast and was at the sink when Trace came through the door. "Morning, Meg."

"Hi there." Nervousness was playing havoc with her stomach. She should've waited until later to eat.

"I had a hard time sleeping last night." He came up behind her, gathered her hair together and kissed her neck. "I was thinking about you. I can't believe I waited so long to ask you for a date."

She turned around. "There's something I need to say."

"All right. I thought I'd make dinner for us. You love my lasagna. How about that along with a salad and a movie tonight? I'll bring everything down here."

She hated doing this to him and felt a smidge guilty, but she didn't want him to think their relationship was going to develop into something romantic. She was surprised herself that it wasn't, but there it was. "Wait. First I need you to hear me."

"Okay. It's not about that guy who was here trying to con us out of the farm was it?"

"No. I had a very nice time with you on our date, but I don't think it's going to go anywhere. You and me, I mean. I love you, Trace, but like a brother, or best friend."

He looked as if she'd slapped him, and for a second, she thought he might storm out. He rubbed his jaw. "Wow. I didn't see that coming. Okay, if that's the way you really feel, I respect that. I guess there's nothing I can do about it."

"I can't say I'm not disappointed. I think we would be great together.

Who knows you like I do? Who knows me like you do? Who knows the farm like I do?" He looked around the kitchen for a few seconds. "Okay, I don't want to make this awkward, so I'll see you around."

"Wait." Meg grabbed his arm. "I'm sorry, really. I thought I had romantic feelings for you too, but they aren't there. I didn't want to lead you on." She couldn't tell him his kiss didn't do anything for her.

"I appreciate it."

"We're good? Still friends?" She didn't want that to change, but she could tell his smile was forced. She loved him like family. Maybe that was the problem, he was family.

"Of course, Meggy. Always."

She watched as he left. She didn't feel entirely convinced that he was okay, but that wasn't anything she could fix.

CHAPTER FOUR

Meg had chosen a navy-blue lace dress with short scalloped sleeves for her date with Nick. She hoped she wouldn't be chilly. Late October nights could be downright frigid in New York state at times. Nude pumps with 3-inch heels, ruby earrings, and a simple gold bracelet completed her ensemble. Her blonde hair was up in a chignon. She was nervous about going out with a man she barely knew, although they'd talked on the phone a few times, and she'd found her attitude toward him softening a little. And she had to admit, that putting on makeup and dressing up—something the cows didn't generally care about—was fun for a change.

Nick was right on time. He looked striking in a bespoke black suit and black loafers polished to a high sheen. His hair was slicked back with gel, and he smelled like an expensive shower gel. It beat the smell of cow manure, that's for sure. She was surprised to suddenly feel excitement about their date.

"You look lovely, Meg."

"Thank you."

He offered her his arm, and she took it. He walked her to his car and opened the passenger side door of his Porsche sedan, and she slid in. She breathed in the rich smell of leather and sank into the buttery soft seat.

"I hope you're hungry," he said as they took off. "This place has a great salad bar, and the best steak I've ever had."

She looked at his profile. "I'm starving."

"I'm a little surprised you agreed to come out with me."

"Me too, actually. I still find what you're doing abhorrent. I'm sure you've seen the bumper stickers, No Farms, No Food."

"I have. I'm not anti-farming, believe me. Most of the farms we buy aren't producing to full capacity, or the owners are looking to retire, and family members aren't interested in taking over."

Meg looked out the window. What would happen to Lemon Meadow when she was gone? She didn't have any children. Of course, at thirty-four she couldn't count out having them someday if the right man came along. What if they hated farming? Would the land be filled with homes and paved streets? The thought made her sad.

"What convinced you to see me?" he asked.

She turned toward him again. She wasn't sure if she should bring this up, she didn't want to open any wounds. Yes, she thought buying up farms was wrong, but he was still a human being, and she didn't want to purposely hurt him. Besides, she felt comfortable with him. Like she belonged by his side, which was terribly weird, not to mention unnerving.

"The article about your wife."

He glanced over at her and even with only the town's streetlights providing light she saw pain and surprise flash across his face. "You read that?"

"Yes, I was researching you."

"You mean internet stalking me." He laughed at her guilty look. "I'm kidding you. I can't blame you. Sorry. I interrupted. Go on."

"It made tears come to my eyes. I can't imagine finding out your wife had early onset Alzheimer's when she was thirty-five. That had to be devastating."

His hands tightened on the wheel. "It was. Alicia was my whole life. But it's been five years. I don't need to bury myself with her. She wouldn't want that. Being alone gets old. Sure, I have friends and business associates, but that's not the same as having someone special in our life who totally gets you and understands you."

Meg's heart went out to him. "You took time off to care for her, be with her. You took her on trips. That's wonderful. I'm so very sorry you had to go through that."

He glanced at her again. "Thank you. I'm not going to lie and say it was a walk in the park. It wasn't, but I'd do it all over again." He smiled a little. "So, I'm not so bad, am I?"

She laughed softly. "No, you're not."

"Do you like jazz?" he asked, reaching for the radio.

"I love jazz, but you already know that. Four-and-a-half stars remember?"

"Squeeeeee!!!"

Meg held the phone away from her ear. "Calm down, Shelby! Good grief!"

"I'm sorry, but this is so exciting! I had a feeling you and Nick would hit it off. How was it? Tell me everything!"

"We had a great time. We had so much in common. This sounds crazy, but it was like I've known him all my life. We had so much to talk about, and we have so much in common, but not so much as to make it boring. It was amazing."

"What about his business? Are you okay with it now?"

"No, I'm not okay with him and his company buying up farms and converting them to housing developments. I still think it's sad and awful. But he took the time to explain a lot to me, and he patiently answered my questions, so he's a little less the evil monster I thought he was."

"Oh, Meg, I am so over the moon happy for you. Wait till I tell, Mom! When's your next date?"

"Next Saturday. He's sponsoring a new young artist at a gallery in Syracuse. He's asked me to spend the day with him."

"Fun! What happened when he brought you home? Did you ask him in?"

"No, believe it or not, we spent an hour sitting in his car talking."

"Talking? Come on, you guys aren't in your nineties. Was gazing into each other's eyes and kissing involved at least? And I mean the good kind."

Meg laughed. "Okay, kissing was involved. The good kind." Yep, the very good kind.

CHAPTER FIVE

"Hello?"

Meg was out in the barn wrapping up one of the dairy inspector's twice-a-year visits. "See you in six months, Dan."

She turned her attention to the visitor. "Hi. Are those for me?"

"If you're Ms. Meg Larson they are."

"That's me."

She took the huge bouquet of flowers. She recognized most of them, sunflowers, pink tulips, green poms, and purple monte. They were gorgeous.

She walked them up to the house to put in water. They had to be from Nick. Her heart thumped. He'd been busy and out of town for a few days, and she'd been at poultry science convention, but they'd talked on the phone, or texted, every night since he's taken her to Syracuse a couple of weeks ago, where she'd had the best time.

They were definitely headed for something serious no matter how much she didn't like the idea. It seemed she had no choice. Her heart was in it for the long run. How could she feel that way about him after two dates?

She put the flowers in water and pulled the note out of the envelope. *I miss you.* Simple words, but they touched her. She set them on the kitchen counter, along with the note. She had to go check on the calves next, but first, she whipped out her phone so that she could send Nick a thank-you text.

Meg woke with a start. She grabbed her phone and tried to focus. She'd been in a deep sleep. She recognized the number. "Jenna, what's wrong?"

"Your barn is on fire! We've called the fire department!"

Meg bolted out of bed, her heart galloping. She flew over to the window and yanked up the blind. She could see the flames and orange glow. Her blood turned to ice.

She heard footsteps thundering up the stairs and seconds later Trace burst into her bedroom. "Meg! The barns on fine! You've got to get out of here. Come one! I've called the fire department."

"Oh my God, Trace. Jenna's on the line. They've called the fire department, too." She felt as if she were going into shock. "I have to go Jenna. Thank you for calling."

"Of course. Be safe. Call me later. Promise?"

"Promise." She disconnected.

Trace grabbed her arm. "Come on. We've got to get out of here! Now!"

Meg nodded and grabbed her jeans and t-shirt that were on her dresser. She slipped them on quickly, not caring that Trace was still standing there, waiting impatiently. She rushed down the stairs behind him to the sound of sirens screaming closer, and an awful thought forming in her brain.

"You cannot honestly think I am responsible for the fire. I have strong feelings for you, Meg. We clicked, and you know it. You have feelings for me. I can see it in your eyes, feel it in the way you kiss me. You trust me. I'm falling in love with you. I didn't want to say that, not this soon, but now it's necessary. Why would I want to destroy you? My God, you could've been killed! Your cows, the apple trees..."

Hot, angry tears filled Meg's eyes. It had been four days since the fire. She had no doubt who was behind it. Thank God the livestock had been spared, and no one had been hurt. But how stupid she had been to trust him.

"Really? All you care about is your housing developments. You thought if you destroyed the farm I'd want to sell to you, but you're wrong. I'm going to rebuild. Trace will help me. I'm sure the police will have you in custody soon. You won't get away with it."

She turned on her heel and marched out of his office. He called after her, but she sped up until she was almost running out the front door.

She could barely drive she was so angry and hurt. How could she have trusted him? How could be have been so vindictive to endanger her life, Trace's life, and the life of her animals?

CHAPTER SIX

"We have a confession. Why don't you have a seat?"

It had been two weeks since she'd stormed out of his office, and she hadn't heard anything from Nick; not that she cared. All she cared was getting Lemon Meadow back in order with Trace's help and seeing Nick in prison. Trace had been such a help with all the insurance business. What would she do without him? She looked up at the police officer, whom she didn't recognize. "It was Nick Garrett, wasn't it?"

"No, Meg. It was Trace Whitley."

She blanched, and the room tilted. No! Oh no. She didn't say Trace. She couldn't have.

"Are you ok?"

Meg's mouth was dry. She tried to speak, but only a croak came out. "But why?" she finally squeaked. "Why would he try and destroy me? How do you know? I was sure it was Nick Garrett."

"Whose Nick Garrett?" the officer asked.

Meg looked at her. "Never mind. How did you figure out it was Trace?"

"We recovered sulfur powder, and potassium nitrate—both potential explosive materials— and accelerants from the basement in his house and he confessed. We arrested him this morning. You weren't at home, or we would've spoken to you then."

"I was at the farmer's market."

She was still dazed by the news. None of this made sense.

"There's someone else we spoke to. He asked to see you when we got his story."

Meg looked at the officer. "Who?"

"Jamie Hawkins."

"Jamie?" Meg gasped. "He works on the farm. What does he have to do with any of this?"

"Stay here. I'll bring him in. I'm going to stay with you while he speaks to you."

Meg nodded her head. This was all too much to take in.

"Meg, I'm so sorry," Jamie cried out when he was led into the room where she sat.

"Jamie, what the blazes is going on? Why did Trace do this? Why are you involved?"

"I saw him set up the explosives. He panicked and told me he'd give me twenty-thousand dollars to shut up. I'm sorry, Meg. God, I shoulda never have agreed. I shoulda gone straight to the police then."

"Why Jamie? Why did you let him give you money?"

"My wife and I are trying to put our oldest through school. The money sure would help. I'm sorry, Meg. I'm just so sorry. After I took the money, I knew I could never live with myself. I came to the police."

"I don't understand why he did it," Meg cried.

Jamie let out a sigh and shook his head. "He was like a crazy man. I was afraid he'd kill me when he knew I saw him. He was ranting about flowers some guy gave you and how you thought you were too good for him. He planned to marry you and own the farm. He thought it belonged to him anyway. He was tired of taking orders from you. His words, not mine."

Orders? Meg never ordered him around. What had gotten into him?

"Can you forgive me?" Jamie sounded on the verge of tears.

Meg looked at him. "Of course. Once I wrap my head around it, I'll come speak to you again."

"I shoulda come in sooner. I'll never forgive myself for takin' his money."

CHAPTER SEVEN

"Nick?" Meg was standing at the doorway to his office.

"What are you doing here?"

"Trace was responsible for the fire. I don't know what to say. I'm sorry, Nick. So very sorry. Is it too late for us?"

His eyes bore into hers, and he lifted an eyebrow. He didn't answer, but his eyes darkened. He looked like he wanted to spit on her, but Meg stood her ground, waiting for him to speak. But he didn't, his attention went back to his computer screen. Stubbornly, she waited for a few seconds, but he didn't look back up. She had no choice but to leave. She'd ruined everything. Tears blurred her vision as she turned and made her way down the corridor.

But by the time she got to her car she was angry, and the tears were gone. How could he not understand that of course she would suspect him? She had no reason to suspect Trace. She still couldn't believe Trace would betray her like that. The thought of what he'd done made her ill.

Once she got home, she made sure all the windows and doors were locked. Trace was gone, but she couldn't take any chances. Maybe she should ask Shelby to stay with her. No, that was ridiculous. She was a grown woman. She wasn't hungry, so she changed into her pajamas, grabbed her book, and built a fire. Settling in on the couch she burrowed under the afghan.

But her mind couldn't concentrate. She and Nick had found a true connection, as silly as it sounded. She couldn't deny the feelings she had for him. Strong feelings. And he felt the same. Should she call him?

Surely, he must still have feelings for her. Could he seriously be so stubborn not to understand why she suspected him?

She shivered under the quilt and thought about Trace. She couldn't help it. He'd never cared for her. It was all a ruse to get the farm from her. She couldn't believe it. He was crazy. Why had he come to rescue her? She had no answers and probably never would. How could she have been so foolish; so fooled?

She jumped when there was a loud knock at the kitchen door. Her heart ricocheted around her chest. Even though Trace was gone, she was still a nervous wreck and probably would be for a while.

She threw off the afghan and went to the door. "Who is it?"

"Meg, it's Nick. Can we talk?"

"Nick!" She whipped open the door and had to hold herself back from throwing herself into her arms.

"Can I come in?"

"Of course." She stepped aside. "What...what are you doing here?

"I didn't answer your question."

"My question?"

"You asked me if it was too late for us."

Meg held her breath. "Is it?"

He swept her into his arms. Her arms went around his neck as he hugged her close. His mouth came down on hers, and as he deepened their kiss and tangled his hands in her hair, Meg knew she had her answer.

12

HARVEST MOON DANCE

PEARL BUTTERWICK

"*H*ow much longer do we have to walk? I'm going to be so tired, I'll not be able to dance!" moaned Ann.

It was too muddy to walk across the fields, and none of the girls could drive, so they had decided it would be fun to walk. They had no choice but to walk along the back lanes, though it would take them almost half an hour more than the usual fifteen-minute stroll over the fields.

They moved in a snaking column of ones, twos and sometimes threes, depending on the width of the lane and who wanted to join in with a particular conversation. They all had a torch, and Iris had stuck hers in her waistband so that it shined where she was walking rather than leading the way ahead. The Harvest Moon was smiling down on them, but occasionally, it hid behind the autumn clouds that were racing across the sky.

Now and again, someone would start singing to keep the pace going, something like *All Things Bright and Beautiful,* Edith's choice, and the others would join in with the chorus. Their breath danced in front of them, swirling around and around as they sang.

They carried their heeled shoes in bags, ranging from swim bags, reusable plastic bags to Iris carrying hers in her old ballerina bag. Not that she ballet danced any more, but she walked with a dance in her graceful steps.

Mary was at the back of the line, daydreaming as normal. Her fingers stung with the bitterness of the cold and so did her feet, she had chosen to wear wellington boots which were good for walking through fields but were not comfortable on the lanes, and they had thin soles. She thought she should have worn socks. The bitterness she felt was not a sad feeling. Her fingers and toes tingled. There was definitely something in the autumn air. She could feel it.

"Aren't we there yet?" Ann moaned again.

"'Obviously, no, we're not," shouted Violet.

"Siiii-eye-lent night," sang Violet.

Ann called back, "It's too blinkin' early for Christmas songs!"

"I thought it was apt with you constantly moaning." Violet chided while thinking that she would take the hint and stop moaning. "You chose a song then..." Violet called back to Ann.

"We plough the fields and sca-teeeer." Ann laughed as she sang. Then she stopped singing.

"If Farmer Jones hadn't harvested his pumpkins and ploughed his fields, we could be there by now!" Ann stamped her feet.

"Stop being so grumpy, Ann," Violet retorted.

"I'm just stamping my feet to warm them up."

"It looked like you were stamping them like my baby sister does when she doesn't get her own way," snapped Violet.

"I'm not a ba..."

Before Ann could finish her sentence, Edith called "Now, now girls, stop the bickering, you both sound like children."

"Oh, no, we don't," said Ann and Violet at the same time. They looked at each other, laughed, linked arms, turned and walked together ahead of Edith.

It was a cold night. Autumn had come quickly, making the air feel like winter with its sharp frosts. The sky was dark, but the moon gleamed bright. Friesian black and white cows were all huddled together beneath the oak tree and an owl was beadily watching them as they wandered past him, their feet crunching on the brittle leaves underfoot.

Mary had only been working at the factory a few days when Ann had called.

"Hey, you! Do you want a ticket for the Harvest Dance?"

She had only spoken to the girls either side of her on the packing belt. Ann was in dispatch; she had glimpsed sight of her through the warehouse doors but had not spoken to her before.

"Everyone goes to it, it's the best night of the yea'," Iris piped up.

Iris worked as 'Time and Motion Administrator' and was often stood watching the various lines at work with a clipboard and stopwatch in her hand. Sometimes her brow would crinkle and then her glasses would slide down her nose making her peer over them, looking for the reason for her displeasure. She was very precise. Everything had to be just right.

"No," she had told them. "No, thank you."

Her mother would be cross if she said she was going to a dance. But once the idea was in her head, she was unable to stop thinking about it. Definitely not what her mother would say! Definitely not! Mary was a working girl now. Surely, she could go?

A week later the girls called out and asked her again, and she had said yes. The words had jumped out of her mouth before her sensible head could stop them.

"That's it then. We'll go together. We'll sort out where we will meet next week," said Iris.

The ticket was safely hidden in her glove, stuffed into her coat pocket. She could still change her mind and not go, tell the girls she was feeling ill. But what should she tell her mother, if she did go?

Finally, she had told her mother that she had to go to the dance. That it was compulsory and if she didn't go, the bosses wouldn't see her in a good light. That did it! Her mother was all for pleasing the bosses and for Mary to do well.

She looked so proud when Mary had twirled around in her dress and touched up her *red* lipstick, which was new and highlighted her bow-shaped lips perfectly. Well, maybe her lips did look as though she was about to kiss a fish, as she pouted, or maybe a frog.

A frog that would turn into her prince, she thought.

Now, here it was. Mary felt that little throb of excitement in her tummy as she thought about the dance as if something was about to change. A sudden wind forced their hair into their eyes, and they all shrieked. The excitement was felt in them all. They were all so happy. Cold and windswept, but happy.

"My hair will be a mess by the time we get there," said Ann.

She was right about her hair though; at the start of the walk her blonde hair was all sleek and rolled at the back into a stylish chignon. Now, the grips had worked loose, and her hair was a beautiful mane, curling all around her face like a lion. Mary thought how funny that the male lion has a more beautiful mane than the female.

Ann does look beautiful tonight. They all do. Everyone had made such an effort. It was a great feeling not to be in their grey work overalls and hairnets. Dressed up to the nines, her mother said. Whatever that meant!

Violet still had her rollers in, held tightly with one of the hairnets like they had to wear at work, except it was yellow, and Ann was sure she hadn't seen any yellow hairnets at the factory.

"Your hair looks lovely tonight," said Violet.

"Thanks, normally it just clings to my head," replied Mary, thankful that today her hair was bouncy and shiny. She had used some of her mother's setting lotion.

"Stop dawdling," said Edith, pulling up the collar on her coat and striding ahead of them all.

The rest of the girls quickened their steps to keep up with her.

"The Harvest Festival Dance takes place every autumn," Violet started talking again. "People come from miles around you know. Not just people from the factory, the farmhands and farmers all come with their wives and girlfriends and some of the accountants that do the books for the farmers."

Mary frowned "Oh, so will we be the only single ones there?"

"Oh, no," Iris laughed "You look so sad, Mary. Did you think you were going to have to dance with us all night? No, a lot of the boys are single. I'm going to get myself an accountant this year. I'm fed up of those good for nothing farm lads making promises and then breaking them and also breaking my heart."

"You're the one who does the heartbreaking. You are so fickle. You get a nice lad who is interested in you, but because he doesn't have a car, you dump him," Edith said.

"There is nothing wrong about me wanting the best for myself. If I had a boyfriend with a car, I wouldn't have to be walking to get to the dance!" Iris said.

"You now sound like Ann with your moaning," replied Edith.

"If you had a boyfriend with a car, you wouldn't be having so much fun with us," said Mary, blushing, as this was the first time she had teased one of the other girls.

The girls laughed, and all spoke at once agreeing with what had been said. Mary glowed inside. She really felt part of the group now. She now had friends. Friends she could tease and laugh with.

Mary had only been to parties given by her Mother's friends. Their sons were all stiff and shy and wouldn't look at her in the eyes. She had tried to look at them as husbands to be and thought about trying to fall in love with them, whilst being watched by their mothers as they sipped tea and ate cucumber sandwiches.

"Do try to look interested," her mother would whisper.

"I *am* trying to look interested," Mary would answer, stifling a yawn and turning it into a grimace.

"Stop smirking," her mother said through gritted teeth.

"Should I laugh then?" Mary retorted.

"I think not. I think not," was her mother's reply whilst raising her right eyebrow in disapproval.

The women spoke about their sons and how proud they were and how they were going to progress with their careers as Managers or Accountants and how they would make good husbands.

Mary suddenly had an unpleasant thought—*Oh no, I hope one of the sons won't be at the dance.* She then laughed out loud thinking, *No, none of the Accountants she had met would ever go dancing!*

The girls plodded on. They were quiet now. The coldness had seeped through their winter coats, through their thin party dresses and into their bones.

Out of the bleakness, twinkling lights began to shine. The girls passed a stone cottage with windows shining brightly, and they could smell the soot that was drifting down from the smoking chimney. As they looked up, they could see the tiles glistening as the Harvest Moon danced with the frost.

"There it is, look!" shouted Edith.

The girls quickened their steps, fighting off the cold, their destination was in sight.

In the distance, Mary could make out the brightness of the hall, and the strings of lights were swaying, as though in time to the music. The lights illuminating the track, showing the way to the entrance.

Taking a deep breath to steady her nerves, she was sure she could hear the beat of the music and the strains of a banjo, and she shivered. Her heart was beating a little faster, not in time to the music, but faster and louder in her head. She followed the girls.

The girls, her friends, were at the entrance, already standing on their tiptoes trying to see into the hall and see who was there that they knew and see if anyone new had ventured to the village.

The doorman, dressed as a scarecrow, welcomed the girls and examined their tickets. When he was satisfied they all had genuine tickets, he stamped the back of each girls hand with a small blue flower. Mary thought it looked like the forget-me-not flowers on her mother's best tea set.

She was nudged by Iris who was saying, "Come on, over here. This is where we can change our shoes."

They perched on a small bench and quickly changed out of their boots and wellingtons into their high heeled shoes. They handed over their bagged shoes and coats to the cloakroom attendant, who handed them a ticket with a number on.

"Don't lose your ticket," said Edith. "Rita won't give you your coat back."

The woman grinned at the girls, whilst nodding her head in time to the music. After hanging their coats onto the rail behind her, she sat down again.

"Go on girls, have fun. My dancing days are over, but I do love hearing the music and seeing you all enjoying yourselves."

"Thanks, Aunty," Edith said as she leaned down and gave the woman a hug. '

"Will do, see you later."

As the girls walked into the hall, they smoothed down their dresses and adjusted their shoulder straps.

"You are not going dressed like that," her mother had said, entering the bedroom while Mary was getting ready.

Mary was confused; she always wore her white blouse with big puffy sleeves and tartan skirt to all the teas with the mothers and sons. Her mother left the room as quietly as she had entered and returned with a sleek black satin dress.

"Try this on."

The dress was divine; it had a sweetheart neckline that hinted at the cleavage it was covering, a tucked in waist that highlighted her curvy figure, and the skirt clung to her shapely hips. Mary had never seen her mother wearing the dress before, though she could tell by the neat stitching that her mother had made it.

All the time that Mary's mother had helped her into the dress, smoothing it down, pulling the zip up and fastening the fiddly hook and eye at the nape, she said nothing. She led her daughter to the mirror and looked over her shoulder. Mary looked at her reflection.

"Whoa, this dress makes me look like a film star. Oh, Mother, thank you, thank you."

Mary turned around and gave her mother a hug, and after a moment's hesitation, her mother hugged her back. For a moment Mary saw her mother's eyes soften and glisten as she took her daughters' hands and looked her up and down.

Her mother's voice, husky, as though she had a cold, said, "Now, stop being soppy with me."

Taking a deep breath and straitening her shoulders, she looked like Mother again, composed with a rigid, straight back.

They walked down the stairs, and her mother opened the door into the drawing room where her father sat reading the evening newspaper. He looked up, and his eyes welled with tears.

"Now don't you look a stunner? She looks just you did, twenty-five years ago, when I first met you at the Harvest Moon dance."

Her parents looked at each other, and a tender look passed between them. Mary felt embarrassed about the look that she had seen, though she didn't understand why.

"Now let's have a twirl," said her father.

Mary spun around to show off her dress, realizing that she couldn't move quickly as the dress was fitted and a bit tight on her hips, but she felt wonderful.

She felt brave enough to now apply her new lipstick. It was a scarlet red, but it looked classy with her sophisticated dress and styled hair.

There was a tentative tap on the door.

"That will be the girl," said Mary. "They said they would call for me as they would be passing."

The four girls were all stood on the doorstep as Mary stepped out with her coat on covering up her dress.

"Have a good time. Be back by..." called Mary's father as the door shut with a bang.

Full of chatter, the girls started walking. Mary glanced back at her house and was sure she saw her mother looking out of the upstairs window. It gave her a warm feeling to know her mother was watching her.

The village hall was a large building with a polished hardwood floor. Oil lamps were lit and hung all around the room. Some with red shades and others with clear glass, giving the hall a look of moonlight and sunset, all at the same time.

Straw bales were scattered around the room, topped with checkered blankets for sitting on. The window shelves were being used as tables for drinks so that there was more room for dancing.

In the corner, on a raised stage, again made from straw bales was the band. It consisted of a banjo player, a violinist and a man with a large drum who was also calling out instructions to the dancers. They wore denim trousers, checked shirts and had handkerchiefs tied around their necks together with cowboy hats and boots.

Mary suddenly felt overdressed.

The hall was already full. People were dancing, and others stood around the edge of the dance floor. The farm boys were wearing neat denim trousers, and multicolored check shirts like the band, but a few lads were wearing suits.

Girls were grouped together, and they all wore dresses; some in miniskirts, others in checked skirts that spun out wide as they turned and twirled on the dance floor. A couple of girls were wearing fitted dresses similar to Mary. Mary let out a big sigh, letting the tension flow out from her shoulders. She hadn't realized she was so tense.

Mary recognized a boy in a suit that was too big for him, his jacket was hanging off his shoulders, and his trousers had been turned up twice. He was from one of her mother's friends' parties. What was his name? Charles? Charlie? It was something beginning with a 'Ch'. Mary quickly turned away before he saw her. Chester, she thought, that was his name!

The music stopped, and so did the dancers. The caller took a big glug of his drink.

"Come on, Mary," shouted Iris. "Stand next to me."

The girls had all miraculously lined up on the right-hand side of the hall, glancing over at the other side of the hall at the boys who too were lined up and looking shyly at the girls. Iris was stood between Ann and Violet and opposite Chester. Mary was at the end of the line, with Edith to her right. Opposite her and to her left was no one. Mary stayed where she was, hoping Chester hadn't seen her.

And they were off! The dancers were galloping like horses up one way and back the other, then down the middle whilst the other dancers clapped their hands. Back up the sides, partners joining hands as they met again at the top of the hall. The couple at the top then held hands, to form an arch with the other dancers bending their heads to get through the arch and then galloping down, around, up and back to the top.

Mary watched, mesmerized, as all the dancers reacted to the instructions from the caller. She was pleased she didn't have a partner as she had never danced like this before. The floor was bouncing beneath Mary's feet, and it was like the hall itself was dancing. The lamps were swaying too, casting moving shadows around the hall.

Dance followed dance, with only brief intervals to quench the participant's thirst.

The boys were moving clockwise around the room and the girls anti-clockwise; linking arms, unlinking arms; skipping around and around and around the hall.

Boys dancing with every girl, albeit it for only a moment as their arms linked, but some couple's eyes watched each other as they danced around the room. These couples were dancing only with each other, dancing with their eyes, although their hands and bodies were touching other people.

"Mary... haven't—you—got—a—partner?" shouted Iris in short bursts as she was struggling to speak.

Her face was bright red, as she had been dancing non-stop. Smiling, Mary shook her head. She had been stood at the bottom of the hall for most of the time, watching. She had joined in some of the dances where you didn't need a partner. But now she was watching someone; intently watching someone.

She had noticed him the moment they had walked into the hall. He was dancing alone, too. Like Mary, he didn't have a partner, but he was joining in all the dances, whether a partner was needed or not.

As Mary and her friends danced together in groups and pairs and other groups of friends intermingled in and out of the dances together, he danced by himself. Sometimes, he was in the middle of a square dance, like playing the childhood game, *Ring a Ring O'Roses.*

He didn't seem to notice anyone else. He was oblivious to everything, apart from dancing in time to the music. He moved with abandonment; his right arm raised at times and his wrist flicking as though his imaginary partner was being twirled in front of him. His eyes were closed, and he was totally absorbed in the music, in dancing.

"Who's that?" Mary asked.

Iris followed Mary's gaze. "We call him Duggie."

"What do you mean you call him Duggie? Is that short for Douglas?"

"No, it's a nickname. You know, it's what they call a motherless calf; a Dogie. Well, he is motherless and looks after the cows on his father's farm. We've always called him Duggie. Duggie Jones."

"Where is his mother?"

"Dunno, she left. It's just him and his father on the farm. We passed his farm on the way here, the one with the cows in the field."

Iris looking back at the dancers. She lost interest in Mary and Mary's interest in Duggie.

She said, "I love dancing. I don't want to stop. I don't want to leave."

Chester, with perspiration on his forehead, appeared in front of Mary and Iris.

"Hello, Mary. It's a great dance, isn't it?"

So, he had recognized her.

Not waiting for Mary to reply, Chester grabbed Iris' hands. They both fell into each other arms laughing and merged into the swarm of other dancers. Perfect and precise Iris, dancing with Chester. Chester who was imperfect and a little untidy but great with numbers.

Mary thought that that was the first time she had seen Chester smile; and dance. He and Iris were having so much fun. So different to when she and Chester were drinking tea and eating sandwiches, under the watchful gaze of their mothers.

Scanning the dance floor, Mary looked for Duggie. He was still dancing alone. Mary smiled to herself, pleased she had spotted him so quickly. Duggie opened his eyes, and he stopped dancing and looked at her. His head twitched, as if in recognition of his audience. He started dancing again but was moving slowly towards where Mary stood.

He stopped so close to Mary she could feel the heat from his body, hear his pounding heart and smell his fiery odor. Licking her lips, Mary could taste him too; he tasted like scorched wood.

Mary's heart was racing, as she looked up to his face.

He stopped, and his mouth opened. Leaning forward and over to her left ear, he nudged some hair away from her ear with his nose. Shocks of electricity went shooting up and down her body. She could hear her heart pounding. She could hear the violin. Then, she heard his voice; deep and velvety, echoing around her head.

"You could come and watch the cows dance."

What did he say? Do you want to dance? Do cows dance? He looked down at her, waiting for her reply. His face was serious, with an intent look on his face as his eyes bore into hers. Whatever he had said, he had meant it and was waiting for an answer.

Mary looked into his eyes, searching for an indication of what he had said. All she could see was his smoky grey eyes with sparks of red from the dancing lamps. She glanced down at his hands. He wasn't holding them out to her like Chester had done to Violet when he took her off to dance.

She felt embarrassed. Embarrassed that she hadn't said pardon, excuse me, or what did you say. Instead, Mary felt nervous laughter welling up inside her. Not like the time at the tea party, when she had smirked, but laughter full of happiness. Before she knew it, laughter escaped from her mouth. Her eyes crinkled as her laughter enveloped her face.

He watched as her serious face dissolved before him into a warm beaming sun. The corners of his mouth twitched, and his brow furrowed, for a second, as she laughed in his face. Not a teasing laugh; like the kids at school, but a laugh that included him. A laugh that made him feel good. A laugh that made him smile back at this girl, this girl who had mesmerized him as soon as she had walked through the door. The girl who he had been dreaming he was dancing with earlier. The girl he had been scared to ask to dance—until she had smiled at him.

Mary finally found her voice and said the first thing that came into her head. "You'd better buy me a drink first."

She had heard the other girls teasing the boys, and that is what they had said. She had never asked a boy to buy her a drink before.

It was now Duggie's turn to laugh. As he did, his cheeks touched his eyes. He shook his head slowly from side to side, shrugged and walked away.

Mary's heart sank. Her stomach churned with a feeling of disappointment, sadness. She chided herself. Why did you have to say that?

He walked towards the bar and stood to wait for his turn. Mary watched him. He hadn't left. He had gone to get her a drink.

Duggie was walking back towards her, with two drinks in his hand. He saw her waiting, and Mary was sure she saw his shoulders relax as though he was pleased she still stood there. He gave her a plastic cup, and they clinked their cups together. They would have clinked if they had been glass, but the plastic just squeaked.

"Cheers."

"Cheers."

Mary saw that the liquid was clear; she guessed it must have been gin or vodka. She didn't like either but wanted to accept this boy's kindness, so she took a deep breath and drank the whole cupful in one mouthful.

She was expecting a horrible taste which would quickly burn her throat, but it didn't; it cooled her throat. It was water. Cool water. Mary smiled with relief.

"Thank you," she said loudly so that her voice would be clearly heard above the sound of the caller and the music.

"That's okay."

He gave his cup a little tilt towards Mary, raised it to his mouth and knocked his back in one drink, too. He wiped his mouth with the back of his hand.

"What's your name?"

"Mary."

"Mary... Mary." He repeated her name in a whisper.

He looked as though he was going to tell her something but changed his mind. They both looked away from each other and looked at the dance floor.

The dance was nearing the end. Mary had no idea how it had passed so quickly. The caller sat down and picked up a large glass and sipped the amber liquid, massaging his throat after all his shouting out orders to the dancers.

The band was playing a slow romantic tune, and the floor was filling with couples holding hands. The boys were leading the girls to the floor for one last dance. Chester and Iris were holding each other close and shuffling around on the same spot in time to the slow rhythm. Ann and Violet stood together at the edge of the dance floor, swaying against each other. Edith sat on the stage, looking up at the caller and her lips were moving; she was singing to the caller.

Mary felt Duggie hold her hand and she found herself dancing. He was leading her around and around the dance floor, small steps, quick steps then slow steps. Her head was leaning against his shoulder. His left hand was clasping her back and guiding her effortlessly around the dance floor.

Mary thought this is how it should be. People coming together and sharing actions that would become memories. Sometimes the people they met tonight would become part of their lives, maybe for months, or years or just a couple of days. But the memories would stay, or fade, depending on the intensity of that meeting.

You could spend your whole life with someone and not understand them. Then again, you could watch someone dance and feel that you had always known them. And when you danced together, you knew that you knew them like you did your own reflection.

Mary thought of her own mother and father as they had shared a look earlier that very same evening. A look that had embarrassed her, without her understanding why. A look of knowing that had passed between them, a look that had not needed words. A look that Mary now understood.

"You look in your own world," said Duggie.

"I was."

"Do you want to join my world?"

"Your world? What world is that?"

"It's a world where I sing to my animals. A world where I get up before dawn to feed the cows. I'm glad we got the cows into the bottom field earlier. My dad said it was going to snow. He always knows. He said the Harvest Moon had told him. "

"The Harvest Moon?"

"Yes, the Harvest Moon shines orange and is the perfect time to harvest pumpkins as we work into the night. Do you want to go outside?"

Without waiting for an answer, he stopped dancing and led Mary to the door. She held onto his hand and followed. His fingers slotted through hers, perfectly interlocked.

If her mother had said to her that this was the night she would meet her true love, without her mother's guidance or friends, she would have said no.

But now, as Duggie helped her into her coat, she thought maybe.

The cold stung their faces as they walked out the door. They walked over to the hedge and looked at the cows, still huddled together at the far end of the field.

"My dad was right, as usual," said Duggie with a smile.

The land looked as though it had been dusted with icing sugar and the air looked as though the bag had exploded as swirls and swirls of fine snow was being blown around by the Autumn wind from the west.

They stood in silence, holding hands and watching the snow dance. The cows were huddled together for warmth against the dancing snow. Every now and again the cows would move, jostling for a place in the middle of the herd. They looked like they were dancing as they moved around. The Harvest Moon was shining brightly on them all.

Mary thought back to the boy dancing, twirling around the dance floor without a care in the world just like the snow was being spun around by the wind.

"What is your name?"

"Douglas, but my friends call me Duggie."

"Duggie," repeated Mary. "I like that."

She turned to face him.

"My answer to your question is yes."

"Yes?"

If he wanted her to dance with the cows, she would. If he wanted her to marry him, she would. Duggie smiled and pulled her into his arms. He looked down at Mary's face, the face he felt he had known forever.

He leaned forward, lips parting just before his reached Mary's. He heard her as she caught her breath, saw her close her eyes just before he closed his. Their lips touched briefly, and then they both opened their eyes.

Feeling warmth and love in each other's arms, they both closed their eyes again. They parted their lips slightly and kissed again. This deeper kiss was full of promise for their future. A kiss under the watchful glow of the Harvest Moon.

The End

DREAMSCAPE

SHAWN MARIE GRAYBEAL

*T*he heat shimmered off the highway creating a haze which muted the stark landscape. A hawk circled in the cloudless sky. The throbbing of the motorcycle beneath her increased the surreal nature of the scenery. She sped up and leaned into the curve.

"Where is he?" she thought as she scanned the road ahead of her. There was no sign of anyone anywhere out here. It just didn't seem possible that he was so far ahead, always out of reach.

She rounded a bend in the road. The scenery was breathtaking. The sun was setting coloring the sandstone cliffs in a dizzying array of reds and oranges. The shadows were just deepening to purples. A herd of wild horses turned their heads towards her and then ran. The hawk, still circling, let out a shrill cry.

Suddenly her head hit the table. She grumbled and sat up and realized she was still sitting at her desk. Looking over at the alarm clock, she groaned. It was 3 a.m. That made four nights in a row.

She took her coffee cup into the kitchen to reheat. As she put it into the microwave, she wondered if she would ever find her nameless, faceless mystery man — the man who had eluded her every night.

Anne was late. Again. Thank goodness for her best friend and assistant, Carol. McConnell's Garden Whimsies would be open, and there would be fresh coffee and cookies.

The bells on the door announced her arrival. Carol smiled brightly at her and then frowned slightly.

"Are you still having those dreams, Anne? You don't look like you slept well at all."

Carol filled a mug with coffee and added cream and sugar and passed the mug across the counter to Anne.

"Every night this week. I wish this guy, whoever he is, would go bug someone else for a change." Anne bit into a chocolate scone. "Oh goodness, Carol. These are amazing. We may need to change the name of the store to Garden Whimsies and Bakery!"

"I've wanted to try that recipe for a while." Carol smiled as she took a sip of her coffee. "There is a guy trying to reach you. He's called twice this morning already. He is a contractor and has a garden he is putting together. He was talking to the guys over at the hardware store who suggested you could help him."

"Hmm, ok. Well, let me know if he calls again. I have a load of pumpkins, scarecrows, and hay bales I need to set up out front. We need to decide what we want to do for the parade, too. The kids are coming by tonight to start working on the truck."

Anne got up and went to the back. She loaded up the wheelbarrow with pumpkins and rolled it around to the front of the store. Whistling as she worked, she cleared the front porch of the summer décor and debris. Hay bales became benches for a family of scarecrows and paper mâché ravens. She walked back into the store to get the autumn leaf garland that she had bought when the rumble of a motorcycle startled her.

She looked up and walked toward the door. The bike slowed and pulled into the parking lot. As the rider got off the bike, Anne felt a jolt. She knew him. He strode to the door with purpose, removing his helmet as he stepped onto the porch.

The door opened. Carol turned to welcome the newcomer.

"Hi! Welcome to McConnell's. May I help you?"

"Hi. I'm Cody Walker. We spoke earlier. Is Ms. McConnell in?"

Anne turned toward him and put out her hand.

"I'm Anne McConnell. What can I do for you?"

She looked up into the bluest eyes she'd ever seen. When they shook hands, she felt the jolt again. She DID know him, but how?

He gave her a strange look and cleared his throat.

"I'm working on a garden. But it's boring. It needs something special, I'm just not sure where to go with it. Bill, over at the hardware store, said you might be able to help me out."

"Sure, I should be able to help you out. Do you have pictures or would you rather I came out to the site?"

He shuffled on his feet a little and cleared his throat again.

"It would probably be best if you came out to look at it. I do have pictures, but it's really a nice little area and the pictures don't show it well." He reached into his jacket and pulled out an envelope. "Here they are. I made copies so I can leave these with you."

He handed Anne the envelope and then took a deep breath. "I have to ask. Do I know you from somewhere?"

"I... I don't think so." She stepped back a half step. "When do you want me to look at the garden. I will be really busy the next week getting ready for the fall festival and the parade but maybe the Monday after?"

"That sounds good. Early is better. Let me give you my card. Call me if you have any questions."

As he handed her the business card, she felt a connection, and when she looked up at him, she knew that he felt it, too. He shook his head and then stepped away.

"I'll see you soon."

And he walked out of the store, got back on the bike, and rode away.

The day of the festival was sunny and cool with more than a hint of fall in the air. The parade had gone off without a hitch, all the brightly colored trucks driving down Main Street behind the marching band.

Kids had pockets full of candy and sticky faces. There was a pie eating contest and people milled around the various booths.

Carol had baked a ton of cookies and was giving them to the passersby. She and Anne started setting the booth up at six a.m. and were finally ready for the crowds that were in the park.

"So, no more dreams?" as she handed Anne a steaming hot cup of coffee.

"No. I haven't had them since Cody Walker came by the store. It felt like I knew him. I wonder if... no that's crazy. But still, I wonder if he is the man in my dreams?"

Carol laughed. "He did ask if he knew you from somewhere. Have you talked to him?"

"Not yet. I did spend some time yesterday looking at his garden pictures though. It needs something... anything. It's just a bare patch of dirt inside a chain link fence."

Carol laughed again and then she turned to talk to some of the high school girls who had walked up.

Anne straightened a couple of the garden gnomes that she had on the table. She looked up and saw Cody walking across the park toward the booths. She raised her hand, and he smiled, changing directions.

"Well hello, Ms. McConnell. How are you on this beautiful morning?" He grinned at her and handed her a muffin.

"What a way to say good morning!" Anne smiled back at him and took a deep, appreciative whiff of the muffin. "Orange cranberry. You must have been talking with Marjorie Jennings."

He laughed. "Of course, I was. Everyone knows that her muffins make the sun shine and the world spin."

"Well, then you must try Carol's amazing chocolate chip cookies." Anne handed him a cookie. Carol had come over, too.

Cody took a bite of the cookie, closed his eyes and savored it.

"Miss Carol, that was wonderful. A man could write songs about cookies like that!"

He grinned again, and they all started laughing. Cody reached over and touched Anne's arm.

"Did you have time to look at the pictures?"

"I looked a little. There really isn't much there?"

"No, I came into this piece of property a couple years ago. I've been building the house but really want to put in a special garden to set the place off. I just don't know where to start."

"Well, the first thing is to get rid of the chain link. A stone wall or a hedge or anything but that."

He laughed and held out his hand.

"Would you walk with me, Anne? I'd just like to spend a little time getting to know you."

Anne looked at Carol who just smiled.

"I have this, Anne. Go enjoy the beautiful day."

Anne took his hand and smiled.

"I won't be long, Carol. Thanks!"

They walked among the booths, stopping momentarily to try a bit of jam, to feel a crocheted scarf, and to talk with people. He held her hand gently, then reached up to brush her hair back off her face.

"I really do feel as if I know you. It's a strange feeling."

"I do as well, but it seems crazy to me. The place I think I know you from is a dream."

He looked at her.

"I have had a recurring dream for years it seems. A dream where I am looking for a man. A man on a motorcycle who is always just ahead of me. I've never seen him, just know that he is slightly out of reach. I haven't had that dream since you came into the store last week."

He turned to face her, took both of her hands in his.

"A couple of years ago, I answered an ad for a piece of land up in the valley. I've spent most of my life in the city, but here I am at a small-town fall festival. I own a small piece of land that I hadn't seen until June. The house plans came to me in a dream. It's almost finished, except the garden. I've just been waiting, waiting for you I think. I'd really like to show it to you."

Anne squeezed his hands. "I want to see it., but I can't leave Carol alone. I will come by first thing in the morning."

She tiptoed up and kissed him lightly on the cheek and then turned and walked away.

As the festival turned into a party, Anne and Carol broke down their booth and took everything back to the shop. It had been a good day. They had sold a lot of the garden décor, and Carol had signed up several people for a baking class she was going to teach.

"So, what happened with Cody?"

"Not much. We walked around the booths for a while. He told me a little about the house he's building."

"Really? With the looks the two of you were giving, I was sure you weren't coming back to the booth."

"Ha! No, we just talked a bit. I do think he is the man I have been dreaming about. Every time I see him, I get this jolt, like 'Oh! There you are!' It's strange. And I feel like I know him."

"So, now what?"

"Well, I am going to meet him at the house tomorrow and see what I can do with this garden. He told me that he bought the land here sight unseen and the house plans came to him in a dream and that he wants the garden to be special."

"Wait. So, the house he is building is his house? I thought he was a contractor working on a house for someone else."

"No, it's his place. I don't understand it, but it feels right. It feels like this is what is supposed to happen."

"Be careful, Anne. It seems strange to me."

"I will, Carol. Go home and get some rest. The shop is closed tomorrow, but I'll call you after I meet up with Cody."

Anne woke early, feeling nervous and impatient. She made herself sit down and drink a cup of coffee before she got ready to go because she doubted earlier is better meant before the sun came up. The pictures were laid out on the table, so she sat and looked at each one carefully, then she closed her eyes.

An image of the garden began to come to her: a stone wall with ivy or honeysuckle, wild roses, daisies, a pond with a waterfall, a tree with a porch swing. This was what she wanted for her garden. She chuckled a little and shook her head. Her garden... that wasn't what she was doing here. This was a garden for Cody's house.

Finally, she decided it was time. It was just after eight so he should be ready. She called his number as she walked out to her truck.

"Good morning, Cody. This is Anne. I was wondering if this was a good time for me to come by."

"Mornin'. Sure, come on by. I'm out on County Road seventy-two. You go about a mile past that old green barn. There's a black Dodge out in front."

"Oh, okay. I haven't been out that way in a while. I'm leaving my house now."

"Great! I'll see you in a bit."

Anne got into her old green truck. He lived almost an hour out of town. She was going to need more coffee. She backed out of the driveway and stopped at the café before she started her drive.

As she drove down the road along the river's edge, she enjoyed the beauty of the changing leaves. Her window was down, the radio on and she sang along. The air smelled of freshly mown hay. This was going to be a beautiful day.

Once she had passed the old abandoned barn, she began to watch for his place. This area had been part of the McConnell land when she was small. It was all cow pastures and hay fields, no houses for miles. Granddaddy had sold most of the land to a neighbor after Grandma died. He sold the rest after Uncle Ben had been killed in Iraq. She hadn't driven out here in years.

She saw a driveway to the right and could see a shiny new black Dodge truck parked up under the trees. She turned, and the dirt drive wound around the trees and a large shed with tractors and farming equipment. She continued on and came to a large wood and stone house which was obviously still under construction. As she stopped the truck, Cody came out of the house and stood on the deck watching her.

She got out and walked up to the deck. He reached for her hand and then pulled her into a quick hug.

"Hi! Did you find it okay?"

"Yes. I grew up out here. Most of the land off this road used to belong to my Granddaddy. He sold it years ago."

"Oh! So, this was once yours?" He looked surprised.

"Well, it belonged to my family anyway. I was ten when he sold the last of it and moved to San Francisco to live with my aunt. But I remember playing in the old green barn and riding the tractor with him."

"Did he have a house out here? I was surprised that there weren't any houses anywhere nearby."

"No. His house, the one Dad grew up in, burned before I was born. By the time I came around, he and Grandma lived in town, in the house I live in. After she died, he gave up on the place. Most of it he sold to the Johnsons. This last bit he held on to I think, hoping Uncle Ben would want to come back home. But my uncle died in Iraq."

Anne shivered a little. Cody noticed.

"Come inside for a minute. I'll show you the house. And then we can come back out and look at where I want to put the garden."

Anne followed him into the house. It was going to be amazing. A lot of wood and natural stone. There was an enormous fireplace in the front room. It took the entire wall.

"Wow! That is going to be nice in the winter!"

He laughed. "That was what I was thinking. I need to get a big comfortable sofa to sit in by the fire. I need to get furniture. I've been working so much trying to get this built that I just have a couple of things."

They turned the corner into the kitchen, a grand, open room with tons of counter space and a huge gourmet stove.

"What a wonderful room. All the windows!"

She looked out the window and took in the view. Mountains in the background, the gold and red of trees along the river. Closer, there was a pasture with cows, the ditch and chain link fence.

"This view is amazing... wait, is that the fence in the pictures?"

He grinned. "Yeah, I don't understand why this little area is fenced in, but yes, that is where I want the garden so that you can look at it from the kitchen." He handed her a cup of coffee. "Do you want to go out and look at it?"

"Yes!"

They walked through the kitchen and then through a room that would be the laundry room. He opened the back door, and they walked out onto a rickety set of stairs.

"I need to finish the deck. I'd like it to wrap all the way around the house."

"Definitely, that would be great."

When she stepped into the yard, she could see her dream garden. There was a huge tree at the other end of the yard that would be perfect for a swing. The pond could go in between the house and the tree. There were already some wild rose bushes along the ditch bank. She turned toward him in wonder.

"This is it. This is the garden I have had in my mind since I was little. I can see it perfectly!"

He looked at her with shock in his eyes.

"I could see it a little, with someone special on the swing. A pond with lilies and roses."

"You are him. The man I have been chasing in my dreams. You have to be."

"I never saw you as someone chasing me but more as just the elusive dream woman who lived here and made my house a home."

They held hands as they walked around the yard, talking about what should go where and how it should be constructed.

"I love that you have used the rocks inside because I see a rock wall surrounding the garden area. A rock wall covered with climbing roses and honeysuckle."

He smiled. "Anything you want here. You obviously have the vision." He turned to face her. "I am starving. Can I buy you breakfast?"

"That would be fabulous. I didn't eat this morning, too nervous." She laughed. "We could cook something."

"We could, but first, we'd have to buy something. I have no food. So, I figured we could skip that part and go to the café."

"Ha! Perfect!"

They walked to his truck and drove toward town. He made a turn before the river.

"I want to show you something."

He looked at her and watched her face as they turned into the canyon. The scenery was breathtaking. The sun was setting coloring the sandstone cliffs in a dizzying array of reds and oranges. The shadows were just deepening to purples. A herd of wild horses turned their heads towards her and then ran. The hawk, still circling, let out a shrill cry.

The End

NEVER AGAIN, MAYBE

DONNA WALO CLANCY

CHAPTER 1

*N*ever again. After a failed eighteen-year marriage and then a six-year relationship that ended with the groom backing out two months before the wedding, men are at the bottom of my list of important things in my life. I consider myself happily divorced.

I have always thought that there should be a separate category on forms that need to be filled out in everyday life. When you check the box next to divorced, you automatically become a loser who couldn't stay married. But, if you could check off happily divorced, then maybe people would look at you and see someone who stepped away from a bad situation and is surviving on their own instead.

After ditching the second loser, I realized that I needed to do what I wanted to do with my life as I wasn't getting any younger. Two weeks later, I moved to the country and began looking for a large amount of acreage to buy so that I could open my own pumpkin farm.

I don't know whether it was luck, fate or God that brought me to Mr. Gregson at the outdoor farmer's market that morning, but I am so glad that he had some mighty fine-looking, polished apples that called out to me.

He was an older gentleman, snow on the roof but still spry for his age. He had an old, beat-up pick-up truck that he had backed into his allotted space. The bed was loaded with apples, pumpkins and all different shaped gourds.

We chatted in between customers, most of all of them he knew personally as he had been born and raised there. He had a farm on the outskirts of town that consisted of a good-sized apple orchard, pear trees, and five acres of land on which he grew his pumpkins and gourds. His parents used to run the farm, and Mr. Gregson inherited it when his dad passed on.

He mentioned that he was getting up in years and was looking to sell his beloved farm to someone who would keep it going and not sell the land off to some money-hungry developer. We started tossing around the possibility of me buying the place as I told him that was what I had moved to the area to do; open a pumpkin farm. The apple orchard was a total bonus.

Two months later we were signing papers, and I now owned my very own, quite large pumpkin patch. That was six years ago, and I have never regretted a single minute of sweat and toil that has been put into running my Smiling Acres Farm. Men…who needs them? I am perfectly happy surrounded by my apples and pumpkins.

October was fast approaching, and the fields of the farm were dotted with orange orbs as far as the eye could see. Anna Bellows stood on her front porch, wrapped in a warm, fuzzy sweater, drinking her morning coffee and looking over her fields, smiling. This year was going to be a bumper crop; her best yet.

Apple picking season had started off with a bang, and she was in the beginning stages of planning for her Halloween hayride and festival that she held every year on the property. Her farm help, all local high school kids, had returned to school and that left just her and her foreman,

Ralph Turner, to do the bulk of the work. The kids would return to work on the weekends to help the customers in the fields and to man the gift shop.

The morning air was cool and crisp. This was Anna's favorite time of year; sweater weather. The afternoon air would be warmed up by the sun to make it comfortable for apple picking and then by nightfall, it was cool again.

Karen Gould, Anna's best friend, worked every day manning the booth at the entrance to the apple orchards. She would spend the day selling the different size bags to the visiting pickers and reading her books between customers. She was an avid reader and loved her seasonal job as it allowed her to read at least four to five books a week.

Unlike Anna, Karen was engaged and going to be married the following summer. She had found Mr. Right late in life and was going to be forty-eight years old when she said her vows for the first time. The wedding was going to be held at Smiling Acres out in the middle of the apple orchard. She was deeply in love with her fiancé, Richard Lewis, and kept badgering Anna to find someone so that she wouldn't grow old by herself.

Anna would smile and laugh it off. She was happy, and everyone around her knew that. Karen was the only one not listening or paying attention to what Anna insisted to be true.

"Good morning, ma'am," Ralph announced, walking by the porch on his way to the barn.

"Yes, it is, Ralph. What's on the agenda for today?"

"I'm going to finish up the hayride path today. I want everything ready for opening day of the festival," he answered.

"Can you put that on the backburner for now? We need to refill all the baskets of the various types of picked apples in the gift shop. This weekend's business just about emptied everything," she requested.

"We can do that," he said, changing directions.

"Have I told you lately how awesome you are?" she asked, smiling.

"Every day, ma'am, every day."

Ralph Turner had come with the farm. He had worked many years for Mr. Gregson, and one of the conditions of the sale to Anna was that

Ralph be allowed to stay on as the foreman. He was a quiet man and stayed to himself most of the time. Tall and lanky, he wasn't one of the most handsome men that Anna had ever seen, but he was a hard worker and knew what he was doing when it came to running the daily business of the farm.

Karen beeped and waved as she drove by the house on her way to the apple orchard. Anna returned her wave and went into the house to refill her coffee mug. Monday was her day for errands and heading into town. She had deposits to make at the bank and groceries to buy.

Her final stop would be at the local five and dime to pick up the twelve new red wagons that she had special ordered for her farm. Last year, she didn't have enough for the pumpkin pickers to use and customers had to wait until someone returned from the fields and emptied their wagon of their purchases. Anna had ordered twelve new ones to add to her existing inventory but would order more if they were needed.

"I'll be back in a couple of hours, Ralph," she yelled to him as he exited the gift shop door. "Do you need anything in town?"

"Nope, I'm good. I'll see you then."

The drive to town only took twenty minutes. It was a peaceful drive past other farms, mostly corn fields. There was one other pumpkin farm in the area, but it was half an hour north of Smiling Acres. Mr. Gregson had built up a good clientele, and his customers had stayed with Anna when she took over the farm.

Minglewood was a small town with a population of less than two-thousand people. The town had all the mom and pop businesses that you would expect to find and a couple of national chain stores that had snuck in over the years. It had been six years since Anna had moved there and was now familiar with most of the locals. They had accepted her as one of their own.

She went to the bank first to deposit the weekend receipts. Tony Longer, the bank's assistant manager, approached her while she stood at the window waiting for the teller to verify the deposit. He had asked Anna out on many occasions, and she had always said no, but he wouldn't give up.

"How's business, Anna?" he asked, leaning in close to her.

"Fine," she replied, backing up a bit.

"It's coming into your busy season now. I guess that I won't bother to ask you out on a date right now," he sighed.

"Yes, it is and good thinking," she answered, tired of his persistence.

"Will you ever go out on a date with me?"

"I have told you before. I am too busy with my farm and not looking for any kind of relationship," she insisted, picking up her receipts and stuffing them in her bank bag. "Have a nice week."

She left the window to the quiet giggles of the two tellers who witnessed the whole scene. Everyone in town knew that Tony had a thing for her, but she had no interest in dating him. He was boring, stuck on himself and couldn't pass a mirror or window without checking out his reflection. He was definitely not her type; not that she even had a type.

The grocery store was quiet, and Anna finished her shopping quickly. She placed the two bags of food in the back seat of her truck and left for Clark's Five and Dime to pick up her new red wagons. She pulled around to the back loading dock and backed up to the platform. Sam, one of the employees, helped her load the wagons. She signed for the order and started to leave.

"Miss Anna, wait up!"

Anna turned to see Andy Brown hurrying towards her. Andy was the best pumpkin carver around these parts. He was only in his late twenties but had already accumulated many awards and recognitions for his artistic carving ability. It was Andy's carvings that could be seen all around the farm during the festival in October.

"Andy, long time no see. How's the teaching job treating you?"

"I love it. The kids are great and very artistic. There is a lot of untapped talent where I teach," he replied. "I have a problem I need to discuss with you."

"What problem?"

"I'm afraid that I won't be here to do your carvings for the Halloween festival at the farm this year. I have been accepted into an accredited art show in Boston, and I have to get all my pieces ready.

This is my first show at a known gallery, and I have to present my best work."

"Congratulations! I am so happy for you. I am sorry that my hayride passengers won't have any pumpkins to look at on their ride this year," she frowned.

"I didn't say that you wouldn't have carved pumpkins this year. I just said that I wouldn't be here to do them," he chuckled.

"So, what's so funny?" she asked.

"I took it upon myself to get someone to replace me. His name is Martin Seavers, and he is just as good at carving as I am; maybe even a little better," Andy replied.

"Is he a local? I've never heard of him," Anna asked.

"He just moved back here a couple of months ago. He was born and raised here."

"Did he go to school with you?"

"Oh, no, he is much older than I am. I believe he is in his early fifties," Andy commented. "But I have seen his work, and it is top of the line."

"Much older..." Anna snorted. "Early fifties are not that old. I'm fifty-one."

"I didn't mean anything by it," Andy mumbled. "I just meant that he is much older than I am."

"It's okay, we must seem ancient compared to someone your age. Am I going to get to meet this carver before he shows up to decorate my farm for Halloween?"

"How about right now?" Andy asked, looking over her shoulder.

Anna turned to see a man walking towards her. His muscular arms and well-defined torso were busting out of the red flannel shirt that he was wearing. His tight blue jeans clung to every inch of his lower body. His jet-black hair was highlighted by silver wisps around his temples. The closer he got to Anna, the more she realized just how handsome he really was.

"Miss Anna, I'd like you to meet Martin Seavers, my dad," Andy announced. "He taught me everything that I know about pumpkin carving."

"Your dad? But your name...," she questioned.

"Andy's mom and I never married. He was adopted by Charlene's husband, thus the different last name," Martin explained. "But I never lost touch with my boy, even when I moved to New York City."

"I used to spend the summers there with Dad, and that's where I learned to carve," Andy informed her. "You think that I'm good? Wait until you see his carvings."

"I don't want you to be forced into my working for you. How about if I come out to the farm and show you a sample of what I can do? Say... Wednesday, ten a.m.?"

"Okay, I guess," Anna replied, still digesting the fact that Martin was Andy's dad.

"It's a date... well. you know what I mean; not a date. Anyway, I'll see you then," Martin announced, turning and hurrying away.

"Weird," Andy said, shaking his head as he watched his dad go up the street and turn the corner out of sight.

"What's weird?" Anna asked.

"Oh, nothing. I'll be in touch to see what you think of my dad's work," he answered. "Talk to you then."

She climbed up into her truck and sat there thinking. There was something familiar about Martin Seavers, but she couldn't put her finger on it. Maybe she had just seen him around town; that had to be it.

Anna drove back to the farm. Ralph helped her unload the new wagons and then she went to check on Karen out at the apple orchard. The parking lot was full, and people were wandering around everywhere filling their apple bags. Karen was chatting happily with the customers. Anna got out of her truck and approached the stand.

"What are you doing out here?" Karen asked.

"I just came out to check on you and to tell you that Andy is not going to be available to carve the pumpkins for the festival this year," Anna replied.

"That's not good news. What are you going to do?" Karen asked, handing change back to her customer.

"He did find a replacement to do the work," Anna stated.

"Someone local?"

"Kind of. I mean, he is now. He used to live here years ago."

"All right...spit it out. Who is he?"

"Have you ever heard of a Martin Seavers?" Anna quizzed. "He's been here for a few months."

"Can't say that I have. Is this guy creeping you out or something?" Karen asked, noticing that Anna was acting kind of funny.

"No, he seemed nice. I only met him for a few minutes."

"So why are you acting so weird?"

"There is just something about him that is so familiar, but I can't figure out what it is," she answered.

"Maybe you just saw him around town," Karen offered.

"That's what I was thinking, too," Anna agreed.

Deep down inside, she knew it was for some other reason.

CHAPTER 2

Wednesday morning arrived, and Anna was up extra early. She sat on the porch, drinking her coffee and watching the sun come up over her pumpkin fields. In the predawn light, the pumpkins looked like bright orange eyes watching her from everywhere.

She had been up most of the night, her mind not able to let go of the feeling that she knew Martin Seavers from somewhere. It was not a feeling of fear, but a feeling of contentment. How could she feel comfortable and content over someone that she didn't know? What was it about that man?

"Morning, Miss Anna," Ralph called out on his way to the barn. "You're up earlier than usual."

"Lots to do today," she answered, not revealing the real reason that she was up before the sun. "Are you almost done with the hayride course for the festival?"

"It's done. I rode the wagon through yesterday to make sure it was good to go," he answered.

"I have a meeting with a potential new pumpkin carver, and I would like to show him the setup to see where he would place the carved pumpkins," she informed her foreman.

Andy's not around this year? He hasn't missed a Halloween since we started this event," Ralph asked.

"He has a big art show in Boston," Anna replied.

"Good for him," Ralph muttered.

"This guy is supposed to be even better than Andy. Do you know a Martin Seavers?" Anna quizzed, fishing for information.

"Andy's dad? He's back from New York?" Ralph asked, raising an eyebrow.

"Do you know him?"

"Used to. We went to school together. His mom just died a couple of months ago. Maybe that's why he came back to town."

"He'll be here at ten. Could you have the wagon ready to go so that Mr. Seavers and I can peruse the course for pumpkin placement?" Anna requested.

"I'll be there," Ralph replied.

"Thank you, Ralph. I don't know what I would do without you," Anna said, returning to her cup of coffee.

At ten o'clock on the dot, Martin Seavers drove up the road towards Anna's house. He hopped down out of his truck holding a leather case in his hand. She was waiting on the porch for his arrival.

"Mr. Seavers, nice to see you again," she said, extending her hand.

"Martin, please. Nice to see you, too. What a gorgeous day!"

"Yes, it is. I had Ralph bring up some different size pumpkins for you to choose from to show me your carving skills. Would you like a cup of coffee before you start?" she asked, smiling.

"I would love some coffee," he answered, looking over the pumpkins that sat on the porch floor.

"Great, I'll be right back."

Anna watched him through the kitchen window while she waited for the coffee to brew. He had picked up a medium-size pumpkin and went to work creating his masterpiece. Martin was quick and precise in every cut that he made to the pumpkin's flesh. In less than five minutes he had carved a witch flying against a full moon.

Anna set the tray on the porch table with the coffee, sugar, and creams. Martin had already picked up a second orange orb and was carving a scary face.

"That smells really good," Martin announced, sniffing the air in the direction of the coffee.

"Cream and sugar?"

"No, thanks. They mask the taste of the coffee," he stated.

Anna had heard that before. Not everyone would answer that way. Most people would just say no thanks, I drink it black. Where had she heard that before and who used to say it?

"What do you think?" he asked, placing the second pumpkin down next to the first.

"I'm impressed. Andy was right; you are good," Anna answered.

"I'm a little rusty. There wasn't much call for pumpkin carving where I worked in New York City," he said, picking up his coffee mug.

"Where did you work? I spent some time in New York years ago."

"I put in thirty-one years at different restaurants around the city. I started out as a dishwasher and worked my way up to executive chef. My mom got sick, and I decided it was time to retire and return home to spend what time she had left with her," he said. "I just wish I had returned home sooner."

"I'm sure that she treasured your time together," Anna said, quietly.

"Yea, I think she did," he replied.

After a few moments of silence, Anna set her mug down and stood up.

"Shall we go take a hayride so that you can see where Andy put his creations?"

"Lead the way. Maybe, I can come up with a few ideas of my own," Martin smiled.

They walked, side by side, through the parking lot and to the back of the gift shop where Ralph was waiting. The hay wagon was hooked up to the tractor, ready for the tour.

"Martin, this is Ralph, my foreman."

"Ralph Turner, as I live and breathe. How have you been?" Martin asked as they shook hands.

"I never thought I would see you back here again," Ralph replied.

"The country called, man. I liked living in the city, but I guess I'll always have the soul of a small-town boy," he laughed.

"I'm sorry to hear about your mom passing," Ralph offered.

"Thanks. It's not quite the same without her here," Martin said.

"Miss Anna, let me help you," Ralph suggested as he held out his arm.

Martin followed her up into the hay wagon and took a seat opposite Anna. They chatted as they went along. Anna pointed out the places where Andy had placed his pumpkins with battery-operated lights in them. She told Martin what scary scene would be on each platform that had been built along the hayride.

He offered ideas about what carvings would benefit each scene. Anna liked his fresh, new ideas and felt that it would definitely be a plus to hire him.

"Let's talk salary, Mr. Seavers," she said out of the blue.

"Please, it's Martin. As I said, I am a bit rusty. If you provide all the pumpkins, I will provide my services of carving for free. Just through in some fresh apples and pears and we have a deal."

"Are you sure?" Anna asked, expecting his services to be expensive considering his skill level.

"I'm sure," he insisted, smiling.

"You have yourself a deal," Anna said, smiling and holding out her hand to seal the deal.

Martin smiled broadly and returned the handshake. The minute their hands met, Anna felt a tingle; something that she hadn't felt in a long time. She pulled her hand back quickly. Martin didn't say anything but noticed how she reacted to their touching.

"We're at the halfway point, Miss Anna. Do you want to stop at the platform and get out and stretch?" Ralph asked, breaking the awkward silence in the hay wagon behind him.

"Yes, please. I'd like to show Martin the highlight of the ride."

Ralph pulled the tractor up alongside the large wooden platform and shut the tractor off.

"I'm going to turn on the display, so he can see what happens here," the foreman said.

Anna and Martin climbed out onto the platform. As they walked the display, Anna told the carver where she would like lit pumpkins placed; the designs could be his choice. The scene came to life around them. Life-size figures darted in and out of doors and windows, wolves howled, and blood-curdling screams could be heard from every corner of the display. Bats flew down over the wagon on hidden fishing lines, along with severed heads.

"This is pretty intense," Martin said, looking around. "I have some great ideas for carvings that can be placed here."

"We also have eight local high school kids that get dressed up and attack the wagon as zombies," Anna chuckled.

"I'll have to ride through here at night to live the full experience," Martin replied.

Okay, Ralph! You can shut it down," Anna yelled.

"It's a lot of work. The pumpkins will need to be replaced throughout the month so it will mean a lot of time here at the farm," Anna said. "Do you still want the job?"

"I'm retired now. I have all the time in the world," he answered.

"Okay, the job is yours," Anna replied.

Ralph had started the tractor and was ready to continue. Martin jumped down off the platform and turned to help Anna. She wasn't watching where she was stepping, and her foot got tangled up in an extension cord that lay along the edge of the display. She fell off the platform, arms flailing. Acting quickly, Martin's strong arms caught her before she hit the ground.

Then it hit her. She knew where she knew Martin Seavers from. Many years ago, in New York City, a young man caught her as she was falling off a subway platform. They spent a whirlwind week together before she had to return to school.

The next year, she returned to the city to find her first love, but to no avail. Back then, there were no cell phones or internet, so it was impossible to track him down. She hadn't thought about him since she gave up on finding him.

"Marty?" she whispered. "Is that really you?"

"I was wondering how long it would take you to recognize me."

"We were so young. I was twenty, and you were twenty-one. It was so long ago."

"It was, but I never forgot you. I couldn't believe my eyes when I saw you in town a few weeks ago. I asked my son who you were, and he confirmed your name. He also told me that he carved for your festival every year. I had to see you again, so I asked him to back out so that I could step in."

"I went back to New York to find you, but you had moved."

"Back then, as I moved up in the ranks of cooking, I worked at a lot of different restaurants. I was never in one place for too long," he admitted.

"Could you put me down, please?" Anna asked, still in shock over who was holding her.

"Do I have to?" he smiled. "The last time I put you down, I lost you."

He set her down gingerly on a bale of hay in the back of the wagon. He climbed up, sat down next to her and took her hand. This time, she didn't pull it away.

"Are you okay, Miss Anna?" Ralph asked from the tractor.

"I'm fine. Let's get back to the gift shop."

The ride back was a quiet one. Martin never let go of his long-lost love's hand.

Anna needed time to process what had just happened. Never in her wildest dreams did she believe that she would ever see her first love again. He had held her heart many years ago, and she didn't know if that hold had ever gone away.

When they arrived at the gift shop, they stood outside discussing their future. Anna told him that she needed time to get used him being back in her life, but she was glad that he was. He told her he would give her all the time she needed; he wasn't going anywhere. They decided to go to dinner on Friday night as a get to know you again date.

Karen was getting herself a cold bottle of water out of the employee refrigerator. She had been on her break from the orchard and was getting ready to head back to work when she saw her best friend and a man she didn't know talking just outside the front door. Not wanting to interrupt their conversation, she stayed inside the shop.

244 | COOL WEATHER, WARM HEARTS

Anna was smiling, and so was the stranger she was with. He leaned in, gave Anna a soft kiss on the cheek and left. She watched him until he got in his car and drove away. She turned to see Karen watching out the door.

"Okay, spill," Karen demanded before Anna even got all the way in the door. "Is that the new pumpkin carver."

"Yes, it is," she beamed.

"Did he kiss you for giving him the job? Kind of forward, don't you think?"

"He kissed me because he found me; thirty years later, he found me," Anna whispered.

"Excuse me?"

Anna told Karen the whole story.

"You still love this guy. Your face tells it all."

"I don't know. We both had to have changed over time. We do have a date this Friday night to catch up and see if we should further the relationship," Anna admitted.

"I thought that you gave up on men. What happened to never again?"

"What about never again, maybe?" she said, smiling as she blushed, touching her cheek where she had been kissed.

The End

Made in the
USA
Columbia, SC